Cola

Gather

To: Scott... the only Barber in Akron who understands "No whitewalls!" Hope you enjoy the story.

Tom Buechler

2-28-14

A Novel By

Tom Buechler

This book is a work of fiction. Names, characters, places and incidents either are products of the author's imagination or are used fictitiously. Any resemblance to actual events or locales or persons, living or dead, is entirely coincidental.

Cover images provided by S McDevitt, Joleene Naylor, Annieannie & Dreamstime.com

Cover by Joleene Naylor

"If our passions are aroused, we are apt to see things in an exaggerated way, or imagine what does not exist."

Arthur Schopenhauer

"We swim, day by day, on a river of delusions. But life is a sincerity. In lucid intervals we say, 'Let there be an entrance for me into realities; I have worn the fool's cap too long.'"

Ralph Waldo Emerson

"You got to get it while you can."

Janis Joplin

ACKNOWLEDGMENTS

Many thanks to Bob Barsan, David Lille, MaryJane Santos, Carolyn Schlafer and Robin Hallum who, conned into reading a ragged first draft, remained steadfastly in my corner. To Melinda Baccus, who for two years did *not* say, "In the name of all things decent, please shut up about that bloody book for two minutes,"…Grazie. To Paul Swan who helped me make the final tweaks and for his honest insights, kudos. To J. Michael Kahle, who let me loiter around his Dayton studio and re-connect with the searing magic of glassblowing, my gratitude. Thanks to Joe Cunningham, whose gifts of hardware, software and humor saved a sinking project. To family and friends who stoically tolerated months of inane babbling and bitchy mood swings and still managed to be unshakably supportive, my abiding affection. For her astonishing artistry and infinite patience in crafting the perfect cover for Cold Gather, I am forever indebted to Joleene Naylor.

Last, but certainly not least, is my brother-in-law and fellow author, Creston Mapes, who challenged me to write a novel. A stalwart mentor while issuing prudent warnings about the ordeal I had chosen to undertake…I cannot thank him enough.

Nor will I soon forgive him.

This one is for Jerry

1

Like a consecrated wafer on the tongue of an anxious Catholic, the disk slid silently into the slot and I was rewarded with the poignant, hard-driving rock and roll jewel that is Bob Seger's "Hollywood Nights."

Having listened to it hundreds of times, I was unprepared for its impact. The blue-eyed beauty who steals the soul of a boy from the Heartland, his instant awareness that he is in for a struggle, his absolute surrender and subsequent desolation… it all had fresh, stark meaning to me after these many years.

For the record, her eyes were brown, not blue. And it happened in San Diego, not Hollywood. Either way, I knew I was too far from home.

From the first time I met her at Neil's "pre-wake" party in September to the following March when she pointed a .38 revolver at my sternum and called me a thief… I was in over my head.

She was mesmerizing. Five foot nothing, built for sin and stone crazy. Just the way I like them.

Neil had warned me she was volatile and unpredictable, a real Jekyll and Hyde-type. In her mid-forties, she had the unblemished face of a fallen angel, a seductive voice and the lithe body of a woman half her age.

Marla Stone was a package so magnetic that I blindly denied the absolute metaphysical *certainty* that she would one day hand me my balls, my toothbrush and the smoldering remnants of my self-respect.

It was going to be a real interesting spring.

Neil Bishop and I met at age seven. Our lives would run on parallel debauched tracks for nearly a half-century.

Learning our chops on the blue-collar near West Side of Cleveland, (labeled "Cake-eaters" by the denizens of other, less desirable neighborhoods), we went to elementary school and dabbled in the dark sciences of the Cub Scouts and Indian Guides. Kennedy was in the White House, men wore hats and One Flew Over the Cuckoo's Nest hit the bookshelves.

A couple of precocious wise asses already, in those early years we learned to compensate for our lack of physical stature; Neil with his relentless energy and flair for artistic creativity, me with my bold sense of humor and mocking cynicism. What Neil did over the course of his life with metal and glass, I've tried to do with language and attitude.

We shared a lifelong fascination with women. Whether it was looking down Mrs. Snyder's blouse in the third grade, trying to cop a feel of Debbie Del Vecchio's budding boobs in sixth, eagerly volunteering for duty in the Sexual Revolution, multiple failed marriages and dozens of bewildering dalliances along the way…from the playground onward, we were shameless. Blessed with extra reserves of testosterone and the blarney necessary to put it to good use, we chose a ridiculous number of ridiculous partners based on the oft-referenced phenomenon of thinking with one's crotch.

His family moved to "the country" when we were twelve, while my parents stayed in town, hoping for the best. We didn't see each other for five years until my family finally bolted to the outskirts. After we graduated high school, he went to Northwestern on a partial art scholarship and I enrolled at a nearby state university.

He pursued a career in art and earned his degree. I dropped out in my sophomore year to become a husband, daddy and writer. Over the next four decades he used his bold talent, flair for self-promotion and often crude displays of ego to become an infamous glassblower and painter.

During that time, I worked a series of jobs in promotions, marketing and advertising...all the while hammering out grumpy eclecticism into essays, short stories, bad poetry and finally a novel that people actually bought.

I developed a reputation as a loose cannon in the world of business, a quirky crafter of tales among the literati and a trusted confidant among friends.

I worked mostly at home writing travel pieces and anything else I could sell, cashing small residual checks and hanging onto a twelve-hour-a-week job at a local DIY place to keep my toes in the mainstream of humanity. I told myself it was anthropological fieldwork.

From the affluent and secure to the common and warped, friends called me for a sympathetic ear when the wheels came loose on their American dreams. I was the guy they phoned late at night, drunk and weepy. I listened, commiserated but rarely told them what they wanted to hear. Some of them still call, though not as often and rarely as drunk.

Regardless of our geographic locations, Neil and I never lost touch with one another. We would meet in Ohio for reunion-type events. He would visit me in LA or Portland or Cleveland or London. I'd fly to Tampa or New York or Jamaica or deep into Appalachia to see him.

We partied on both coasts and points in between. We were big fish in small ponds. We drank firkins of whiskey, bathtubs of beer, smoked bales of ganja, cords of hashish and snorted yards of blow. We pursued a parade of women, all willing and fair. For a couple of trolls from Ohio, we sure got laid a lot.

Neil once got on the phone with a young lady I was trying to seduce and told her, "Jack's a mensch. He never forgets his friends. Never. And I've never known him to lie. He's probably far too honest and decent for you, but he'll treat you like a queen… or like a whore, if that's your thing." Three days later she moved in with me.

We proudly shared the honor of bailing each other out of jail…twice. We burned with the phosphorescent intensity of young stars and crashed across thousands of twisted nights. We never mentioned "paying the piper", although we knew he was out there.

Neil's lifestyle was, by design, glaringly more bohemian than mine…more bohemian than just about anyone else I've known. And I've known a lot of people who marched to lost drummers. He took great pains to reinforce his image as the wild-eyed artiste. His gaucheries were overlooked. He blazed through several fortunes in his short, crazy life. He was an absolute genius and a visionary artist.

He could step into a barn full of dusty crap that anyone else would set out as trash, and emerge, exhausted and grinning, two days later (subsisting on eggs, pita bread, papayas, hot sauce, ostrich burgers, Bombay gin, and lots of weed) with a fully-operational Mardi Gras float, a twelve-foot-high, phallic stars-and-stripes calliope that roared "Don't Fear The Reaper", a half dozen Halloween costumes, nine new recipes for omelets and a cure for the blues.

I have often said that Neil "saw" the world in a way entirely different from our way. In visions the rest of us cannot imagine, his eyes were tuned to new kinds of perception and his mind processed those perceptions in unique ways, giving birth to fantastical objects.

Neil was Sui Generis. Born without brakes, he lived the artist's life to the hilt.

Twice married, father of two children and twice divorced by the time I was thirty-five, I spent twenty years in Southern California and in the Pacific Northwest. Broken up briefly by a four-year stint in Ohio, (my second marriage to an insanely jealous, carnally accomplished Sicilian who tried to kill me with a carving fork), I spent most of those two decades drinking, smoking pot, chasing tail and writing.

I'd had several other star-cursed live-in arrangements; a wild Irish nurse in Palo Alto, a blond who was a year younger than my daughter, a Czech poetess-welder-junkie in Tucson, the mayor of a small town in New Hampshire, a cop in Cleveland. Sometime in the late 90's I experienced an epiphany of sorts. I grew fatigued of the non-stop debauchery and ultimately allowed the German strand of my DNA to demand a time-out.

I stopped smoking in 1990. Six months later I stopped drinking. Not a drop for ten years, finally having a glass of wine in 2000. I now enjoy a beer or a Maker's Mark on the rocks occasionally. I don't use drugs anymore either...well, except for a few weeks when I smoked some medical grade, state-approved marijuana with Marla. But that's getting ahead of the story.

While I was cleaning up my act, Neil continued to rattle and hum down his road to ruin until finally the alcohol, the drugs, the exchanged bodily fluids...and god knows what else...brought him Hepatitis B, along with cirrhosis of the liver. He would later develop both Hepatitis A and C, completing the trifecta of liver killers.

He called me from Jamaica to tell me about the Hepatitis and asked me to keep it to myself. I did. He continued smoking all manner of substances and, despite the clear and persistent warnings of every doctor he ever saw, drinking like a goddamn fish.

At various times there were rumors he was in debtor's prison in Honduras, that he'd been chased out of Puerto Vallarta for compromising a fourteen year-old, and that his visits to Bangkok had resulted in sweeping revisions of local vice statutes.

That July, after we all thought the Hepatitis was under control, the bottom fell out. Phoning from California, Neil told me he had liver cancer. "The quacks tell me I might have six months." He delivered the news with his usual bravado and nonchalance, but I heard the fear in his voice. The piper had kicked down the door.

I don't remember any other details of the conversation. I'm sure I said something inane, something useless. He told me that Marla, the woman he was living with in California, had become a wonderful caregiver. He sounded upbeat for a guy who had just been told to get his affairs in order.

Although Neil described her to me many times, my first exposure to Marla was a photo he emailed me.

She had surprised him with a three-day stay at a luxury spa near Calabasas. In the photo, framed by colorful Mexican tile, palm trees and a fountain, they are wearing huge, white terry-cloth robes. Neil is grinning like a cretin and she is looking into the lens with a half-smile. He was dying. It was as if, at the instant of the shutter's click, Marla had been sucker punched by the full realization of their situation. It is a disturbing photo, but she is breathtaking in it. He and Marla had been together for a little over three years at the time of the photo.

At my first sight of her I said under my breath, "You lucky bastard." That is what I also said to him on the phone and again later, in person. We never pulled our punches. The frankness with which we spoke to one another made a lot of people squirm.

My email reply to him was four words. "Screw you. Send her."

I'm not sure if "smitten" quite says it, but I was a goner. The moment I saw the enigmatic expression on her exquisite face, I wanted to be the man who would protect and comfort Marla after Neil was gone. I owed it to him and I owed it to myself. It's what old friends do. I owed it to her.

Neil had told me about Marla's vile temper. He told me about her kindness and generosity. He extolled her energy and passion. He did puzzle me with his comment, "And she even lets me have sex with her."

There was nothing right about that. That did not sound like Neil.

The thing he mentioned most often…aside from the epic sex…was her volcanic anger. He described to me a sweeping, unreasoning rage like none he had seen before. "She is two different people, man. Two completely different people. One minute she's pouring me wine, kissing me, baby talking and tending my wounds. The next minute she's screaming at some imagined insult or telling me what an ungrateful, useless piece of shit I am. It's disturbing and demeaning, but the sex is worth it."

As the craziness of my time with Marla recedes from memory, I recall other things I wish I had paid more attention to. He said she was the only woman who had ever intimidated him. Though at the time I thought it was just more of Neil's hyperbole, today I know all too well what he meant.

I have an old friend, a dentist by trade, who some time ago determined that I was that most rare of breeds, the romantic curmudgeon. I have always been a romantic; hoping that every woman will be "the one", that love conquers all, that two-hearts-beating-as-one-can-overcome-anything, etc, etc.

To be a romantic in Twenty First Century America is the hallmark of an idiot. I had suspected so, but not until the events of these last few years landed on top of me like a cartoon anvil was I convinced.

I can be a sharp-tongued, opinionated prick. But the curmudgeon has always prevented the romantic from piercing its ears, buying a raffish hat and riding a Vespa to spend Friday nights with the world-weary poseurs at the local coffee shop.

After a couple near-death experiences, two bankruptcies, one STD, broken hearts, broken promises, duplicity and dishonesty heaped on...I thought I'd pretty much seen it all.

But nothing had even remotely prepared me for the shit storm that awaited me.

The romantic curmudgeon writer was about to run headfirst, full-throttle into the narcissistic vamp. The collision would scatter Eros and wreckage from coast to coast.

A few days after Neil told me about his death sentence, he called again to ask for my help putting together a party, a sort of hometown wake/reunion. He planned to make a couple stops around the country, places he had worked and exhibited and taught. He called it his "Pre-wake Tour." I told him I would get right on it.

He and Marla were living in Olinda, California, a small suburb on the outskirts of San Diego, "close to the Bay" he always said, as if I knew what that meant. Over the next six weeks, via phone and email,

I contacted old friends and classmates from all over the country. He contacted more people from his place in California. We stayed in close touch, emailing and comparing notes. By September we were set for a bash at Gilhooley's, a small neighborhood bar on the Cleveland's Near East Side.

We were delivered a sunny, end-of-summer day for the party. I rode over with my dentist buddy, Painless, and his wife. I was gratified to see the parking lot full.

We went in and Neil was standing right inside the door, his back to us, talking to a group of three or four people I didn't recognize.

When someone in the crowd called out my name, Neil wheeled around. We exchanged a long bear hug and his eyes welled up. "Jumpin' Jack! Wow, man, you really outdid yourself here. Look at this place! Thanks, man. Thanks." I hadn't seen him in three years and, although he'd lost weight and was the color of expensive mustard, he looked better than I had prepared myself for.

I said, "Hey...you only die once, right? You must have done some serious legwork, too. I don't know half of these folks."

Pulling me toward the bar, Neil's next question was one we had asked each other probably a thousand times over more than four decades, "What are you drinking?"

When the leggy, redheaded barmaid bought my Black and Tan and his double Bombay, Neil prodded me, "Come on, Scanlon...give me your best Irish toast."

I recited;

"Here's to a long life and a merry one,

A quick death and an easy one,

A pretty girl and a true one,

A cold bottle and another one."

I told him he looked good. He told me he felt pretty good, that he had a great, sexy nurse in Marla. Then he began to enumerate the medications he was taking for the cancer and all of their ugly effects. In addition to the morphine and other serious painkillers, he had a steady supply of (legal for a change) marijuana.

As Neil continued this maudlin inventory and more people came in, he got distracted. When he got around to discussing suppositories and stool softeners, I began to look around the room.

There wasn't much to the place. Neil's contingent easily outnumbered the townies five-to-one. There were a half dozen regulars on their stools, one couple playing pinball, the jukebox blessedly silent. Knotty pine paneling and a black and white checkerboard floor. Curtained windows on three walls let in enough light. A large curved oak bar, a fine selection of beers on tap, three pretty barmaids. No ferns, no yuppies, no faux-Irish "theme" shit. It was an honest gin mill and the vibe was positive.

I said, "Where's this woman I've been hearing so much about?" Some new arrivals had approached and Neil was off on another round of storytelling and drinks. But he had heard my question. While talking to the newcomers, he looked at me and nodded to his left. With slightly raised voice, "She's seen your picture. I told her to look for you."

I turned my head in the direction of his nod and saw Marla.

Everything unflattering Neil had told me about her...the maddening unpredictability, the combativeness, the moodiness, the fits of blind, crazy rage...all of it vanished, like steam.

She was talking to a small group of people when we made eye contact. I gave her a smile and a nod. I sensed a note of recognition in her glance and the slight reciprocal nod of her head. I recognized her from the white robe photo.

11

Raymond Chandler once wrote, "From 30 feet away she looked like a lot of class. From 10 feet away she looked like something made up to be seen from 30 feet away."

Not this woman. She wore no make-up, no jewelry other than a small pair of stone earrings. In tight jeans, a simple white blouse and sandals, with shoulder length brown hair and brown eyes, Marla was slim, tanned and alert. She immediately had my undivided attention.

She smiled and spoke softly to guests. She graciously accepted, no doubt for the hundredth time, their introductions and condolences.

Her jaw firm, she moved with a gentle dignity, her posture elegant, her smile warm and inviting, and her body obviously perfect beneath the unassuming clothes. Every man in the place turned his head when she entered his field of vision. I swear to God, I could hear necks rubbing against collars.

I know a little about body language and it was clear that Marla was treading water furiously to hide her weariness. In a fishbowl surrounded by strangers, playing hostess at a wake, she was a study in nervous energy, graceful under pressure and magnificent in her bearing. She picked up and arranged glasses, delivered drinks, shook hands, hugged strangers and fussed with small details. She was continually scanning the room, tapping her foot, looking for and finding things to do. She needed to stay busy.

She was distractedly wiping a tabletop when I saw her cast a second, small smile my way. I thought she was looking at someone behind me, when…just beneath the surface of her beautiful composure…I saw a hint of panic. The expression in her widening eyes screamed straight at me, "Are you just going to stand there and drink or are you going to help me out here?"

I dropped Neil like a burning turd and headed straight for her. I extended my hand and said, "I'm Jack Scanlon."

With a sunburst of a smile she said, "Oh, I know who you are. I'm Marla," and we shared a quick dispassionate hug. Our bodies were a nice fit. Months later, she admitted she had felt it also.

Taking her hand, I told the group holding her hostage, "I need five minutes," and we walked to a pair of empty barstools.

"Thanks for rescuing me. They're really sweet people but it's a little overwhelming. Neil's told me about all the help you've been in putting this thing together. He really loves you."

"He really loves you, too. I'm glad to help out. How are you holding up?"

"I'm fine. It's really hard. But we'll get through it. Thanks for doing this."

Sitting knee-to-knee, I could see only her face, hear nothing but her voice.

That naturally ultra-feminine voice. The same voice she'd had at seventeen. None of the affected, little girl nonsense or forced cuteness women employ to manipulate guys. There was no resisting it.

"I wanted to get you out of that scrum and talk with you."

She patted me gently on the back of my hand, pulled me down into those peanut butter brown eyes and said, "Yes. Let's talk."

Her skin was lightly tanned, unblemished. She was revealing only her lean forearms, her neck and face. She was small-chested, small-waisted without being gaunt. She had curves, I was confident, under those threads.

Her hair was luxuriously thick and full. I wanted to touch it. Naturally sculpted eyebrows and long lashes framed pupils dilated just enough to signal that she was listening to me and ready to communicate.

They weren't lustrous, Marla's eyes. I recall thinking that whatever flame had once burned brightly there had been reduced to a flicker. They were deep, but deep with immense sadness. I would discover that the light within was reflected off the bleached bones of old pain.

She had high cheekbones, delicate ears, a jaw that declared her a formidable person, a woman to be reckoned with. Her mouth was small, lips forming a cool smile. From that moment forward, Marla's smile never failed to stop me in my tracks and turn me around.

Only her hands betrayed her age. They were small and feminine and all they should be. But they weren't as youthful as the rest of her. They say that's how carnies can judge a woman's age…the neck and the hands. She was a dozen years younger than me.

This woman had it all. The word I always return to in describing her is "striking."

I wanted to put my lips on hers, fold her into my arms and tell her to not worry about anything, that I would make it all better and that her life would go on in fullness and joy.

Instead I said, "It's nice to finally meet you. You're as beautiful as Neil said you were. I've been talking to him on the phone for weeks. Now, I want to know how *you* are doing."

She touched me again, now letting her hand rest on mine for a moment. I felt a change in my breathing.

"I'm hanging in there. It's been hard because he's in so much pain. You can't see it now because he's numb from meds, booze and all this love and attention. Our refrigerator is half-filled with serious, heavy-duty narcotics. I love him so much and he's…dying."

Her face began to dissolve. The corners of her mouth folded in as her head fell slightly forward. Her eyes filled, one tear escaping to quickly run down her left cheek. I caught it gently with the back of my right index finger as it reached her chin. Taking a bar napkin, she dabbed at her cheek. Then very tenderly, as if I had been the one crying, she wiped her tear from my finger. I felt something electric happen behind my kneecaps.

I said, "Marla, there will never be a time when you can't call me. Come to me for anything. The next few months are going to suck and you've already been through a lot. I've talked to Neil about this. I don't want to keep you from your guests, but it's important that you know this."

"They're Neil's guests. It's Neil's day. Thanks for doing all of this for him. Thank you for getting me away from it for a minute. They're lovely people, but I don't know anybody except his family. I feel comfortable with you already. After everything he's told me about you, I feel like I've known you as long as he has."

"I hope he didn't tell you everything." I really did hope he hadn't told her *everything*.

Marla's eyes were fixed on mine as I implored, "Don't go through this alone. Anytime, anywhere, anything. It's never too late or too early to dial my number."

She looked squarely into my eyes for a few seconds. She seemed unsure, a little confused. I don't think she'd ever heard anything like this before.

She said softly, "I'm sure I will need you. I'm sure of it."

This was not me bullshitting some hapless roundheels in a bar. It was not the opening salvo of a seduction siege. I meant every word and she knew it. Let there be no misunderstanding--I wanted her. But if that was ever going to happen, we all had a lot to get through first.

We talked for ten minutes. I don't remember much of the conversation. I do clearly recall that when it ended, I would have eaten broken glass for her.

I let her resume what she had been doing…trying to not think about Neil dying and schmoozing all these weirdoes. She went back to magnificently picking up after the rest of us, keeping her interaction diplomatically minimal and winning us over with her sinuous beauty and her quiet strength.

I spent the balance of the evening talking with old friends and killing defenseless brain cells with that delectable concoction of Bass and Guinness. I had abandoned any effort to be inconspicuous as my gaze lecherously followed Marla around the bar.

I had several chances to drag Neil aside so we could talk. He was drinking gin and being Neil; pinching barmaids, spinning tales and holding court as only he could. At one point he stood up on a chair to thank everyone and to reminisce a little. There were few dry eyes left when he climbed back down.

Every time Marla came within arm's reach I would try to get her to sit with a group of us but she preferred to keep her elbow rubbing (and bending) to a minimum and let it be Neil's show. As far as I had observed, she'd had only a glass or two of wine.

Confident and determined, her movements seemed effortless. She worked the room without getting bogged down in the trivia. I quite literally could not take my eyes off of her.

The dentist snuck up on me and said, "So, Scanlon…you like what you see there?"

By that point I was well lubricated and said, "What's not to like? She's frigging breathtaking. Painless…I think I'm in love."

This is always an "uh-oh" moment for my friends. Here goes Jack again. Painless cautioned, "Watch out. Neil says she is a dedicated man-eater."

By about nine o'clock the crowd had thinned out to a dozen hangers-on. I was sitting at the bar with Neil. He was working on what was probably his eighth gin and I'd had an equal number of Black and Tans.

Two old warriors, sitting in a decent tavern, manageably drunk again, arms over each other's shoulders and trying to not say goodnight. This one would be our swan song.

With me in Cleveland, busy as a pair of jumper cables at a hillbilly picnic, and him in San Diego, running out a three-month hourglass to a date with darkness, we both knew that this was the last time we would see each other. We lied.

"I'll try to get out there to see you soon, brother," I said.

"I might be back for Thanksgiving," he replied unconvincingly.

It was quiet for a few minutes. We drank. I continued to blatantly and shamelessly leer at Marla as she gathered up detritus and assisted the barmaids.

Neil was closely, with affectionate amusement, watching me watching her.

Catching me red-handed, he said, "Isn't she fucking remarkable?"

I turned to my dear friend, this man with whom I had howled at the moon and raised so much hell across the years and said, "You do realize that as soon as you're cold... I'm coming after Marla."

He squeezed my shoulder, smiled broadly and said, "I hope you do. She'd be good for you."

He had never been more wrong. But sometimes you hear only what you want to hear and I could not ignore the gravity of an imprimatur like this one.

Shortly thereafter we all said our fond farewells, and headed back to our separate realities.

I promised Neil and Marla I'd be in touch and charged them to do likewise. After hugs all around, she clung to him as if she could keep him here on Earth by the sheer power of her will. Promises were confirmed and things turned toward the new normal.

Everybody went home, hoping that, if it didn't mean too much ugliness and pain, Neil might see one more Christmas.

He didn't.

Fall came early. The oaks and maples of America's North Coast presented those of us lucky enough to live there with an outrageous palate, brisk nights and sunny, colorful days.

October flashed by like an ornate flying carpet and before we had adjusted to the end of summer, Thanksgiving was upon us.

I was busy inside my house in Cleveland, writing my third novel, editing two others, living on the small advance, and writing reviews. For a guy who had lived paycheck to paycheck for thirty years, one broken arm or catastrophic illness away from living in a public park...my life was more comfortable. I was slightly less poor.

With no woman in the house, and not having been in a committed relationship for some years, I was focused on moving my life forward. I was waiting for someone to tell me what the hell "moving forward" meant so that, in the unlikely event I ever "arrived", I'd recognize it.

I visited my daughter and son-in-law in Boston, friends in Montana and Oregon and spent a lot of time with my son and my parents in Akron, about 40 minutes away.

My spare time was spent screwing around. I re-read Conrad, Bellow, Chandler and Tom Robbins. I played poker with some pals one Wednesday a month, becoming something of a local legend as the guy with the second-best hand. I volunteered with Special Olympics. I tried to learn about wine.

There were two women on the periphery of my life: Miriam, a former co-worker now a friend and confidant; and Elaine, an RN who dabbled in local theater. Miriam was a thorny Phi Beta Kappa from Berkeley who critiqued my writing and manifested a curious jealousy of Elaine. Elaine periodically applied her professional knowledge of human anatomy to implement some robust lovemaking.

I cared for both of them but it was clear that one was a buddy, one was a lover and that was that. I wasn't after their hearts and they weren't after mine.

It was a good situation, but as I wandered aimlessly through middle age I had begun to suspect that there was something unstable about both of them. I extrapolated that these traits seemed to be universal, in slightly varying degrees, among women.

They seem incapable of abstract thought. Their wiring always needed work, shorting out and misfiring at the most inopportune and critical times. They used methods of reasoning that were glaringly unreasonable.

These revelations had turned me into less the romantic and much more the curmudgeon. I was crusty and funny. Or so they told me to my face.

I called Neil and Marla at least twice a week. Marla generally answered, but was reluctant to engage in any but the most cursory chatter before handing the phone to Neil. I was not offended, but hearing her voice always left me wanting more.

He was deteriorating. By Thanksgiving his voice was weak and it was clear the drugs were slowing him down significantly. He often praised the quality of the medicinal marijuana he was getting. If it was good enough to get praise from a man with an experience the breadth and depth of his...it must have been some killer weed.

He was having considerable difficulty getting around. The morphine had made it impossible for him to work anymore and not being able to make glass was an indignity he railed against.

Marla was still working, but missing increasingly more time so she could care for Neil. She expressed fears that her company might go under within a year. She began to take me into her trust and talked a little more openly each time I called.

On those occasions when I called and Neil was asleep, (he didn't really travel much beyond their garden anymore), she would talk at great length about their bungalow and her treasured garden.

A few years earlier, Neil had built a fence around the yard and planted a big garden in front of the tiny place. Like some weird Amazonian bird, he filled it with all manner of flowering plants, cacti and pieces of his glass to attract Marla and entice her to move in with him. It took a year, but it worked.

They sent me photos of the garden and the front of the place. I remember thinking how fortunate that they were both small people because the place looked tiny.

The garden looked to be as big as the bungalow. The photos were great, lots of brightly colored stuff outside their front window. I could tell from her descriptions that the garden was her refuge and her sanctuary. They had turned their love shack into the nearest thing to home either of them had known for a long time.

All of Neil's efforts, working so hard to make it beautiful for her, fortified her love for him. What I got from him during those last months was bravado, brutal honesty and stories of her beauty, her strength and her explosive instability.

What I got from her was lamentation about his pain and detailed descriptions of the bungalow. Always, the bungalow.

The garden was keeping her together. If she wasn't working or shopping or tending to Neil, she was playing in her beloved magical garden... digging in the dirt, grooming, and watering. "Putzing" she called it

This scenario, this whole phenomenon of Neil finding a love nest and feathering it elaborately to attract females had been his modus operandi for years. Although it had proven largely successful as a method of wooing mates, in the long term it had a dark history of generally being disastrous for his partners.

As far as I knew, his first wife was living in her car and with assorted family around the country. His second wife, a painter Neil brought to America from Budapest, was living above a biker bar in Key West and determinedly drinking herself into an early grave.

Marla had left behind two married daughters, some grandkids and a good paying gig in North Carolina to be with Neil in San Diego. This was a definite pattern and I worried about her.

Neil's Bacchanalian lifestyle caused his painful death and it had certainly led to the detrimental treatment and disposition of some of the women in his past.

There was also the matter of "the freak show" as I came to call it.

Since college, he had encouraged the attentions of the most bizarre and dangerous people he could dig up. They had a way of finding him and he reveled in the mayhem and drama they added to his already edgy life.

Former porn stars, ex-convicts, recovering junkies, thieves, bums and losers of every stripe found their way into Neil's world and he welcomed them all. He never met a person he wouldn't get drunk or high with. He trusted too many people and he was now paying for these misplaced trusts.

I'd met a number of these players over the course of my friendship with him. I am not a fearful man. I consider myself an adventurous sort. But some of Neil's hangers-on were just plain scary. Not the kind of people you would want to share a table or a cab with, they all ended up stealing from him.

Neil had formed a whole new squadron of edgy wing nuts and pharmaceutically altered knuckle-draggers in San Diego. Or, rather, one had formed around him.

There was Enid, the Danish immigrant neighbor who mowed the lawns at the bungalow complex, lived on the dole and was obsessed with Neil. Enid was always angling for his glass.

There was Sasha who had known Neil for a long time, currently sleeping in his cousin's garage and supporting himself by hitchhiking around the country taking surveys and doing "petition work." Sasha seemed to be spending increasingly more time around the bungalow as Neil's demise drew near. Marla described him as, "a little weird but loyal to Neil" and "a big, gentle guy with bad motor skills." What I heard was "burned-out drifter."

There was Marla's son, Ben. I recall Neil's visceral anger with Marla for bringing Ben to California. He had described him as a "parasite." She described him as "Twenty-two going on fourteen."

They had both talked about the rest of the cast of Southern California-style wack jobs: the security guard across the street who talked to himself and had no ID; the perennially angry mailman; the next door neighbors, resentful of the fence and garden; the members of Ben's band and their girlfriends; the family of nudists down the street.

It was a non-stop surreal circus. It had never been anything less with Neil. I was not swayed by Marla's insistence that she loved it that way.

I would soon join the menagerie.

2

In my favorite verse of Dylan's "Buckets of Rain", he sings the praises of a woman's smile, her touch, her speech, her allure and ends with the observation that she is bringing him nothing but misery.

Although I believe that to sum up a person's life in one sentence is callous...I have always been a fool for love. The fuel for this masochistic behavior is a wicked brew of misplaced trust and undiluted testosterone. The spark is maddeningly complicated females.

I invite misfortune by aligning myself with women who harbor complex self-esteem problems. Part of their baggage results from horrific childhood experiences, some from abuse and mistreatment at the hands of past husbands and lovers, and some is due to lack of pride or issues concerning physical appearance.

It is true that most of the women I've fallen for I have encountered at points in their lives when they were down and confused. I find these qualities to be irresistible. I'm not a predator. If they just happen to be attractive and bright, then I shift into another gear and curiosity becomes desire. Desire brings to the fore the most ruinous of my weaknesses – denial.

I have an innate need to comfort people. I spot a damsel in distress and am compelled to bind her wounds. I am good at it and I am sincere about it. I have often compared myself to an off-ramp on the freeway, "Rest Area Jack." They pull their leaky, clanking lives into my station. I fix the flat, top off the fluids, check the belts, wash, wax and vacuum.

I get them back in college, help them find work, rebuild their confidence, surround them with an atmosphere of affection and security. I offer sanctuary, respect and the time and space for them to stop spinning and come back into the world.

I fall in love with them. They tell me they love me. They call me "Honey", "Sweetie", "Baby." They tell me their feelings, their pasts, their dreams, fulfilled and crushed...the deepest, darkest secret things.

Four weeks, four months, four years later... they are gone. All. Gone.

I am not warped enough to believe that sex is last on this list. I have repeatedly allowed my genitalia to act as a divining rod. But I never have been unfaithful in thought, word or deed to a partner.

I have struggled with the unappealing concept that these impulses reflect less altruism and more my primal urge for fornication. I have a robust libido and a clear conscience about its application. Two consenting adults entered into these alliances. Although they are dynamic, sensuous intermezzos, they all end with me coming home to an empty house and making the bed alone.

The awful part is that I did love them all. I always think it will last. More precisely...I never think about it ending. This, I am told, is the definition of denial.

I would soon willingly transition from stern critic of those who live in denial to an accomplished and dedicated practitioner.

Marla and I spoke more often and more freely now. She came to accept that my concern for her and for Neil was genuine and she opened up to me.

By December, Neil was sounding weaker and less lucid each time I called. Marla revealed that he was only taking calls from me, his immediate family and Jenna Lehman, a mutual friend from Monterey.

Jenna was another treasured old schoolmate. A noted and widely published shrink, she was planning to visit Neil. Marla said Neil had rallied in anticipation of Jenna's visit.

Jenna was a real force of nature in her own right. Equal parts Tinkerbelle, Anna Freud and Ethel Merman, she is caring and flamboyant. We have bolstered each other through rugged valleys over the years and formed what turned out to be my first real platonic friendship with a woman. I named my daughter after her.

She called me on her way back home to Monterey after two days with Neil and Marla. She told me Neil was close to the end. Although the three of them went to brunch once and talked extensively, she said he was failing rapidly.

"He's yellow, more like orange. He is very thin and has a lot of trouble getting around...very unsteady on his feet. And his concentration, which was never much good anyway, is continually broken by the pain and the meds. He's dying, Jack. It is just so sad. He is like a little old Indian man."

"Should I fly out there?" I asked.

"If you're both happy with the good-bye you shared in Cleveland, then I'd leave it at that. Marla is amazing, one of the strongest women I've ever met. But you can see that she is exhausted."

"She's one of the sexiest I've ever met."

"Darling, you really are a pig. She told me Neil enjoys your calls and looks forward to them. She finds your voice consoling, so stay in touch with her. She's really going to need you when this is all over."

We talked a while longer, but there was really little more to say.

The cancer was killing Neil quickly now. The level of his pain spiked, as did the application of painkillers. Hospice people were now involved and we all knew what that meant.

Neil's deterioration was such that, by mid-December, I asked Marla if I should stop calling. I sometimes felt it was too much effort for him.

"No." she quickly said. "As rarely as he feels like talking, he looks forward to your calls. They take a lot out of him, but you seem to wake him up and get him interested. The rest of it is just pain and managing pain. Oh God, Jack...I don't know if I can do this."

I reassured her,"You're already doing it and you are magnificent. Hang in and remember what I told you at the party. Use me."

"I see why he kept you and Jenna close after all these years."

"He's always had questionable taste in friends."

Marla's laugh was small but genuine. "I'll need that sense of humor of yours later. You can always make me laugh."

"Anytime, kiddo. I'm at your disposal. Is the old boy up to a little chat?"

"He's sleeping. He sleeps in spurts of an hour or so. I can wake him"

"No, no. Tell him I called and I'll try back later."

A small silence and then, "I am so frightened, Jack. He is so weak and in so much discomfort. No matter how he moves, he can't get comfortable. It's like watching him being tortured."

"Don't be frightened. You have lots of support, ready to help whenever you need us. Are you sure you don't want me to come out there?"

"Thanks but, no. We'll handle it. Will you please call later?"

"I promise. You stay strong, OK? He needs you now more than ever and you are the best thing that ever happened to him."

She then said, softly, "What do people call you? I mean…do you prefer Jack, Jackie…John?"

I said, "I'm one of those lucky people who actually likes his name. My given name is John, but I've always been Jack."

She said, "Would you mind if I called you Johnny? It just seems right."

It was like honey poured over bells. Johnny. It was warm caramel in her mouth, as if in a language I'd never heard.

I said, "You can call me anything you like. Johnny sounds good to me."

I could hear her smile through her weariness. "Bye, Johnny. And thanks."

"Bye, Marla."

I spoke to Neil a few more times. Marla called me on the nineteenth of December to tell me he was fading very quickly. I spoke to him for perhaps five minutes. I joked with him. I choose to believe he knew I was there. His responses were slurred and disjointed. He could no longer speak.

She marveled that he actually tried to talk at all and told me, "I think he's leaving very soon. I'll stay in touch."

On the twentieth she called me briefly to tell me she didn't think he'd make it through the night. I did not ask to talk to him.

In all the time I spent with Marla she never referred to Neil's "death" or to him having "passed away." To her it was always, "After Neil left."

Although the hospice folks did what they could to mitigate Neil's suffering and members of his coterie of kooks tried to assist, Marla had been his principal caretaker through his last six months; bathing, feeding, changing dressings on the oozing sores of his legs, changing his soiled clothing, hearing him cry out in pain. When times demand it, we either rise to the challenge or crumble. When it really counted, this woman did not waiver.

Midday on the twenty-first, I got an email from Marla, sent to myself and about a dozen others. Neil was gone. He had breathed his last in her arms.

She and Sasha had moved him, washed his body, dressed him in orange Keds, turquoise shorts and one of his trademark Hawaiian shirts and laid him out on the sofa to await the arrival of Eva, Neil's estranged daughter. The people who would handle his cremation had been notified.

I called that evening and Marla was, predictably, a mess. Neil's body was at the mortuary, Sasha was still hanging around, Enid had been caterwauling and making a pest of herself all day and Eva and her husband had just arrived on a one-way ticket from Seattle, giving Marla no clue as to what they wanted or how long they intended to stay at the bungalow.

She was having a cigarette, walking up and down the sidewalk out front. Her voice was as fragile as a junkie's promise. Hit by successive waves of abandonment, panic and utter exhaustion...it was clear she was just barely hanging on.

"Oh, god, Johnny. I can't do this. I can't do this. When I really need to be alone, all these people are here. I need to rest. I only met Neil's daughter once and she's a weirdo. Her husband never speaks. I'm letting them sleep in my bed and I'm on the couch. I know they are really here for the glass. And they won't say how long they plan to be here. What am I going to do? I can't do this. I have to have space to grieve."

I spoke softly and calmly, asked a few questions, made her take three deep breaths, and gave her the best advice I could. She and I had gone over Neil's Last Will and Testament some days prior and it was simple; everything went to Marla.

"Don't commit to anything, don't give Eva anything you want to keep. Call me when you want to talk, day or night."

I made a small joke that evoked a small, weary laugh. She said through tears, "You have to pull me through this, Johnny. You can always make me laugh and you're always calm when I'm not. I don't have any friends here. All these people are Neil's friends."

"You're not alone. Remember what I said...no fear of this daughter. All the glass and everything in that house belongs to you and nobody else."

"I'm afraid, Johnny. I don't know what she wants and I'm so tired."

I felt impotent, frustrated. Not being able to take her in my arms was terrible.

"Talk to her like you would talk to any grieving daughter, not like an adversary. She's as confused as you are. Don't see her as your enemy. Try to get some rest and call me when you can."

"I don't know if I can do this."

"I will be with you every step of the way, kiddo. Take it five minutes at a time. Take it thirty seconds at a time, if you have to. Be as strong as you were for Neil. Pace yourself. Picture my arm around your shoulder."

"You're an angel."

"Jesus...you could not *possibly* be more wrong."

Another tiny laugh. "Can I call you later?"

"You can call me at four AM. You can call me every five minutes. You can stay on the phone for six hours if you need to. Get some rest, take three more deep breaths and stop thinking so much."

She said, "That's exactly what Neil always told me...'You think too much.' I am going to be leaning on you."

"I can handle it. Let's hear three deep breaths."

"I'll do that in a few minutes."

"Let's do them now." I insisted, "In through the nose, deeply and all the way out through the mouth. Let's go. Number one..."

She gave me three good, long breaths. I could hear the exhaustion in her voice but also the relaxed smile as she said, "Thank you. I'll call you later."

"Marla?"

"Yes?"

"Keep that beautiful chin up. Don't go blue on me now. Promise me."

"I promise, Johnny."

I dug through my music and found Albinoni's Adagio in G Minor. I poured three fingers of Maker's Mark, put on the disc and allowed the Berlin Philharmonic to ring a few tears out of me.

He was really gone. It's always a shock to hear someone has died. But in Neil's case, no surprise. He had lived fully, if not wisely, on borrowed time for years, and during the journey created some of the most unique, bold and exotic blown and sculpted glasswork ever made.

Next morning Marla called and left me a message. She was effusive in her thanks for my advice.

"Johnny, I did everything you said, just the way you told me to and everything went beautifully. I can't thank you enough. You saved my sanity and I just wanted to tell you how great you are. I wouldn't have made it this far without you. You are awesome. Thanks again and I'll talk to you soon."

When she called, we talked about Neil's daughter who was finally heading back to Washington with plans to return in the spring. We discussed the Holidays. She had cancelled plans to visit her daughters and grandchildren in North Carolina for Christmas. "It's just too much, Johnny."

We talked about Neil. She was lost and heartbroken and I guiltily coveted my role as life preserver. She was in need of guidance and friendship. I gladly did my best to provide these things for her.

Christmas passed, as did New Year's, with little hoopla from my corner. I had reached a point in my life, as so many right-thinking adults had, where Christmas was little more than a cloying, grinding pain in the ass.

Marla and I became more comfortable with each other. She said she loved my voice as much as I enjoyed hearing hers. We consoled, amused and helped each other. She was eager for my advice and counsel. We talked and sent emails every day, often several times a day.

I had been in contact with Jenna who suggested that it might be good for Marla to get out of that sad little bungalow and spend some time with friends.

Marla had not been exaggerating when she said she had no friends, only the borderline psychos Neil had left behind. Jenna called Marla, with my blessing, and pitched the idea that she come visit me for a few days.

As Jenna later related it to me, she told Marla, "Jack knew Neil longer than any of us. You need to talk about it with someone and Jack's a wonderful listener. He's a true gentleman under that cheesy desperado facade he puts on when he's chasing a woman. It would be healthy for you to spend some time away from that tiny place. Go where you can be still and safe and valued for a while."

Marla called me to talk about it. She was hesitant. I did not push but told her that I agreed with Jenna. I further reassured her that I would not try to jump her bones. I felt a responsibility to help her regroup and a powerful sense that I could be instrumental in getting her through this awful time. Go figure.

"I am going to be pretty busy so you'll have as much time to yourself as you need. If you want more company, I will change my schedule. Come to Cleveland. You'll have your own bedroom, lots of quiet. Give your head a rest."

She said, "Are you sure I wouldn't be in your way?"

Knowing that Neil had been a real terror in the kitchen, I asked her, "Can you cook?"

"Of course I can cook, silly."

"Are you excessively flatulent?"

"I wouldn't call it excessive." she chuckled.

"Do you juggle knives or set small fires when you're nervous?"

"No! God, you make me laugh."

"Then you will not be in my way."

So it came to pass that during the second half of January, a few days before my birthday and more than a month after Neil's death, I was driving through a frosty Sunday evening toward Cleveland Hopkins Airport to pick up Marla. She would be my guest for five nights, leaving the following Friday morning.

She had sworn me to secrecy. Neil had family close by and she didn't want them to get wind of her visit. She said she never wanted anyone to think she was a "floozy." I filed that one away for further inquiry.

I was five minutes from the airport when Jenna called, asked me to keep her updated. She joked, "Marla is very, very fragile right now. Try to not molest the poor woman, will you?"

I said. "I will be the perfect gentleman. You can trust me, you know that."

"Yes, darling, you are a prince. But you are a pervert, too. I have seen this girl and I know keeping it platonic is not going to be easy for you."

"What am I, chopped liver? Who's to say she won't grab my tush at the airport and demand a turn on 'Mister Johnny's Wild Ride' right there on the baggage carousel?"

"I'm hanging up now."

"Love you."

"Love you, too. You're doing a good thing. Have fun."

There was a steady lake-effect snow settling in. The forecast was for three or four inches by the next afternoon. Getting out of the car at the airport, I felt an odd, unsettling mix of opening night jitters and protective instincts.

Big stuff, here. Big stuff, I kept telling myself.

"Holy shit..." I thought as I entered the baggage claim area, "What must be going through *her* mind right now?"

I checked the monitors to find her flight information. It looked like she had landed while I was parking the car so, I wouldn't have a long wait.

I stood a good forty feet back from the front phalanx of greeters. I unbuttoned my jacket and tried to look nonchalant. I had a moment of concern when I couldn't conjure a distinct mental picture of Marla's face. It had been four months, after all. I knew every nuance of her bewitching voice, but suddenly I worried that I wouldn't recognize her.

After fifty or sixty people had come down the concourse, merging with friends and families, the flow of passengers stopped. Maybe she'd had a last minute change of heart and bolted before she boarded the flight from San Diego. I was sure she was sitting alone in her kitchen, trying to bring herself to call me.

Then I saw a form that looked like it might be her. Her hair was a little more auburn, less brown than I'd remembered. I'd forgotten how tiny she really was. She had lost weight.

She came down the last one hundred feet of the long corridor with a furrowed brow looking nervous, almost agitated. She got closer and spotted me. Her smile of relief and recognition ignited mine.

She was pulling a small, wheeled bag and carrying a big purse. She wore a short denim skirt, low-heeled shoes and a red silk blouse under a suede jacket. She had everything necessary to pull off this look in the middle of a Cleveland winter. But her face belied a "fish-out-of-water" unease.

We walked up to each other and embraced, holding on for a few seconds longer than that first time at Gilhooley's. The top of her head met my cheekbone. I felt her relax, release, as if she were growing lighter in my arms. She put her face next to mine, softly said "Hi" into my ear and pecked me lightly on the cheek.

I made the usual "how was the flight, did you eat, how ya feeling" chatter that nervous men make in the presence of beauties getting off planes.

"God...you look terrific," I managed. "I'm glad you decided to come."

"I've lost almost fifteen pounds." She gave me the quick once-over and said, "You look pretty good yourself."

She had not checked any luggage, so I took the handle of her bag and we headed out of the building.

On the way to the car, we kept looking at each other and smiling. It all seemed so unlikely but felt so right. I was very much aware of the pride I felt as every guy we passed looked at her.

She shivered and said, "Wow, I haven't seen snow in a long time."

"Fifteen pounds? Where did you find fifteen pounds to lose? Seriously, you look absolutely great." And she did, though I could now see that her face was thinner. She was stunning.

"You're so sweet. It's all the stress. I haven't had a real meal in weeks."

"It's early. How about we stop somewhere for a bite? Little Italy, Brother's, Great Lakes Brewery. There's a nice little place not far from me, The Larchmere. What are you hungry for?"

She touched my arm as I tossed her bag in the trunk. "That's the problem. I don't feel like eating...ever. I just have no interest in food. Would you be mad if we just went to your place so I can slip out of these shoes?"

I have always been a leg man. Holding the door open as Marla got in the car, I got my first real look at her gams. Tanned, toned and smooth. Perfect. This week was going to be a real test. I resisted the impulse to blurt, "Baby, you can slip out of whatever you want. No need to stop at the shoes on my account."

What I *did* say was, "We'll get a fire going in the fireplace, pour a little wine, have some cheese and fruit and let you unspool. Sound good?"

She grabbed my hand and chirped, "You have a *fireplace*?"

"And wine. And hot and cold running water. And a place to rest your feet."

She hit me with a smile that made me want to write bad checks. "Sounds so good," she purred.

It was near sundown and Sunday traffic was light. The flurries had turned to real snow. I made my way back onto I-71 and headed home. About halfway there, her phone rang. It was her son and she seemed less than thrilled.

"Yes, Ben...I just got here, Ben...How much do you need? No. I just gave you fifty dollars this morning...well, then don't go to Laguna...Honey, I'm still in the clothes I left San Diego in and I don't want to talk about this…Ben, no. I'm with Neil's friend, Johnny...I explained all this to you yesterday." After several more minutes of the same she hung up.

I didn't ask any questions. She volunteered, "My son, Ben. I love him more than anything, but, Jesus, he's such a dumbass sometimes."

Taking our time and enjoying our conversation, we got to my place in twenty-five minutes.

In Northeastern Ohio, if the weather dorks tell you three to four inches, it might just as easily be hip-deep by sunrise. It was really coming down now in big, slow flakes. I pulled the car up the driveway and into the garage.

The house was a drafty old beauty and Marla was wowed. "This is your house? It's beautiful, Johnny."

To myself, and a few close friends, I jokingly refer to my house as "Windfall Manor." About four years before, I had been the beneficiary of two unexpected and astonishing infusions of capital. These windfalls provided me the means with which to buy my first house.

The wealthy mother of an old friend died and left me, to my shock and amazement (and to the bitter chagrin of her family), ten thousand dollars. She had always doted on me and been a good friend of my mother's.

Less than a month later, a group of twenty-four employees from the DIY store split a Lottery prize of just under a million. My four-dollar investment netted me, after taxes, close to thirty grand. I paid off my credit cards and my car, bought my parents a huge TV and put most of the rest down on the house.

Only a handful of people knew the whole story of my good fortune. The rest of the world attributed this new lifestyle to income from my work as a writer. I was happy to let people believe what they wanted to believe. Truth told...I was hanging onto the part-time job at a DIY store and still scrambling to meet the bills each month.

"Yup," I answered Marla's inquiry. "Just 316 more payments and it's all mine. You should see it with grass and leaves. Let's get inside and get those shoes off. We'll get you settled then I'll give you the five-cent tour."

The house is typical of North Coast brick and stone homes built in the Forties and Fifties. It sits back sixty feet from the street, two massive beech trees dominating the front yard, a border of twelve-foot arborvitae running along both sides of the property and lots of juniper below the windows along the front of the house.

With old-fashioned radiator steam heat and poor insulation, it was a bitch to warm through the raw Cleveland winters. But the place suited me from the first time I walked through it and I felt at ease there.

The front door is solid oak and has a small leaded glass window. The foyer walls are oak, the floors are oak, the stairs and railings to the second floor are oak. Oak throughout. As you enter, the living room is on the right, dining room on the left, stairway to the second floor straight ahead.

The kitchen is through the dining room. There's a half bath off the kitchen and stairs leading to the full, finished basement. Off the living room are a sunroom and my office. There's a full bathroom adjacent to the office. More oak.

At the insistence of my friend, Miriam, I had grabbed two bunches of flowers earlier in the day to stick around the house. I put one in the living room, one in the bedroom where Marla would sleep.

Marla had dropped everything on the sofa, walked out of her shoes and was rejuvenating herself with buoyant, cheery "oohs" and "aahs" and "ohmygoshes" all through the place. She was a toucher, this one, gently running her fingers over fabric and wood.

"And flowers!" she laughed.

Putting some kindling into the fireplace, I heard Marla make a sound that was part purr, part growl when she turned from the dining room and saw my kitchen. I listened and smiled as she turned the water on and off, opened the fridge, peeked into a few drawers and cupboards, asked me where I kept the coffee.

I hung up our jackets and joined her in the kitchen. She was beaming. The first floor had met with her approval. It made me feel good, seeing her happy and a bit more relaxed.

"Oh, am I ever going to cook you some meals, buddy. This kitchen is four times the size of mine. Neil would have loved it."

"I'll call Burger King and tell them they can close early this week." I opened my arms and gave her a short, friendly hug.

"I'm so glad you're here." I meant it. Already the place was transformed, alive in a new way with her energy.

"I'm glad I'm here, too."

I led her to a small rack holding a few bottles of wine, showed her the glasses and the corkscrew. "Take your pick, pour two glasses and I'll meet you at the fireplace."

The living room is big. It had taken nearly everything I had in my old apartment to furnish this one room.

Two large, soft chairs, my recliner ("The Big Chair"), a loveseat and a long sofa. The rest of the décor I had turned over to the amazing women in my life--friends, family, and neighbors. They picked out drapes and rugs and vases. Left on my own, there would likely have been a lot of plastic milk crates, beanbags and a futon.

The fireplace is on the immediate right as you enter the house, so when you sit on the loveseat or sofa, you're facing the fire and the front yard. There are two six-foot high windows on either side of the fireplace. It's my favorite spot in the house.

I set a match to the kindling in the grate. In thirty seconds it was popping and snapping. The elemental aroma of smoke moved something primitive in me. I was in full hunter-gatherer mode and once the fire was sufficient to trust, I confidently tossed on a couple pieces of well-seasoned beech. The flue was drawing perfectly, the bark had burned off and the wood began to catch. I had done well and the woman would be impressed.

Just then Marla tipped on bare toes to my side and handed me a glass of wine. "I hope Cabernet is OK."

"Always."

"Well, here's to the snow...and to us."

"And to a restful week for you."

We touched glasses and she asked if she could see the upstairs. I grabbed her suitcase and we started up the staircase.

She asked, "I saw some glass pieces. Are they Neil's?"

"I have six pieces of Neil's stuff; two penguins, a Christmas ornament, a candle holder, a bird and one that requires a little explanation."

With great interest, "I saw the candle holder and the bird."

I took her to a sideboard in the dining room where the round, tri-colored ornament sat in the top of an old beer stein. "I've seen a few of these before," she remarked.

I was aware of how very careful we were being to avoid touching each other.

At the top of the stairs was the master bedroom with its full bath. To the left and right, two more bedrooms, the left unfurnished, the right with an inflatable bed, a desk, chair and nightstand. At the end of the hall to the right, another full bath.

I opened the door to the master bedroom and put her bag on the bed.

"This is your room. Clean sheets, clean towels, king-size four-poster bed and a nice view of the back yard. Extra blankets, pillows and towels in the closet."

It was a big room with high ceilings, crown molding, beautiful overhead fixtures and French doors leading to a small balcony. I had scrubbed the bathroom till it shone like a diamond in a goat's ass. Her response was what I had hoped. "Oh...Johnny."

Marla walked all around the bedroom, smoothed the bedspread, looked out the French doors, touched the books in the built-in cases. She breathed hard on one of the windows of the balcony door and slowly drew two eyes and a smile in the fog she'd made. She stood there for a long few seconds, lost in thought.

On my dresser, she found the two glass penguins. I told Marla that at some point in my youth I had expressed my affection and fascination with penguins. The word got out and I now had about thirty penguins of all types. I am not a collector by nature, but I seem to have a lot of penguins.

"Tell me a little about these."

"The small clear one, Neil let me take the gather from the oven and pull the glass to shape the wings and beak. He did the rest. This big, heavy one, with black and white inside the clear glass outer shell, he and his ex-wife made for me as a birthday gift about ten years ago. It's the king of my penguins."

She held them gently, reverently. "And the sixth piece?" she asked.

"It's on the bookcase in the bathroom."

We went into the bath, where she caressed the towels and looked into the shower that was inside an old porcelain, claw foot tub.

Inquisitive, she was learning the terrain and making sounds of approval. Marla approached the bookcase. She saw Neil's glass and drew a sharp breath. She stopped dead in her tracks and seemed reluctant to approach it.

I explained, "There are seven deadly sins; Lust, Envy, Gluttony, Sloth, Greed, Anger and Pride. Neil planned to make all seven. This one is Lust. I don't know if he ever finished the other six or not. He gave it to me years ago for safekeeping. But things kept getting in the way and the last time we talked about it, I think he had only finished four or five."

It was a large piece for one of Neil's freestanding sculpted works, weighing easily thirty-five pounds. Blood red, cerulean blue with flecks of yellow spread throughout, "Lust" could not be ignored. It was a starkly minimalist rendition of two human bodies intertwined in the unmistakable act of lovemaking. It was a powerful object. I had always viewed it as a totem and it was the most prized object in the house. I was sure it had some value on the market, perhaps increased now with Neil's demise, but it was not for sale.

Marla stood motionless and silent for a good thirty seconds. She tentatively, as if it might bite, moved a half step closer to the piece and finally, slowly put her fingertips on it. "No," she whispered. "He finished them."

She seemed shaken and I asked, "Are you OK?"

After another long silence, her hand still delicately on the piece, she said softly, "I think I'd like to take that shower now. But I have lots of questions about this piece."

"Sure. I've made some space for you in the dresser and the medicine cabinet."

She turned to me, smiled contentedly and said, "It's perfect, Johnny."

"If you want to shower now, go ahead. Or we can have some wine and sit by the fire for a while."

"Yeah," fatigue in her voice. "A hot shower would be great. And you can go play with fire."

She had been through a lot in the four months since I'd last seen her. She was thin, tired. Her boyfriend had died in her arms. She'd been left to fend for herself in a community of freaks. It was seventy-four degrees when she left home. It was twenty-four degrees in Cleveland. She'd been on the move for seven hours. She needed a little R&R and a warm, comfortable bed.

"Give me a holler if you need anything."

"I think you've thought of everything."

I closed the bedroom door on my way out, then stopped short in the hallway.

"Marla?" I called through the door.

"Yes?"

"There's a big, poofy bathrobe hanging on the bathroom door if you need it."

"Thanks, Sweetie."

Knowing that a woman requires time in the bathroom, I went downstairs, put on some music, poked the fire and settled into The Big Chair with an old copy of <u>Another Roadside Attraction</u>.

The chair and sofa sit at right angles to each other; the sofa facing the fire and the chair facing the right end of the sofa, a modest coffee table in front of the sofa.

It only took fifteen minutes to have a great fire going. The room was toasty and the sounds and smells of the fire permeated the house. About ten minutes later I heard the shower shut off.

Six pages and two sips of wine after that, the bedroom door opened. Marla walked out and started down the staircase. She said, "Wow! What a beautiful fire. I'm impressed."

I looked up from my book. I think...but could not swear...that I said something like "How was your shower?"

I am fairly certain she said something in response. I know her lips moved. But if she spoke to me, I heard only the pounding of blood through my head.

She had my bathrobe over her left arm and a bottle of some kind of lotion in her right hand. She was wearing baggy green socks and a lime green terrycloth thing. It had elastic at the top, resting just above her breasts and it came to about two inches above her knees. It was basically a towel, stitched up the back. Had she been six feet tall, it would have been a tube-top.

Her dark jungle of hair was still half wet. Looking at her shoulders, arms, legs and ankles...I suddenly understood the real meaning of "petite."

45

I was fully extended in The Big Chair. She passed between the sofa and me, touched my bare foot and squeezed my big toe. "God, that is a great bathroom, Johnny. I feel much better," and she stood in the light of the fire, warming her back.

I, meanwhile, had lost the power of speech.

She smelled delicious. Coconut and mint. Scrubbed squeaky clean and glowing. Fresh. New. It had been a long time since I'd known the complex pleasure of having a beautiful woman in my home. I was now certain that her body was as perfect as I had imagined. And if I never saw all of it, this would have to do.

I finally managed to say, "That is...uh...some outfit there, kiddo."

"Oh, this? Well, I love your robe, but after that hot shower it was too warm. I always put this old thing on after my shower."

She took a sip of wine and sat down at the end of the sofa nearest me. She removed her socks, leaned forward and shook her hair from side to side. "God, I hate my hair. It's like a black girl's hair...so damn thick and curly. I spend half an hour every day, brushing and straightening it with a hot comb."

She squirted a big glob of white lotion into the palm of her left hand, rubbed her hands together and began to massage it into her right leg, from her foot to her calf to her thigh and back to her foot, slowly and thoroughly. All the while Marla was demurely cautious to sit turned, her knees slightly away from me.

After what must have been several mute minutes, I managed to croak, "You're killin' me."

She sat up quickly with a look of concern, "What's wrong?"

"If you're gonna wear that thing and do this every night, all bets are off."

"Oh, grow up." She flashed me a big smile and winked. "Jenna assures me that you're a gentleman. I feel safe here with you." With that she began to languorously apply lotion to her other magnificent leg.

"Honest to god, Marla...seriously...you are **killing** me over here."

"Oh, alright, I'm almost done," she laughed. She put lotion on her arms, elbows and neck. She took another swallow of wine. "The fire is so pretty. Thanks."

This was a woman fully in touch with her own allure and sensuality and aware of the perquisites and pitfalls incumbent with wielding that kind of power.

"You are a breathtakingly beautiful woman."

"No. Stop it," not scolding with her small, almost childlike voice.

Marla and I spent the next six hours talking, picking at berries and grapes and Brie and crackers. We polished off the bottle of red and started a bottle of white. I tossed on two nice pieces of maple and the fire hissed and popped.

For six golden hours there was no world outside. We were warm and safe and smiling.

I felt a sensation of nourishment when I made her laugh. She needed to laugh and she did it in a way that energized and rewarded both of us.

We talked about her son (a parasitic nitwit), her job (she was pulling down fifty grand per annum and was convinced the company would fold by the end of the year), our friendship (it seemed filled with promise), the "freak show" (they were wearing her down, but she needed to hold onto some of them out of necessity), and Neil.

She claimed that there were times she wasn't sure she really wanted to go on living without him, but those feelings had dissipated in the past week. She generously gave me some of the credit for that and thanked me lavishly for my support and for helping her to find strength.

"You probably saved my life, Johnny. That sexy, smooth baritone voice in the night, your jokes, your encouragement, your excellent advice. Just always being there. I think you really are saving my life."

We told Neil stories. I saved a few. She seemed a little surprised that he had talked about her temper. She brushed that aside with bemusement. "Oh sure, we had disagreements. But Neil and I never really fought. It was more like a debate."

This triggered a small but clarion bullshit alarm. Neil argued with everybody and he had often described their raging and rancorous battles. I let it pass.

I told her the truth about my perennially precarious financial straits, how I got the house and a little about my past life and loves. She told me about her job, her family and her sorrow.

I brought up the topic of the Seven Deadly Sin pieces, but she demurred. "Can we maybe talk about that later?" she asked and I let the subject drop.

We spoke a little about Neil's drinking and the physical problems it caused. Neil had told me more than once of doctors' warnings that if he did not stop drinking, it would kill him. Marla nodded, but did not comment. She told me that he seemed to handle it pretty well and that her participation was mostly social.

"I have a glass of wine or two in the evening. Occasionally more. But it's not a problem."

We had an open and warm exchange. She revealed, "I feel like I've known you for a long time." Mostly, I just let her talk.

She made three trips onto the back deck for a cigarette during the evening. She said she normally only smoked a few a day, but had been smoking more "since Neil went away."

Marla shed a few tears that evening. Periodically, she sat silently for several moments and her smoky brown eyes glazed over every time she mentioned Neil.

The disconnect was evident. It seemed clear that her mind was back on the couch in that bungalow, Neil slipping away, his head in her lap and her tears falling on him. Kissing him and stroking his head. Neil breathing that last, weak half-breath. Her recalled terror and emptiness were palpable and genuine.

Midnight came and passed. The fire had died down to a few quiet orange coals under the ash. I would stir them one last time and, in a few minutes, close the flue. We both yawned big, noisy yawns at the same time and laughed.

"Time for bed?" I asked

"Yeah, that's probably a good idea." She stood up. "It'll take me an hour to get the knots out of my hair."

Topping the stairs, as I entered the bedroom and opened the linen closet. I said, "OK. I'll grab a blanket and my pillow."

She looked at me blankly, "What for?"

"I think I'll sleep on the sofa instead of the inflatable in the guest room."

Her jaw set and her voice was softly stern, "That's silly. I'm not going to throw you out of your own bed. I'll sleep on the sofa."

"No, you are my extra special guest and you'll sleep in a proper bed while you're here. I've slept on this sofa many times and it's very comfy," I lied.

"Why does *anybody* have to sleep on the sofa? Is there some reason we can't sleep in the same bed? It's huge. Don't you trust me?" She was indignant. "Maybe we could just put a big board down the middle of the bed."

"It's not you I'm worried about." I was being honest.

With a look of impatience she said, "What does or doesn't happen in that bed is up to me. Do you really mean to tell me you've never been in bed with a woman and not had sex with her?"

"Not yet. So...I'll take the couch and you'll sleep in the bed. Alright?"

"Do you mean you don't trust yourself? Are you some kind of rapist?"

Neither of us could keep a straight face. We had a good laugh at this sleepy, goofy exchange.

"OK, Mister Irresistible. I'll take the bed, but I think this is stupid. There have been several times I've slept in a bed with a man and not had sex with him."

"Was I one of them?"

"Oh, forgodsake. I still say it's silly for you to sleep on the couch."

"If you play your cards right, you'll see me do all kinds of silly shit during the course of our friendship."

She liked that and gave me the thousand-watt smile. "Thanks so much, Johnny. You're a good friend."

"I'm really glad to have you here."

"Thanks."

I turned to walk out of the bedroom.

"Good night. See you for coffee."

"Sleep well, butterfly," she said softly.

Every life is a dance. Some wrenchingly short, some agonizingly long.

We enter dancing and only with the greatest of good fortune do we leave the same way.

Light on our feet or crashing around on two left feet, we all dance.

Fuzzy spots in a petri dish and whales; dogs and snakes and peacocks, mice and men and jaguars...we dance.

From a Polish wedding to the running of the bulls. From the high school prom to boot camp to pall bearer...we dance.

The mystique of dancing permeates every culture, every language.

We danced in our caves.

Fast dance, slow dance. We dance around a problem. First dance. Last dance.

Ladies Choice.

We dance with death. We offer our dances to the gods.

Some dance feverishly, some futilely, some divinely.

Some hate to dance and some live for "The Dance." Some are fancy dancers, some are dancing fools.

When a man and woman meet, when there is electricity present at their first contact, the man and the woman enter into a dance.

Marla's partner in a gruesome *danse macabre* had slipped away to parts unknown.

I felt weightless, unencumbered. I felt bewitched, graceful.

I was dancing with Marla. She was dancing with me.

I was a cranky knot by six AM and finally, softly cursing, got up to put on the coffee.

The sofa was narrow and hard and I got maybe two hours of real sleep. I'd have to try the air mattress in the spare room tonight.

Old houses have a music all their own. Once you learn the music, you can tune in to movements in other parts of the structure. From any place in the house I could tell whether the sound of running water was the washer, a toilet, a shower, *which* shower, a sink or the dishwasher.

The third, eighth and tenth steps going up the stairs from the living room (sixth, eighth and thirteenth coming down) squeaked, unless you were light or walked on the very edges of the steps. In the basement, I could tell whether the person in the kitchen above was at the sink, table, stove or fridge.

A floorboard in the hallway and two in the dining room, floorboards on both sides of my bed and at spots throughout the house--all betrayed peoples' whereabouts. Each creak and groan has its own peculiar pitch. The doors each have their own unique sounds, opening and closing.

I knew that Marla had not moved from bed all night, getting some much-needed sleep. That helped me to forget, momentarily, that I might never again be able to stand erect. Goddamn sofa.

It was seven-thirty. I'd started my second cup of coffee and was taking a bite of English muffin when the oak harmonics signaled that my guest was stirring.

Four inches of snow had accumulated overnight and it was quite a picture outside. This was corroborated moments later by a squeal from the bedroom of, "Oh... it's beautiful! Johnny! Have you...?"

The bedroom door swung open. Marla in my robe, barefoot, hair all crazy, glee in her shining eyes. "Have you looked outside? It's so pretty!" Like a little girl on Christmas morning, she came downstairs, hugged me quickly and got some coffee. She went from window to window, looking out at the new snow.

I asked, "How'd you sleep?"

"Oh, like a baby. I brushed my hair, brushed my teeth, fluffed up the pillow and that's all I remember. I slept great. I haven't slept like that in six months."

Then, sarcastically, she asked, "How was that comfy sofa?"

"It was fine. Just fine."

"Bullshit. I can tell by your eyes you didn't get enough sleep."

"You've never seen my eyes in the morning, Sherlock. How do you know I didn't sleep as well as you did?"

She said, "Seriously, Johnny...you can sleep in your own bed. Don't make this visit unpleasant for yourself. Please?"

"I'll try the Aero Bed in the guest room tonight. Everybody seems to love that thing."

"You're impossible."

"Yes…yes I am."

Her irritation seemed genuine. "That's just foolish. Are you trying to insult me?"

"Nope. I thought I'd save that for after breakfast."

She declined my offer to take her to Big Al's Diner, so we made scrambled eggs, sausage, toast and juice and ate on TV trays in the living room. Marla picked at her food, ate about half of her eggs, a piece of the sausage and some toast. "Still not much appetite, but it's tasty."

She loved my kitchen and was suitably impressed with the way I handled sharp objects.

I told her that I had a pretty full day planned; doctor's appointment at nine, lunch with some publishing people (hoping to land some more editing or reviews), and a three hour stint filling in for a sick friend at the store. I guessed I'd be home around five, sooner if possible.

Marla was OK with that plan, saying she would read, nap and put together a shopping list. "Can we go to the grocery store tonight?"

"Sure. I'm going to get cleaned up and get out of here, Gorgeous. Do you need to use the bathroom?"

Once I got clearance, I shaved, showered and dressed. When I came back downstairs, she was sitting on the sofa, staring out the window at the freshly fallen snow. She was two thousand miles away.

"Is there anything you need before I go? Anything you want me to bring back?"

"Will you call me later?"

"Of course I will. What time?"

"I don't care. Just so you call."

"I promise." I trudged to the garage. "Make a snowman!" I yelled back to her.

She smiled a wistful smile from the front door and with a distant look, waved goodbye as if we would never see each other again.

My day went smoothly. The doctor said I wasn't dying of anything, there was the likelihood of some more writing work and then three hours of selling bolts, rope and ladders.

I called Marla twice and she sounded bored and lonely.

During the second call, I said to her, "I've fallen into the habit of calling you little pet names like 'Gorgeous', 'Kiddo', 'Sweetie.' I hope that's not a problem for you. I know some women hate that and I should have asked you before. It's becoming second nature to me, but if it bothers you, I'll knock it off."

There was a small pause and then, "I can't explain to you why...but it doesn't bother me at all. From most other guys, it would aggravate me and I would tell them so. But with you it seems natural. Truth is...I've missed it."

"So we're OK?"

"We are more than OK."

"Excellent. See you soon."

"Johnny? Don't forget we have grocery shopping to do."

In my best henpecked voice, I said, "Yes, dear" and was rewarded with that wonderful laugh.

I got home about four. No more snow had fallen, but it was colder and the midday slush had turned to jagged concrete.

She was coming out of the kitchen as I came in the front door. She handed me a glass of red wine to match hers. She was wearing hiking boots, brown corduroy pants that appeared to have been applied with a paint sprayer and a snug, long-sleeved beige turtleneck top.

"Honey, I'm home!"

She rolled her eyes with a twinkle. "Can we go to the store? I want to make this new Asian shrimp dish for you, but I did some snooping and you don't have any of the stuff I need."

"Really...so it requires more than salt, mustard, wine and ice cubes?"

"A little," she grinned.

"What did you do today? By the way, you look fantastic."

She flatly answered, "I did nothing. I just sat around."

That's why I'd brought her there. Shopping was a promising sign. I was encouraged that she wanted to get out of the house.

She seemed perturbed. "My son called about three times and Sasha called twice."

This Sasha character had called her several times since her arrival and was mentioned frequently in about half the phone calls we'd shared.

"Aah, yes...Sasha. I'm working up a distinct dislike for this fella. Why would he call you here?"

"Something about some pieces of Neil's glass in the garage. Birds, some other small things. He knows someone who might want to buy them, but I don't think I want to sell." Then, her face suddenly hardened. With an unmistakably confrontational tone I'd not heard before, "Are you jealous of Sasha or something?"

"No reason to be. I'm in no position to feel jealousy toward any of the men in your world. I just am a little tired of hearing his name. He knows you're here, at my house, right?"

"What difference does that make?" her voice raised, and for the tenth time, she told me, "Sasha was there for me when Neil was dying. He was the only one around when Neil left. He helped me move his body and clean him up for the crematorium people."

"I understand that. And your loyalty to him is admirable. Timing is everything. Let's not forget that I did ask you if I should come out and you told me not to. I'd have been there if I could have been there. You know that."

"I know you *say* that."

"And you don't believe me?" It was my turn to confront.

"I guess I believe you. I just don't see why you have this animosity toward Sasha. I don't know what I would have done those last two days without his help."

57

"Well, from what you and Neil have told me about him, it's not like he had anything else terribly pressing to do. He's basically a drifter, isn't he? Homeless?"

I saw her neck flush and her eyes narrow and knew I'd said enough. In a split second, tension ruled the room.

"Sasha has been helping Neil sell things for a long time, especially when Neil was destitute a few years ago. I know he's creepy and has a lot of problems, and Neil sometimes indicated Sasha had been less than honest with him, but I know he'd never let anyone hurt me."

"Neither would I. Never mind, OK? It's not important. Anything else interesting happen today?" I moved on.

"I arranged your Tupperware," she volunteered.

"Wow, thank you. Because, about a year ago I just started putting everything in sandwich bags. You poor thing. You must be exhausted. The last woman who took a shot at that job ended up in rehab. Let's go get you some shrimp."

She dispelled the icy air with her warm laughter.

"That's the first time I've laughed all day, Johnny. God...you know how to make me smile."

"And it's a beautiful smile. You're a beautiful woman."

"No. Stop that."

"Nope. Not gonna stop. I'm going to tell you the truth until you at least acknowledge that I believe it. Then we'll work on you believing it. You are an exquisitely lovely woman."

"And sometimes you piss me off." We were back to Sasha.

58

"Sometimes my candor and lack of grace angers people. I'm working on it, all the time. You are the last person I want to make unhappy."

"I can hear the shrimp getting freezer burn while you're screwing around here."

"OK, we'll go to the store. It's not a very exciting grocery, but they'll have what you want."

I had dodged a bullet. I'd finally seen the flame and smelled the smoke from that fire Neil had so often tried to describe. I knew the discussion of the topic of Sasha wasn't over. Marla's anger lay beneath the thinnest of surfaces. It was clear that, when she unleashed it, it would be consuming and devastating.

Yes...I was jealous. Rightly or wrongly, I wanted Marla's undivided attention.

Shopping with this woman was a true learning experience. I found out about Chinese Five Spice, sesame seed oil and couscous. She not only introduced me to Jasmine rice, but later taught me a foolproof way to cook it. Determined and focused, she dug through every single bag of shrimp in their freezer until she found one that met her approval.

I reveled in an odd mixture of pride and lust as we made our way, joking and conferring, through the store. I was shocked and a little unsettled to realize...I was happy.

I told her, somewhere in the bakery aisle, that whenever I was walking behind her, she could safely assume I was looking at her ass. She smiled and shook her head. "You're bad."

She insisted on paying for the groceries, refusing to acknowledge my protests.

Back at the house, I got a good fire going. We lit white tapered candles in pewter holders and decided to eat at the dining room table, "like civilized people." She encouraged me to assist in preparing dinner. We joked and elbowed each other and enjoyed the work. She was a demon in the kitchen.

The vibe and the body language were crystal clear; we were quickly becoming more at ease with one another. Learning the ropes. Something more than shrimp was cooking.

It was one of the most interesting and exotic meals I'd ever eaten, prepared with spices and tastes entirely new to me. I lavished praise on her and toasted the chef repeatedly. I teased her into taking a small bow and was pleased when she ate a fair-sized portion.

After dinner, we did the dishes. She said that she never went to bed until the dishes were done. The morning before she arrived, I had washed a large, aromatic mound of greasy, gray dishes, most of which had been in the sink for over a week.

After the clean-up, she ducked outside for a smoke. I poured wine for both of us and headed for the fireplace.

Our second night together started much like the first, only this time I showered first.

I was once again treated to the incredibly erotic moisturization ritual of the night before. About halfway through her treatment, she stopped, looked sideways at me and asked, "No funny remarks tonight?"

"I swallowed my tongue about five minutes ago."

She smiled and shook her head. "You're a nut."

"And I have the papers to prove it."

"So, you suppose we can trust ourselves to sit on the couch together tonight?" she asked, mock-seriously.

"I think that's the best idea you've come up with yet."

We settled into the sofa. It is dark blue and very comfortable...as a sofa. I sat at the left end, Marla at the right end, facing each other.

The sofa is every bit of nine feet in length. We're not tall people, so if I put my feet at about the level of her knees and she did likewise, we could put throw pillows under our heads and relax. We had plenty of room. Inevitably, someone's foot would touch the other one's leg.

Both in our robes and socks, sharing a heavy afghan, it was relaxing and just intimate enough. To emphasize points during the conversation, we touched the others' feet. Learning new steps of the dance.

We topped off the wine and talked about all manner of things. She didn't bring up Sasha or Ben, for which I was grateful. Lots more about Neil, of course. It was fairly early, but I was sleepy.

Out of nowhere, she rested her hand on my ankle and said, "I'm a little nuts, you know."

I said, "Sweetheart, I know that. Hell, if you weren't a little nuts you would never have hooked up with Neil...or stayed with him...or come to Cleveland in January to spend five days with a guy you hardly know."

Marla looked at me for a couple of seconds, smiled and said, "No...I mean I really am a little nuts." Her expression was serious, mouth thin and eyes darkened.

"We're all nuts. I doubt you're any nuttier than anyone else I know. I'll make the necessary adjustments."

"You're really something, you know that? And you..." she paused and took a breath, "you have the most beautiful eyes. Hazel, but they have flecks of blue in them." She seemed relieved. "I've wanted to tell you that since the first time I saw you, but didn't want you to get the wrong idea."

"Thank you. That's very sweet of you...and not nuts at all. So, should I go ahead and get the wrong idea now?"

Ignoring my inquiry, she said, "Your birthday is the day after tomorrow?"

"Right and I'll probably be late, maybe ten or eleven."

We decided that we'd get out of the house the next day...bookstore, movie, lunch, the mall...something to get some air and keep her active and not obsessing.

She asked, "Are you really going to sleep on that awful air mattress thing tonight? Why are you doing this? Come sleep in your own bed. You're going to end up with two sleepless nights in a row and not be worth a damn tomorrow."

"I'll be fine. You'll see."

"God, you've got a hard head."

"Takes one to know one. Speaking of bed, I think I'll turn in."

She said, "Me too. I sure hope I sleep like I did last night. That is really a great bed...and it's all mine," she crowed.

"Enough," and I started up the stairs.

"I'm going to finish my wine and I'll be right up."

"OK, goodnight."

"Sleep well, butterfly."

Stopping at the bottom of the stairs, I had to ask, "Where does that come from?"

She replied, "That's what I always said to my kids when I tucked them into bed at night. It seemed right for you." She grinned.

"I like it. Sweet dreams"

"Sleep well, butterfly."

There was more snow falling as I turned right at the top of the stairs and headed to the spare bedroom. It was the coldest room in the house in the winter and the hottest in the summer. Prior to Marla's arrival I had put flannel sheets, a blanket and spread on the air bed. Ordinarily that would have been sufficient. The temperature was going down to twenty-two degrees.

I had not taken into account that the room had been closed up all day. The result being that the air inside the bed was as cold as the air outside the bed. No amount of body heat was going to significantly change that. I pictured sides of beef hanging.

As I heard Marla come up and close her door, I laid down on a bed that was, for all practical purposes, an ice cube with sheets.

After a couple hours of miserable tossing and turning, fairly sure Marla was asleep, I grabbed my blanket and pillow. Being careful to walk lightly on the edges of steps six, eight and thirteen, I made my way to the sofa for a second night of dismal twitching.

I was up first around six, having again slept only a few hours. I heard Marla moving around near seven.

She came downstairs not long after, dressed and ready to get on with whatever the day held for us.

"Good Morning, Johnny." Looking at the mess in front of the fireplace, "Did you sleep on the couch again? What the hell?"

"Let's just say I was no butterfly. That air bed's as cold as a witch's titty, so I came down here. Did you sleep well?"

"Pretty good, actually. I had a dream about Ben…that he was in some kind of trouble." She would have called him right then had it not been for the three hour time difference. That and the fact that he slept until noon.

We made waffles and bacon and fresh grapefruit juice for breakfast and talked about things we could do. Marla ate more than the day before and I was encouraged.

We agreed that we'd drive to Hudson and stroll around. Then to Loganberry, one of my favorite bookstores, followed by dinner in Little Italy at La Dolce Vita.

We left the house around ten. Walking from shop to shop in Hudson, she held tightly to my arm as we bent into the freezing wind. Once she put her icy hands on my neck and yipped when I jumped. Touching was becoming less taboo and I could see no downside to that. She bought a small doodad for her key chain and I bought a set of four black lacquer chopsticks.

The cold air and the exhilaration of being with Marla made me forget how tired I was. The very act of being a man and a woman together in public was just what the doctor ordered for both of us. She relaxed. I beamed.

There were a few minutes of tension when she asked me if I visited Hudson often. I told her that I had last been there with my past live-in girlfriend, Nikki, a few years before.

Marla stopped on the sidewalk and said, with none of her characteristic lightness in her voice, "I guess no one ever told you that it's rude to keep mentioning your old girlfriend to the woman you're with."

My gut reaction was to remind her that she managed to bring up Neil's name about every ninety seconds, but thought better of it. Of course, she was right and I said, "You're right. I apologize."

She wasn't ready to let it go. "I know I talk about Neil a lot, but I loved him and he died in my arms a month ago. Is Nikki dead? Were you there when she died?" A hint here of the twisted logic Neil had tried to describe to me.

"Look," I replied, "I don't know if Nikki's dead or alive. Don't honestly give a shit. I'm with you right now and I like it that way. You asked me a question and I answered it. Don't drag Neil into this. You will never hear me mention Nikki again. Is this the tone you're going to set for the day?"

We moved on, and Marla Stone never again heard me speak Nikki's name.

Back in Cleveland, we went to the bookstore and spent at least an hour wandering around. For a dollar, I picked up a copy of <u>Daniel Webster; American Statesman</u> by Henry Cabot Lodge, circa 1883. Marla tried to pay for the book, but I waved her off.

She asked me "Will you read that?"

"Probably not. I'm just a sucker for funky old books," I admitted.

"And pretty young girls?"

"I'm here with you, aren't I?"

"Oh, brother...you are sleep-deprived," and she laughed that amazing laugh that lit me up like a pinball machine.

We'd grabbed a snack earlier, but it was nearly sundown now and we were getting hungry.

"So, Italian is alright with you?"

"I love Italian," she reassured me.

Little Italy is my favorite part of Cleveland. Italian food is my favorite food and we were starved by the time we got there.

We threw caution to the winds and ordered the "Chef's Feast." It is six courses per person; two appetizers, one pasta, one risotto, veal or fish, salad and dessert. Marla made a beeline for the restroom.

Back at the table, she patted my knee. She insisted that, even though my birthday was not for another day, this would be my birthday dinner. "It's my gift to you for your guidance and friendship."

We ordered a bottle of Chianti and giggled like kids. Marla sat close to me in the curved booth. I ordered the fish, she ordered the veal. When the salads came, our waiter asked if we were celebrating a special occasion.

She looked to me, puzzled and lost for a response. So I said, "The lady's here from California and it's her first trip to Little Italy. Why do you ask?"

"No reason. Just that you both look very happy. Enjoy your salads."

We looked at each other, aware that something had shifted. We were projecting an image to the outside world.

"Should I be feeling a little guilty about this, Johnny?" she said slowly.

"We're just having dinner. No reason for you...for either of us...to feel guilty about that. It's Italian food. Don't overthink it."

"We both know this is more than just dinner. This is not just Italian food, Johnny. Maybe I meant is it OK to be having this much fun?"

"The simple answer is yes. And Neil would be happy to see that two of the people he cared about most have formed a bond and are having fun."

"Do you really think so?"

"I've never been more sure of anything."

"I guess you're right," a hesitant relief in her voice.

We toasted Neil and our new friendship. The meal was magnificent. We were magnificent.

Later, sufficiently stuffed, two waiters brought our desserts; the first bearing Marla's cannoli, the second carrying my tiramisu...with a single lit candle in it. Our waiter bent down and said, quietly, with a nod toward Marla, "Sir, the lady has informed us that tomorrow is your birthday and that you would not want any fuss. A very happy birthday to you."

It seemed so unlikely, so unreal, that she was right there, her left leg against my right, smelling like a garden and as sexy and beautiful a woman as I'd ever seen, glowing with satisfaction and wine. She'd done this sweet thing for me. She had made this loving gesture. And now she was looking at me and smiling in a new way, waiting for my response.

I fought back the words, "I'm falling in love with you, Marla" and said instead, "You are a real piece of work, Stone. Thank you. You're a very special woman."

"You're delirious from no sleep. We should get you to bed."

"I'm sleepy, but I meant every word." I knew she had a pretty good idea what I had *wanted* to say.

We got back to the house around ten and, as we walked in the front door, her phone rang. Sasha again.

I said nothing, hung up my coat and went upstairs to shower and brush my teeth. I could hear Marla talking, but not what she and Sasha were discussing.

As I dried off, toothbrush in my mouth, Marla tapped on the bathroom door. "Johnny? Are you mad at me?"

Jokingly, "Oh jeez, Marla...did you break something?"

"Seriously. You just kind of stormed off and left me hanging."

I was fatigued and when I get that way I can be curt. Sardonic, you might say. I thought better of it.

"Stormed off? I **stormed** off? Really? Honey, I just wanted to get showered and out of those clothes. I'm not mad at you. Have you done something that I should be mad about?"

"I don't think so, but it seemed a little odd that as soon as Sasha called, you disappeared." Her tone was one of concern but there was a discernible edge to it. Was she actually looking for a fight after the great day we had shared?

I fudged, "I assumed, since you walked away from me, into the kitchen, speaking in hushed tones, that you and Sasha needed some privacy."

A full minute of silence.

Then Marla said, "I have something for you."

"I'll be right out." I rinsed the toothpaste from my mouth, tested my breath in the palm of my hand and went into the bedroom.

All manner of vivid ideas were careening across my mind...several of a decidedly depraved nature. But I pushed them away, took a breath and opened the door.

Marla was already in her robe. Maybe I had been hasty in ruling out an ending to this day far beyond anything I had expected. I found it titillating that she had obviously undressed and put on the robe with only the bathroom door between us. The look on Marla's face was clearly playful.

"Are you ready?" she teased me. She was really enjoying this, brown eyes aglow.

"I guess so." I had no clue what she was up to, but I kept an open mind.

She gave me a sly look and gripped the top edge of the bedspread.

The devil on my left shoulder hollered, "Hot Damn! Happy Birthday, Dude!"

She whipped the spread back...and I saw it.

She explained, over my laughter, "I've been thinking about something we discussed the night I got here. I'm afraid if you don't get some sleep soon, you'll collapse before I leave. So I found the solution to our problem in the basement."

There, lying straight down the middle of the bed, was an eight foot-long two-by-four. She really had put a board in the bed. It was so utterly incongruous there, like Charlie Manson at Wimbledon.

"You are unbelievable. That is hysterical. You win. I'll sleep in here tonight. I am too tired to argue. And my back is sore."

"Well," she clarified "It's not a win or lose thing. You need some sleep, and it's cold as hell in this room. I can use the extra body heat."

"I can do that."

She smiled a pleased smile and, her little sermon notwithstanding, she clearly saw it as a victory. I was out on my feet and only too willing to acquiesce.

"I'll be right back." She closed the bathroom door and I heard the water run while she brushed her teeth.

I took off my robe, put on a fresh pair of boxers and a t-shirt. I usually sleep in the buff, but my part in this thing had to be unambiguously non-sexual.

Before I could get into bed, she opened the door. She was wearing, under her robe, a pair of purple satin boxers, bright orange socks and a dark blue, long sleeved cotton t-shirt. God, those legs would be the death of me yet.

"So...do you think we can get along without that?" pointing to what would forever after be called simply "The Board."

I picked it up and stood it carefully in the corner. "I'll leave it nearby in case you feel yourself being overwhelmed by my charisma."

"You should live so long, hotshot."

"I am a patient man, Marla. A patient man. Which side do you want?"

"It's your bed, Johnny. Which side do you usually sleep on??

"The right."

"I'll take the left."

We got in the bed, pulled the covers up to our chins and let out a collective, "Aaaaahhh."

I said, "Oh, Bed. How I have missed you, Bed. I will never leave you again." It felt so great to be off that sofa.

We were like a couple of kids in a tent in someone's backyard. We talked for at least on hour. We again laughed uproariously at her asking if I was a rapist. We talked about love and devotion and friendship. It seemed perfectly natural to be doing exactly what we were doing.

She told me that she could be very jealous. I assumed she was talking about Neil and said, "Glad I don't have to worry about that."

To which she replied, "Well...no. I guess not."

It was pitch dark in the room. As the conversation wound down, we both started to drift off. I turned onto my stomach, said "I'm going to sleep, kid. Sweet dreams."

Marla said, mockingly, "Thanks for not rejecting me again tonight."

"My pleasure. I don't want you to develop a complex."

She swept her leg in a playful effort to kick me and missed. "My god!" She sat bolt upright and put her hand on my back. "Are you on the very edge of the bed?"

I had purposely placed myself as far from her as I could get. "I always start out way over here and generally wake up on my back, clear over on your side."

"Jesus."

"What?"

"Do you mean to tell me we can't keep each other warm without getting you all aroused?"

I answered honestly, "How the hell would I know?"

"Can I move a tiny bit closer to you, then?"

"Sure."

She rolled to the center of the bed, her face a foot and a half from mine. "Much better," she said.

She rolled onto her right side, facing away from me and said with sleepy contentment, "Sleep well, butterfly."

I was on my right side, behind her. I could smell her hair, see her slight shoulders rise and fall and feel the warmth of her wonderful body.

"Sweet dreams, Gorgeous."

I have never desired anything, before or since, more than I desired Marla Stone. But the agreement was upheld and I honored the fact that she was making the decisions regarding how much or how little intimacy we would share. Truth told, when morning came, I was proud of myself—of both of us.

It had not been easy. The one thing Marla needed now, as she had often reminded me, was someone she could trust and I was determined to earn it.

At different points during the night, I awoke to find we were holding one another. The first time, Marla simply rolled over into my arms. Once she backed up to me, both of us on our left sides, and we "spooned" for who knows how long. Later, I found myself close enough that my nose was in her hair and I just put my arm on her hip. Each time, one or both of us would become aware of the configuration and pull away with a mumbled "Sorry" or a grunt.

It was innocent. The bed had gotten uncomfortably warm, off and on, all night. One of those "kick-the-covers-off, pull-the-covers-up" nights. Even though we moved around a lot...I got probably six hours sleep, more than the two previous nights combined.

I woke up on my side of the bed, Marla's back firmly against mine. When I got out of bed Marla made an "Mmmmmm" sound that I thought had elements of disappointment in it.

I peed, threw some water on my face, and came out of the bathroom. Marla had opened her eyes for a second and gave me a tiny yet hearty, "Happy Birthday."

"Thanks." I sat down on the edge of the bed. "Don't get up 'till you're ready. I'm going to make us some coffee."

"M'kay"

I didn't stand up right away. After a minute she opened one eye. "What?"

I said, "You even look terrific when you wake up."

"You're goofy," and she rolled over.

She truly did look great when she woke up. The more I looked at her, the more beautiful she became. She was in my bed and it was my birthday and this day was getting off to a pretty damn decent start.

Putting on the coffee, I tried not to think about Marla's departure in a couple of days. It was fun having, not just someone to share good times with, but a beautiful, sexy, smart woman in my home.

I realized I was smiling a lot more. I was infatuated with her. There was no doubt that her interest in me held some possibility of becoming a romantic one. The previous night she had told me that her bungalow ("You could fit it in your living room") had no air conditioning and that in the heat of the summer, she often pulled all the blinds and did her housework in the nude.

She mentioned the loneliness of going to the beach alone in "my little black bikini." She was no fool. She knew that, with my imagination, I would take these mental pictures to all sorts of lasciviously twisted places.

Her new found ease with our very gentle contact, her increasing willingness to truly relax with me... Marla indicated trust and perhaps an interest in exploring scenarios beyond a short stay in Cleveland. She was smiling more, too.

She had been borderline catatonic when she arrived. She was now humming in the kitchen, building fires, cooking... sometimes morose and distant, but undeniably coming back to life. I took pride in seeing that Jenna and I had been right; Marla needed to be here. She was healing. I was trying hard to not fall in love with her.

I had to be in Columbus at two thirty to attend the funeral of the wife of an old friend. I did not even ask Marla to go along. She'd had a belly full of death. On the way home from the funeral, I was to have a quick visit with a friend in Mansfield, then a short stop in Akron to do a favor for my parents.

Not the perfect birthday, and I'd be home too late for us to really do anything. Some of this stuff had been planned before her trip, so I was committed.

Marla came down and into the kitchen. "Happy Birthday again!"

"Thank you, Ma'am. How did you sleep?"

"Some guy kept grabbing me," and she gave me a mock-sultry stare.

"Point him out. I'll kill the lucky bastard with my bare hands." The caffeine was working.

"Actually...it wasn't that awful. So, you're going off and leaving me all alone on your birthday," she teased.

"I have to, kid. I'd much rather be here, but duty calls."

"You're a good man for doing it. Any idea how late you'll be?"

"I'll haul ass back here just as soon as I can. I want to spend at least part of my birthday with you. I imagine sometime between nine and eleven."

"Will you call me later?"

"Of course I will, probably numerous times. If you need me, call me and I'll turn around and head straight back here."

I would leave around noon, so we had time for a nice leisurely breakfast and conversation before I left. We made pancakes with poached eggs and ham, moving in concert, as if we'd done it a thousand times. We ate on TV trays in the living room and she cleaned her plate.

In response to my question about her readiness to go back home, she said, "I'm having a wonderful time here with you, Johnny. You've removed all the reservations I felt about doing this." Then, testily, "But I have to get back to the work that's piling up on my desk and I feel a little guilty about leaving Ben out there this long."

"Guilty? He's twenty-two years old, Marla. You talk about him as if he was ten."

She said, defensively, "He's my child and I worry about him. And he is more a child than a twenty-two year old."

"It's only been three days. You're dragging around all this guilt. Guilt about someone seeing us together and thinking you're a 'floozy.' Guilt about Ben. Guilt about what Neil would think. I understand that you are going through a lot of shitty stuff right now, but try not to make this heavier than it needs to be. You just have to let some of that go."

"I know...I know. Neil was so pissed off that I brought Ben to California with me. He told me a hundred times that Ben would never become a man until I forced him to fend for himself."

"I remember him saying that to me and he was absolutely right. You're not doing Ben any favor by letting him stay a baby."

"Just how much did Neil tell you about me?"

"More than I'll ever tell you. A lot. Everything."

She said, "Neil said my only fault was that I liked country music."

Taunting her now, "Wow. That ain't the way I heard it." It wasn't.

"Tell me."

"Maybe another time. I have to get ready to go."

I shaved, showered and dressed. Marla asked if she should make dinner for us later.

I told her, "I don't know how hungry I'll be. There's a reception kind-of-thing after the funeral and I'll call you from there. Believe me, I'll shorten this day up as much as I can. I promise I'll stay in touch."

"Can I use your pick-up if I need to go out? I think I might need cigarettes later." I had a ten year-old truck in the garage. It was used rarely, but I kept it in good running condition.

"Of course. The gas tank is full and the keys are in that basket in the kitchen. Use it anytime you need it. You know how to drive a stick?"

"I'm a country girl. I can drive anything."

The trip to Columbus was about two and half hours and it was getting close to noon. I said, "I have to run. Call me if you need anything, promise?"

"I promise. I'll be fine. Please drive safely," and she gave me a solid hug.

I found myself with one hundred and fifty minutes, give or take, with little to do but think about Marla.

It was abundantly clear that she had a hell of a temper. She had kept it pretty well in check. But I'd seen flashes of it, mostly when she talked to her son or Sasha or when she spoke about Neil's family. They seemed to have an inordinate interest in the glass Neil had made while he was with Marla...and most aggravating to her, glass she claimed he had made just for her.

77

She was obviously still on the ropes from Neil's awful decline and his prolonged death. They had known each other for fifteen years, but had both been with other partners. There had been a long-denied tension, an unspoken longing and interest. And now, after all that waiting, in less than four years…it was over.

She was the most beautiful woman I had ever shared this much time with and her presence had changed me. Those things that I normally hated to do, I enjoyed doing with her. I was completely taken by her femininity, her beauty, her voice, her bearing, her sensuality, her vulnerability and her toughness.

She had let it be known, in her own version of subtlety, that she had been doing some thinking about me as well. She acknowledged that, unlike most men, I actually listened to her and gave proper weight to her words and feelings.

She had made it a point to inform me that she had tested negative for any signs of Hepatitis, both when she first went to San Diego and after Neil's passing. She reinforced for me that she could be very jealous. It was important to her that I fully appreciate that.

Although our hugs were short, they were warm and firm and seemed to be mutually sincere. She called me her lifesaver, her lifeboat. I had taken to calling her "Beautiful Girl". She did not object. She sometimes called me "Sweetie" and I glowed every time.

Marla also mentioned, during one of her somber reveries about Neil, that they had called each other "Baby." She related this as if to accentuate the exclusivity of its usage. I took note of it.

It had been confirmed the previous night that physically we fit together like a hand and glove. We were gentle and sweet with each other. I hadn't had sex in months and holding her was a rush of every primal emotion to which man is prone. When she was in my arms, it felt as if part of me was holding her, part of me was just barely holding onto reality. If she chose to associate me with stabilizing her world, I was eager and ready to make any sacrifice to do exactly that.

Although the subject of things sexual was not approached, the events of these few days together (added to what Neil had told each of us about the other), there could be little doubt that we were attracted to each other. And that, if the flame were fanned, the resulting fire would be something truly transcendent. Big egos, big libidos...big stuff.

Traffic on I-71 was manageable. I navigated the engineering abortion that was Interstate 270 and made it to the funeral home on time. I called Marla.

"Hey, kiddo. What's going on?"

"Are you there already?"

"Yeah. No problems at all."

"Will you call me and let me know if you're going to want a meal when you get home?"

"You mean birthday cake?"

"Dream on, buddy."

"I'll let you know. Gotta go. Bye, beautiful girl."

"Bye, Johnny."

The service and burial over by five, we all went to my friend's house for a nosh and some refreshments. It was all very civil, not at all somber and we all had a few laughs...just the way his wife had planned it.

I worked the room a little, ran into an old lover who pretended that we had parted as friends. This despite the facts that I had caught her screwing her Tai Chi instructor and she had stolen my vinyl jazz collection. She was now married to the biggest Isuzu dealer in the tri-county area and had bought herself the petrified face and phony tits that had become "new money" *de rigueur* and confirmation of her newfound affluence. Looking like a mummified hooker, she was about one more facelift away from a goatee.

Around six fifteen, I said my farewells and got back on the road northbound. I called Marla.

"Where are you now?"

"Just leaving Columbus. I think I might call my friend in Mansfield and beg off that stop. It's nothing real important. Nothing I can't do another time."

"You're still going to stop at your parents' place, right?"

I could tell she was moving around in the kitchen. "I'll get to their place in about an hour. Are you baking my birthday cake?"

"Seriously...you really need to let that go. I can't bake. Grab yourself a package of HO-HOs on the way or something. Actually, I went to the store and I'm slicing some fruit to make a nice fruit salad for us."

"Cool. I don't think I will be too late, maybe ten. Will you still be up?" I wanted to have all the time I could have with her. Tomorrow would be her last full day with me.

"I don't know. I'm pretty tired. I might go to bed early."

"I'll be there before ten thirty for sure, sooner if I can. But I won't call on the way in case you're asleep."

"OK. See you later."

Damn it. This birthday was going to end up sucking. A funeral and no evening with Marla. I called my friend in Mansfield and changed our plans. He said, "Hot date?"

I said, "Well, as a matter of fact, I have a drop-dead gorgeous house guest from California and it's my birthday."

He said, "And you were actually going to stop *here*? Get your ass home, man!"

I rolled into my parent's place around eight. My father's memory got shorter every day and my Mother was getting more arthritic all the time. But they still managed to run a house with a little help.

We chatted for a while. I checked their water softener, shoveled their sidewalks, put salt on their driveway, found some lost receipts for my Mom and helped Dad with his crossword puzzle. I gently turned down the obligatory six offers of food.

As I was getting ready to leave, my sister in Georgia called and we all talked to her family for about twenty minutes. I got on my way home around nine thirty, with all the manifold warnings about my Mom's greatest fear...winter driving.

I did not call Marla for fear of waking her. There had been a small fender-bender on the highway, which added time to the trip home. As I turned the corner onto my street, I could see that my house was dark. She was asleep. I said "Shit." I'd have some peanut butter crackers and call it a day. I assumed I would be sleeping in my bed again.

It was about ten thirty. Tired, hungry and with no expectation of quality time with the beautiful girl, I devoted that last block and a half to cursing my foul luck and grousing about what a lousy birthday this had turned out to be.

As I glumly dragged myself out of the car, closed the garage and started to the front door…I noticed a glow coming from the back of the house. Passing the dining room window, I looked in and saw a light coming from under the kitchen door.

I opened the front door to the aroma of something delicious going on in my kitchen. When I looked left, I saw the dining room table beautifully set for two. In the center of the table was a chocolate layer cake with "Happy Birthday Johnny" on it.

"Hello?" I offered.

Marla called from the kitchen, "I'm out here."

I walked into the kitchen and saw Marla, at the stove, a dishtowel tucked into skin-tight corduroys, stirring something remarkable in a skillet.

"Happy Birthday!" she said with a huge smile. "Surprised?"

I'm sure my mouth was hanging open. "Holy shit...what's all this?"

"All of this is for you, Birthday Boy. Cake, Graeter's Ice Cream and Chicken Fettuccine from scratch."

I walked over to the stove, grabbed her, kissed her lightly on the cheek, and repeated, "Holy shit." I opened the freezer to confirm the Graeter's part of her story.

She was smiling like I'd never seen her smile before, eyes bright, cares gone. She was proud, she was competent, and she had taken me completely by surprise. "Well?"

"From scratch? Where the hell did you find Graeter's? You did all this today? Holy shit! And cake!"

"I've been a busy girl. I got the cake first, then the ice cream. I know you love Italian, so I thought I'd experiment on you with this. Never made it before. Are you hungry?"

"I am now. You are incredible. I thought you were asleep and I'd have a crappy birthday."

"Well, your timing is perfect 'cause this is going to be ready in about five minutes. Why don't you open a bottle and pour some wine. I finished that bottle we opened last night."

I hugged her from behind and kissed her on the temple. "Thank you so much for all of this. What a great surprise."

"I hope you like it." she said. "It smells alright."

"It smells like an Italian restaurant in here." I put my finger in the sauce and tasted it. It was perfect. "Molto Bene!"

"Please tell me that doesn't mean 'holy shit' in Italian."

"Oh, Marla...this is wonderful." I wanted to gently take her face between my hands and kiss her full on the mouth.

She said, "Let's eat." We dished up the fettuccine and took it to the table where I poured Chianti.

Marla jumped up and yelped, "Garlic bread!" We both ran to the oven to find the bread perfect.

The dinner was a thing of beauty. Her cooking skills were unquestioned. The fettuccine was magnifico and I made all the appropriate noises to show my appreciation. The wine was grand, the cake was moist and the ice cream was wonderful. We talked about our respective busy days. She insisted on washing the dishes while I took my "birthday shower."

When I returned downstairs, we retired to sit at opposite ends of the sofa in our robes. We'd become accustomed to this configuration which put her feet against my hip and vice versa. This day that had looked like a dud had become, instead, the best birthday of my life. This complicated, magnificent woman had reached beyond her grief and touched the center of my heart.

"Did I miss the application of the moisturizing cream?"

"Sorry. I took my shower before you got home."

"Damn."

We let our hands rest on the others' feet, sometimes rubbing, sometimes just enjoying the simple gift of touch. I massaged each of her toes, one at a time...minus the "this little piggy" malarkey. That and the wine had unwound her as much as I'd ever seen her, and it made me feel that this whole effort had been worthwhile. We had another day and two more nights and I was a happy man.

After a lull, she said, "I've wanted to ask you something since I got here and this seems like a good time for it."

"Sure."

She bit her lip, pulled her knees up. She was struggling to formulate her question.

"Ask me anything, Marla. You may not always hear what you want to hear, but I won't lie to you."

She paused a second longer to add, "Understand this is not necessarily about you and me."

"I understand...a hypothetical."

Marla nodded, "If you tell someone less than the entire truth, is that lying? I mean, if you are truthful but don't tell them the whole story, is that the same as telling a lie?"

My first thought was, "Where the hell is this coming from?" I reflected for a minute and said, "I guess it would depend on who you were talking to. If I were in that position, I would ask myself 'How important is it to this person that they can trust me?' It's probably not a lie, technically. But it sure isn't the truth."

She had been watching my face intently and shown no reaction to my response. "That's not really an answer, Sweetie."

"There is the sin of omission. And it is probably the kind of thing that could come back to haunt you. But...is it a lie? No...I don't think I would say it's the same as lying."

She looked at me with flat, brown eyes and set jaw. Then her face relaxed into a smile, the lights came back on in her eyes and she said, "Now, that's a much better answer. Thank you."

I was tired. "My mouth tastes like wet dog. I'm gonna brush my teeth and hit the sack."

She agreed, "Sounds good to me. I'll tell you a bedtime story."

Intrigued, I asked, "Really? And what is this story about?"

"It's my life story...condensed, of course."

Neil had alluded to Marla's dysfunctional childhood and upbringing, but without a lot of details. It was obviously something she wanted to share with me and I wanted to feel closer to her.

"I can't wait, Kiddo."

It was sixteen degrees outside and the bedroom was chilled. We brushed our teeth at the same time and got into the bed, wearing what had become our regular nightclothes.

The sheets were icy cold. I took my usual position on the right side. Marla quickly moved to put herself flush against me, her back to my belly. We were close, not embracing, warming up the bed and ourselves.

Then...something new.

She reached behind her with her left hand, grabbed my left wrist and pulled my arm over and around her. She pressed the palm of my hand firmly to her chest, above her breasts, just below her throat. She held onto my hand with both of hers. She made a sound of relief, a small release of breath from her nose. I was in a state of sheer bliss.

"This is nice. Are you OK with this?" she whispered and turned her head to show me a questioning smile.

"I am definitely 'OK' with it. Thank you."

"Thank me for what?"

"For trusting me"

"I trusted you the first time I heard your voice." She lightly kissed my hand. "Are you ready for your bedtime story?"

"I guess I'm as ready as I can be. Go ahead," and I held her slightly closer.

For nearly an hour I listened with horror as Marla told me of an upbringing a weaker person could not have survived.

Raped by a stranger at the age of eight. Sexually molested by two adult family members throughout her childhood and adolescence. The death of her mother from lung cancer when she was ten. The murder of her father when she was twelve. Foster homes. Physical abuse. The suicide of her big brother. A loveless marriage. A growing alienation from her daughters. Her son's legal and drug problems. And now, Neil's illness and death.

I kept silent. A few times, Marla stopped, gripped my hand tightly and looked back over her shoulder to ask, "Are you still awake? Should I stop? I'm afraid I'll scare you away."

Each time she stopped, I kissed her very lightly on her shoulder or the back of her head and gently reassured her, "I'm fine. You're not going to scare me away. Please. Keep going."

When she finished, she thanked me for listening. I praised her honesty and thanked her for confiding in me.

She turned once again for a lingering look into my eyes, then said, "Sleep well, butterfly."

I whispered, "Good night, Beautiful Girl."

We fell asleep in the same position; her lissome body pressed to mine, my hand just above her heartbeat, her hands holding onto my hand. Exhausted, she needed the kind of sleep they used to call a "slumber." I would process all of this information after she left town. I wanted tomorrow, her last day with me, to be a good one.

Her story had shocked and unsettled me. Slipping into sleep, the phrase "shipwreck in a bottle" floated through my mind.

Marla's last day in Cleveland flew by before we had a grip on it. I finally convinced her to go to breakfast at Big Al's Diner with me. She loved the place. We had a great meal and a good start on the day.

Her phone rang all day; her son three times, her work twice, Sasha twice, her son three more times, her work once more. We never really had a chance to relax. I was a little pissed off at all the needless, trivial interruptions, but I said nothing.

I showed her Severance Hall, the ballpark (always Jacobs Field to me), The Flats. She had been to the Rock and Roll Hall of Fame once before, so we passed on that. She was blown away by the Arcade. We had a great hour at the West Side Market then shared a wonderful lunch at Great Lakes Brewing. Against her adamant insistence, I picked up the check and we headed back to the house about four o'clock. Marla was quiet during the drive. I chalked it up to fatigue.

She did a little laundry and as she began to pack said, "I'm sorry I can't pay attention to you all day, every day, Johnny. This has been a lot of fun and I am glad I came. But I have a busy life at home and it's time for me to get real about it again."

I'd come to recognize this tone of her voice. It was always less *what* Marla said to you than the *way* she said it. She had long ago mastered confrontational inquiry and the condescending snarl.

I said, "What the hell are you talking about?"

"You've been pouting ever since...I don't know...most of the day."

"I haven't been doing any such thing. If you noticed some disappointment, you're right. I'd hoped we would have more time for us...to just relax and talk, that's all. But it's fine. The day went well and you have to get ready. I get it."

"I don't need to apologize to you if my son or my job or my friends call me. If you take that as some kind of insult to you, then we've got a problem."

She was in the mood for a fight.

I countered with, "When did I ask for an apology? I never said a word about your phone calls. If you think I'm going to hide my feelings from you, you're sadly mistaken. Friends aren't supposed to do that. I've been open with you, so why don't you tell me what you're really pissed off at."

"You're moping around like a little boy whose feelings are hurt."

"If I'm moping around, it's because I don't want you to go."

"Well, I *have* to go!"

"I understand that." Walking off, I said, "I'm going to get a glass of wine. I'll bring you one and then I'll leave you alone to pack."

"I'd like a glass of wine, and I don't want you to leave me alone. I just don't appreciate you trying to make me feel guilty about being on the phone."

It was time to let her know that I was unafraid to make my point and ready to engage when necessary.

"I was not trying to make you feel guilty. Every one of those phone calls today was bullshit…bullshit you could have handled when you got home and bullshit you didn't have to bother with. The apologies should be from your people in San Diego. I am not going to fight with you about this, Marla. If you want your visit to end on this note, that's up to you."

"Fine. I don't want to fight either. Can I still have that glass of wine?"

"It's on the way."

We went to the sofa in front of a small fire. Tense at first, we snacked on cheese, crackers and fruit since neither of us was "dinner hungry."

Feathers smoothed, we talked about weather and work. Her flight left at eleven in the morning. Even with a two-hour layover, she'd be back in her bungalow in time for dinner.

I confessed, "I miss you already."

"I miss you, too." she said softly. "Will you come visit me? There is lots of fun stuff we could do."

"Just say the word and I'll be there."

"I might do that. There's a lot of cleaning up and rearranging and organizing to do and you are good at that. I have to get on with my life, Johnny."

"I hope you'll save a corner of it for me."

"Oh, come on...you know I already have. We've made huge impressions on each other. I need your friendship and affection and help."

"You'll have them as long as you want them."

We talked a while longer, both yawning and stretching. It was only a little after nine, but she headed for the shower and I poked the coals around to get the fire down as the day wound to a close.

Marla came down from her shower and asked, "You going to shower now?"

"I thought I'd wait around and watch you put on your lotion," I leered.

"You really like it that, huh?"

"Yes, ma'am...I really do like it...very, very much."

So, while we recounted all the things we'd seen and done, Marla rubbed white lotion thoroughly into her flawless legs. I watched, for what might be the last time, with a hunger that satisfied itself.

As I went up to shower her phone rang again. Searching through her purse, she said, "Sonofabitch...now what?"

I continued to the bathroom, no longer interested in her phone calls.

We were in bed by ten, joking about how old we must be getting.

"Hold me, Johnny."

"My favorite three words." As I pulled her into my arms, now confident enough to put my hand on her chest where she had placed it the night before, my hips to her astonishing butt, my chest to her delicate shoulder blades, Marla put her legs to my knees, her feet on top of mine.

I could hear the grin in her voice as she murmured again, "Hold me, Johnny."

"I've got you."

She held her lips to the back of my hand for several seconds. "Sleep well, butterfly." That quickly, she was asleep.

I whispered, "Goodnight, Beautiful Girl."

At that instant, I knew I was inextricably involved in something tangled and strange and dangerous.

I didn't care. I was going to do whatever it took to be with this woman.

Friday morning found us up and busy at seven. Marla took a quick shower and spent lots of time with her hair preparation. I shaved and dressed while she finished packing. There wasn't a lot of talk.

She was ready to get back to whatever was left of her life out there. I was trying to be helpful and unobtrusive. I did not want to betray my sadness at the thought of coming back from the airport to an empty house.

Allowing the recommended ninety minutes for baggage check, security and boarding...we had a light breakfast of English muffins with jam, fresh fruit juice and coffee and left the house at nine.

It took forty-five minutes to get there, but she had only one carry-on so we made it in plenty of time. We had printed out her boarding pass the night before and the lines were not long. The time had come.

When we got to the security area, she said, "I'm going straight to the gate. I hate long goodbyes. I can't thank you enough for putting some sanity back in my life, Johnny. You are a wonderful guy."

"You deserve the thanks. You've brought some warmth to the coldest season of the year and you lit up my home. I can't remember the last time I've felt this good. I hope you had fun."

"I had a great time. I'm going to go. Be safe driving home."

"I'm going to just hang here until you're all set. Call me when you get home?"

"I promise."

She gave me a strong hug and a peck on the cheek. She took a half-step back and looked into my eyes for a few seconds, smiled and started through the queue. After she had retrieved her belongings and put her shoes back on, she walked about twenty feet and stopped. Then she turned to smile, wave and throw me a kiss.

For the first time in thirty years...I threw a kiss.

And she was gone.

3

It's all about the heat.

Six thousand years ago, a Phoenician merchant ship carrying a cargo of nitrate sailed along the coast of the Mediterranean in the region of Syria. Back then, nitrate was used to make soap.

As night began to settle, the captain moored his vessel ashore so his crew could prepare dinner and get a night's sleep.

With no stones on which to prop their cooking pots, they rested them on blocks of nitrate over the roaring fire.

When they awoke in the morning, they found that the intense heat from the fire had partially melted the blocks of nitrate. This super heated flow had acted as a flux to melt the sand, which had then formed an opaque liquid. The liquid had cooled to form small, jewel-like ribbons and beads.

They had discovered glassmaking.

The Roman Era saw the biggest developments in glassmaking. The earliest man-made glass objects appeared around 3,000 BC in Mesopotamia. These small baubles illustrate the struggle to achieve sufficient temperatures for glassmaking. Advancements in furnace technology were slow.

The Egyptians, around 1,500 BC, developed a process of dipping a mold of sand into molten glass and then turning the mold so the glass would adhere to it. Pharaohs brought glassmakers to Egypt as prisoners after a military campaign in Asia.

The big breakthrough was the discovery of glassblowing by the Syrians around 50 BC, and the long, thin metal tube used in their process hasn't changed much since.

In the course of my friendship with Neil, I'd spent many hours in his studios and it was always a singularly intense and elevating experience.

The first things you notice is the roar of the furnace, the high ceilings, the ash in the air, the exhaust fans, and then…as you get deeper into the space and approach the furnace…the enormous heat strikes you full in the face. Your eyeballs go dry, your face gets hot, your breathing is interrupted as your nose, throat and lungs are assaulted. You stop moving in the direction of the danger. It's the "fight or flight" response.

Adrenaline, cortisol and catecholamines squirt all over your reptile circuitry as the brain reverts to the intuitive choice between running or facing the fire. Your heart races. Your sphincter tightens. Blood vessels in your arms and legs dilate so more blood is available to them. Salivary and tear glands close up shop. Your hearing is diminished and you begin to experience tunnel vision.

At a temperature of two thousand four hundred degrees, the furnace turns a mixture of sand and flux into a pool of molten glass the consistency of warm honey. With the searing heat of the furnace on the hands and arms, the artist takes a five-foot metal tube close to the furnace and dips it into the molten mass. He then has a few seconds to coax the molten glass onto the pipe, as the enormous heat gets less tolerable.

It is a high-risk balancing act from there. Everyone in the studio is aware of his or her position in relation to that of the gaffer. The gaffer removes the glowing orange blob from the furnace…turning, turning…constantly turning the glass to prevent it from drooping or falling off the rod on its way from furnace to bench.

This is the "gather."

Everything begins with the gather. Glassmakers overcome the impulse to flee for the sake of the gather. It is the seed, the embryo of glass art. In the hands of the gaffer, using gravity, temperature and air, this Ur-glass comes to life. One must be willing to bear the terrible heat to collect it. And, if the temperature of the gather is not maintained, if it cools too quickly…it ends up as just so much broken glass.

We are willing to dance with fire, to risk being burned, for those things that bring us joy and comfort and beauty. We do it time and again, knowing that anywhere along the way, in an instant…it can all shatter.

The winter wasn't particularly vicious. No worse than normal for a windy city on the shores of the Great Lakes. It had been made immeasurably more livable through my continuing contact with Marla.

She called while waiting for her connection in Denver. She called as she was putting her purse on the kitchen table at her place in San Diego. I called her that night, we talked for two hours and the pattern was set.

We talked every night. We e-mailed every day. We sent text messages and she even called me from work occasionally. We exchanged videos and music via computer. For several days we spoke of the prosaic and safe things, but gradually, easily, our conversations took on a warmer, more conspiratorial tone.

We touched lightly on the possibility of my coming to her place to help clean up the mess Neil had left behind and other things that she had been unable to handle in her spare time. I confirmed my commitment to her.

Our nightly calls were lengthy, heartfelt affairs, filled with playfulness. Often, she was depressed and lonely and I did my best to console her. Concerns about her job, about her mendicant son, about

Sasha's constant talk of Neil's glass and pressure from Neil's family dogged her. I could tell that, as she was talking to me, she was putting away a few glasses of wine. One evening the conversations took an interesting twist.

Marla had alluded several times to a bothersome topic, one that she was not comfortable discussing with me. I let it go, telling her that if and when she felt the need, I'd listen.

On a Saturday night about two weeks after she got home, half an hour into our nightly call, she said, "Johnny, something weird has been eating at me. I don't want you to think badly of me. I don't think I could deal with that."

There was a long pause. I finally said, "Just tell me what's bugging you. I won't be upset if you're honest with me."

With a sigh of resignation she said, "Sweetie, Neil and I had a very active sex life. It's been a long time and I'm a woman and I have needs and it's getting to the point where I think about it all the time. It's effecting my concentration at work and I'm not sleeping. Enid thinks I should just pick up a guy in a bar, go to a hotel and get it taken care of. None of the guys I know here are even remote possibilities. A lady at work says I should call an escort service. I feel like I'm going crazy. Am I crazy?"

She was making an indirect connection between me coming to visit and a solution to her "problem." Once I had turned down the roaring noises inside my head, I responded, "Enid is a cretin. I hate both of those plans. You would be putting yourself in risky situations. Risky in lots of ways."

Graphic thoughts caroming off each other in my brain, I decided to go for broke. "I think you are probably overlooking the obvious alternative, Honey... one that doesn't jeopardize your safety or require batteries."

Quickly, she informed me, "I'm not a battery girl." Marla then added to this odd exchange, "Johnny, you should know that I can be a very jealous woman sometimes, OK? Would you be able to handle a thing like that?"

This was enough to send my mind close to overload. She had considered a level of intimacy between us wherein she could become jealous. Others who would try to lay claim to our affections would be in for a rough go of it. This was getting very interesting very quickly. She was thinking seriously about a relationship with me. Holy shit.

I flashed on Steely Dan's song about loving a little, wild one who would bring you only sorrow.

Then, aside, she exclaimed, "Hi guys! Johnny, can I call you back in a little while? Ben and his friend, Kevin, are here and they're probably hungry."

"Sure, kid. I'll be around."

"You're a sweetie."

"I'm a sap." It was eight PM and I felt my heart slipping into the keeping of this small, untamed woman.

The three-hour time difference was a pain in the ass. No longer the dedicated night owl, I tend to get up early and fall asleep during the late news. By the time I was yawning into my beer, Marla was showered, having some wine, still full of steam and putzing in her garden.

She called back about eleven. "Sorry, sorry, sorry. Those boys just didn't want to leave and after they did, I fell asleep on the bed for about half an hour."

"It's no problem."

"I had a dream about you."

"Please tell me it had something to do with what we were talking about earlier."

"I'm too embarrassed. Maybe later. I really should get off the phone. The sheer amount of all this stuff I have to do here is freaking me out."

But she didn't hang up and we talked until after midnight, when we both started getting punchy. She was overwhelmed with concerns about getting rid of all the heavy medications, cleaning the garage, wills, taxes, probate, and the hundred other things that had gone unaddressed while Neil was sick. Not to mention all of Neil's amazing glass and who would get it.

I said, "I wish I could be there to help you."

There was a pause and then Marla blurted out, "I dreamed you were here with me at the bungalow and we were naked together in my bed...and I was just riding you and riding you. I woke up sweating and embarrassed and breathing like I'd run a marathon. This thing is driving me nuts. You must think I'm a complete whore. God, why did I tell you that? I'm so sorry. Please just forget all of that, will you? Pretend I never said that, OK? Please, Johnny? God. I am so embarrassed."

I managed, "If I live to be a hundred, I'll never forget what you just said. I don't think you're a whore. You are a vital, attractive woman and this is natural. I'm proud to be in your dream...especially *that* kind of a dream."

"You shouldn't be surprised. We've slept together already."

"Not like *that*. I'm relieved to hear I'm not the only one thinking about it."

"You too?"

"Are you kidding me? From the first second I saw you across that barroom and every day since."

I opened another beer. Marla poured a little more wine. We brushed up against the topic of sex a few more times and finally, giddy as a couple of sixteen year-olds, we plunged into what now seemed inevitable.

"Maybe I should come out there to help out with...whatever you decide you want me to help with."

Marla giggled, "Would you be willing to do that? I need somebody I can trust. They've been telling me at work that I came back too soon and I should take some time. I'll have to work Monday, but the rest of the week will be ours. Are we really doing this?"

I replied with a smile, "I think we really are."

Within five minutes...both of us online checking flights from Cleveland to San Diego and trying not to wake the neighbors with our crazy laughter and noise...it was done.

I would be in San Diego on Monday morning and stay for five days. She would have to work Monday and Thursday, I would leave on Friday morning. We'd have lots of time to spend together. Marla put it on her credit card and said not to worry about paying her back for now. I balked at that, but she said, "First things first."

She was beside herself with anticipation and nervous energy. I was in a mild state of shock but absolutely wired. We exchanged "ohmygods" and "holyshits" for another quarter hour before we finally said our sleepy goodnights. We could hear in our voices the big smiles on our faces.

She said, "Are we crazy? We are actually doing this!"

I said, "Yes and yes. Let's get some sleep. I've missed you and I can't wait to see you. Make a list of all the things you want me to help you with out there. Everything. I want you to put me to work."

"I will. And I've missed you, too. What do I tell people?"

That shit again--the Floozy Factor. "Tell them the truth; I'm one of Neil's oldest friends and I'm coming to help you out of the hole you're in."

"Honey," she said, "this really is crazy!"

"Ain't it cool? Sweet dreams."

"Hey, Johnny?"

"Yeah?"

"It really was a hell of a dream. Sleep well, Butterfly," and she made a tiny squealing sound as she hung up.

During those days while my natural pessimism and stolid skepticism were feasting on a veritable banquet of bad news--my country taken over by thugs, the calamity of capitalism more apparent every day, environmental cataclysm edging to center stage, the brute facts of life brought home by the deaths and illnesses of people I loved and by my own creeping decrepitude--to make this decision inviting more uncertainty into my life was surely madness.

John Bunyan said, "Passion will have all things now."

Boarding my six AM flight that Monday in Cleveland, I was hoping to catch a nap on the way to my connecting flight in Houston. I would arrive in San Diego at eleven, local time. Marla would leave work to pick me up and take me to the bungalow.

As the jam-packed Boeing banked West over Lake Erie, I settled in. In my window seat, I had a business-type Yuppie on my right and a Goth zombie on the aisle. I've always been able to nap on planes, but the non-stop movies of Marla rambling across my cortex were clearly going to impede sleep.

She had several times lauded the quality of her life in Olinda. She expressed hopes that I might overcome my dislike for Southern California and love it as she did. It was important to her that I be comfortable when I got there. She wanted to take me to all of her favorite places.

Because of her family back East and the uncertainty of her position at work, she also mentioned she wasn't sure she would stay in California forever. She did not want to move back to Carolina. "Too much baggage. Too much drama."

This emboldened us to float the possibility that, if she were to leave California, she might consider living someplace nearer to me and nearer to her daughters and grand kids. Virginia was mentioned. We could see each other, find out if there might be a future for us and allow her access to family without being too close.

She even volunteered, "That would put us within a day's drive of each other instead of two thousand miles apart."

To my surprise, we discussed this possibility several times and the very thought of having this electrifying woman more readily available made me a little crazy.

As my visit approached, our conversations had taken on a more and more suggestive tone. In the last hours before my trip, they crossed over into the salacious.

We had connected on several levels, but I was unsure which Marla I was seeing; the Marla she had always been, the Marla she had become under Neil's spell or the grieving Marla who seemed to be drinking and smoking more and who needed help putting her life back in its orbit.

I had told her about my "Rest Area Jack" theory; a slow parade of wounded women taking what they needed and then leaving me in the lurch once their needs were met.

She instantly rankled at the idea. "That's a shitty thing to put on me. That's not a good start. Do you really think I could do that to you?"

I told her, honestly, "How would I know, Marla? All I know for sure is what is past. I very much hope there's a future for us. Let's just see how it plays out...one thing at a time."

She was clearly a resourceful and intelligent woman. She had revealed enough of the temper and volatility Neil had described to cause me concern. I had to wonder if at some point, she would turn the full heat on me. Maybe Neil had exaggerated. She was carried a lot of anger inside, but I attributed her less appealing qualities to her current state of upheaval. Marla was a very full plate.

Since her visit, she had shown clear indications of careless decision-making and confusion and I was concerned about her. I would be expected to clean out the narcotics from her house, help her take care of the paperwork aftermath of Neil's death, clean out the garage, comfort and guide her and be her lover without compromising the trust we were building. I hoped she might one day see me as the logical successor to Neil's vacated throne.

The connection in Houston went off without a hitch. I called Marla at work to let her know about my progress. "I still can't believe we are doing this! I'm excited. Are you excited?"

I admitted, "You have no idea. I can't wait to see you."

Her office was not far from the airport. "Call me as soon as you land and I'll be outside the baggage area when you get there." She described the kind of car she would be driving.

I dozed fitfully on both flights and imagined Marla's body; how it would look, how it would taste, how it would feel pressed under my hands and against my body with no fabric or pretensions getting in our way. Each time I awoke smiling. I wanted to be with this woman in every possible sense of the word.

I had lived in Los Angeles County for sixteen years from the Seventies into the early Nineties. I had only visited San Diego twice during that time and then, only briefly. I knew little about the area other than the constant chorus about its perfect climate and how "It's different...not like LA."

I hoped Marla was right about San Diego. Los Angeles had that cloying whiff of decay on it when I first got there in 1973. During a business trip there thirty-six years later, it had the gagging stench of death. The white flight to Oregon, Washington, Idaho and Arizona continued to accelerate. Trapped lower income residents (the middle class having bailed out or planning to leave soon) had to either accept the rapidly burgeoning reality of living in a true "New" Mexico or follow the lead of ultra-conservatives and arm themselves to the teeth in preparation for Helter Skelter.

My experience had taught me that Southern California is a lie. The cynical myth of the laid-back lifestyle is bullshit. The atmosphere is one of relentless competition and fear. It is dog-eat-dog, take-no-prisoners, all day, every day. The only real sin in Southern California is to be poor. It is a grand illusion and a nasty little trap.

I remember as a kid growing up in Ohio watching the Rose Bowl festivities on New Year's Day. While the temperature outside our house was in single digits, the people at the game and on the parade route in Pasadena were in shirtsleeves and shorts, wearing shades to protect their fragile retinas from the very same sun that had abandoned us at Thanksgiving.

It's this image and all the other hackneyed, threadbare hokum about California used in every car commercial and sun block ad that lure the poor, frozen suckers from Detroit and Youngstown and Altoona and Newark – only to find that the schools are shooting galleries, the highways move like glaciers and the streets are owned by heavily-armed platoons of sociopathic Third-World mutants.

What finally drove me back East was my own "cost-benefit analysis" of living in LA. Every year, on every level, the quality of life declined measurably. Every year the cost of living and doing business increased. Simple math and common sense prevailed.

As soon as the plane landed, I called Marla. She excitedly said, "I'm on my way, Handsome! I'll look for you in front of the baggage claim area."

I hate airports and the one in San Diego was about what I expected; functional, crowded and bland. Although my ratio of good airport experiences to unpleasant ones is about equal, all airports blend the worst aspects of bus depot, shopping mall and hospital waiting room. I believe the majority of travelers rushing through airports aren't so much scurrying to catch planes or cabs as they are simply trying to find the nearest exit.

I walked out into the sun. It was eleven AM and seventy degrees, at least fifty degrees warmer than what I had left behind. My first impression of Southern California after a twelve-year absence was one of underwhelming ambivalence. I was here for the girl, not the palm trees or the beach or fun in the sun. I positioned myself as far from other travelers as possible to make myself more visible to Marla and, about five minutes later, I saw the car she had described coming around the corner.

She pulled right up to me, flashing that great smile. I opened the back door.

She said, "Welcome to San Diego!"

I said, "Thanks," tossed in my bag and hopped into the front seat.

After an odd second of indecision on both our parts, we exchanged a big hug and off we went.

Marla was wearing a dark blue two-piece business suit, the skirt slit halfway up a flawless thigh and a tastefully low-cut lacy white blouse. She was even more beautiful than I had remembered. She was an intense, aggressive driver and the ten-minute haul to her place was a crash refresher course in the realities of California freeway survival.

Twice I lifted her hand from the gearshift to kiss it. Twice she reached over to gently stroke my arm or leg and say, "I can't believe you're really here."

I could not take my eyes off her. And she kept looking back at me and saying, "What?"

"Nothing. I just love looking at you, that's all. Any chance you can take the rest of the day off and we can just lie around the house and get re-acquainted?"

"I really can't, Johnny. I'm still catching up from my trip to your place."

I said, "My god, you are gorgeous."

"Oh, stop it." She had been grinning since I got in the car. "I'll take you to the bungalow and get you settled in. You can take a little nap. I know you must be tired. I'll be home around five. We'll go to the store and make a nice dinner for ourselves."

I was having fun with her. "I don't know...I'm way too tense from all this travel to take a nap. So...there's no possible chance you can give your boss some jive story and hang around the house with me...help me unwind?"

Marla gave me a crooked smile, narrowed her eyes, and in her best Lauren Bacall voice said, "Plenty of time for that later, Sweetie."

Olinda is a seedy, nondescript "beach" community; half commercial, half residential. We passed a lot of bars, liquor stores, car lots, restaurants, aging apartment complexes and past-prime single-family homes. Take away the climate and native vegetation and you had another sad, failed swipe at the good life. A crappy little town stuck between two big cities. Granted, there is the bay and the area surrounding it, but the overriding feeling is one of a near miss. At every turn, in every car, on every building and on every face...the ubiquitous, desperate need to be *seen* that quantifies life in Southern California.

Your huddled masses yearning to breathe cool.

Marla pointed out the bay, her favorite Thai restaurant and, in the distance, Sea World. It was clear that she loved the area and was determined to convert me. "It's so pretty here, Johnny, and it doesn't get cold. I know how you feel about Southern California, but give it a chance. If you try to be open-minded, you might actually like it."

Ten minutes later we turned onto her street. It was narrow with vehicles parked bumper to bumper on both sides. Her neighborhood was a mix of prosaic commercial office space and squat, beige living spaces with sparse vegetation. These weren't bungalows in the strictest sense. I had expected places with a pointed roof, shutters...like little houses. These were drab, cookie-cutter stucco boxes. More like duplexes, but with the twin units back and front, instead of side by side. I never, even in the worst of times, pointed out to her that she did not actually live in a "bungalow." I knew she was only repeating what she'd been told by Neil.

She ground out her cigarette in the ashtray and said, "If there's no room on the street, I have my own space in the alley behind the bungalow."

As she slowed down, I saw on the right, a place decidedly unlike the rest of the dreary little boxes. Twenty-five feet from the street, it had a lath fence in the front. In front of the fence were a couple of eight foot-long planter boxes jammed full of brightly colored flowers. Behind it a jungle of plants, small trees, more flowers and the front of the bungalow. This had to be Neil's place. It had more color and life to it than the rest of the houses on the street combined.

Marla groused, "No place on the street. We'll park in the alley."

We went to the end of the block, made two quick right turns. We pulled up the alley to a block wall next to a garage, behind her place. I grabbed my bag from the back seat as Marla came around the rear of the car and opened a wooden gate attached to the garage. A dog-ear fence ran from the gate along the back and side of the bungalow.

There were two small grassy areas split by a narrow sidewalk. The sidewalk went for about forty feet between two identical units, ending at another gate. Marla's bungalow was the second half of the unit on the left. She stopped with her hand on the latch, looked at me with wide eyes and said, "I really hope you like it here. I want you to be happy here." And she opened the gate into her beloved garden.

As she pulled her mail from the box and unlocked her front door, I admired the work she and Neil had put into the place. It was an oasis of brightness and lush color amid all the bland brown sameness of the surroundings. He had lured her with a garden and she stayed on to tend it in his memory and to maintain her sanity...such as it was.

Some of Neil's smaller glass pieces were mixed with the potted plants and in the planter boxes and hanging baskets. A round stone table with stone benches and an umbrella were right outside the front door. Everywhere were ferns, geraniums, impatiens, daisies, snapdragons, begonias, six foot-tall hollyhocks, the outrageous Bird-of-Paradise and an herb garden. It was inclusive and shady. It was a haven and I now understood why Marla spent so much time here, putzing. It was a beautiful refuge for a beautiful woman, a place to decompress after work. It had become her sanctuary, somewhere to cultivate and preserve memories.

The front of the bungalow had a small portico. To the left, a picture window to the living room and on the right was a smaller window to the kitchen. The storm door had a heavy metal grate over it. Marla opened the door and I followed her in. She sang, "Here's my bungalow."

The whole place couldn't have been more than 800 square feet...about the same size as the garden. A borderline claustrophobic, I instantly saw how this place could get very small in a big hurry if things weren't going well. I tried to imagine spending weeks jammed in here, watching your mate die, unable to run away. How cramped it must have become during the many knockdown, drag-out "debates" she and Neil surely had.

We entered a small living room, simply and inexpensively furnished. A long dresser along the left wall doubled as storage and entertainment center, a large television on top. A floor lamp with a fantastical shade of Neil's glass in white and green, a nondescript oval coffee table and the cheap black vinyl loveseat where Neil had breathed his last, all rested on a large green and yellow woven rug. On the loveseat were Day-Glo green and orange throw pillows and a Mexican serape.

Marla led me to the loveseat, pointed to a barely discernible discoloration of the rug in front of it. "In the last weeks, Neil had these awful open sores on his lower legs that constantly drained. I swabbed and cleaned and dressed them a hundred times. But sometimes, when I was away, they would drain onto the floor. At that point he couldn't get around or even lean over. I can't get it out of the rug, so I rarely sit there."

A set of three-foot high shelves in front of the picture window displayed a dozen of Neil's pieces. They were bright and fanciful, as his work tended to be.

Several of them were familiar to me. Marla later explained that the other pieces had been made while she and Neil were together…most of them created for her. Neil's paintings, sketches, glass and photos of him covered every wall. Marla's place was a colorful, unapologetic and straightforward shrine.

Pointing to the middle shelf, at a square black box that appeared to be covered in black felt. "Those are Neil's ashes. He wanted me to have them mixed with glass and blown into goblets."

The small kitchen was to the right and as Marla set her purse on the kitchen table, I let out an honest and uninhibited, "Wow."

"It's tiny, but it's home. Let's get your bag put away. Unfortunately, you have to go through the bedroom to get to the bathroom."

The bedroom was straight ahead. Like the rest of the place it was very small and crowded with old photos, drawings, more glass and other reminders of Neil everywhere. A queen-sized bed, a white wicker nightstand, two small desks—one with a computer on it-- and a plain dresser filled the room. The bed was immaculately made with a Delft blue comforter and three sizes of pillows, a Venetian-blinded window just above the head of the bed. There was just enough room to walk between the bed and dresser.

Marla opened the sliding door on the built-in closet and said, "You go ahead and unpack whenever you're ready. I cleared two drawers in the dresser in the living room for your stuff and we'll put your bag up here, in the closet."

I put my hand on the bathroom doorknob. "I have to pee," I said.

She grinned, "Take a deep breath."

She had told me a week before that she was going to paint the bathroom a brighter color to welcome me. It was yellow. As yellow as it could be. I mean, psychedelic-space-chicken-egg-yolk yellow.

I chuckled, "Damn. You weren't kidding. That is bright."

"Too much?" she asked with amused concern.

"Absolutely not," pretending to shield my eyes. "I love it. This will wake me up in the morning."

"I might ask your help painting the trim and helping me pick out a new shower curtain, if you're interested in doing that."

"I like to paint." I was struck by how accommodating and reassuring I was with Marla. I wanted to make this woman, above all other women, happy. I closed the bathroom door, did my thing, threw some cold water on my face and washed my hands. There was a large green glass penis and one of Neil's candleholders on top of the medicine cabinet.

When I came out, Marla was still in the bedroom. She opened a drawer in the small computer desk. She reached all the way to the back of the drawer. She withdrew a plastic baggie filled with marijuana and said, "Here's the pot Neil used for pain...and I use it sometimes for relaxation. It's there for us to share if you want or not. You and I have never really talked much about it. We can do that later, but I wanted to be up front with you."

"Cool. Thanks."

Back in the living room, I began to put things in drawers and Marla went into the kitchen to grab a bite.

"Are you hungry, Sweetie?" as she re-entered the living room.

We were in the middle of the room. I walked to within a foot of her, put my hands on her hips, interrupting her perpetual motion, and said, "I'm going to kiss you."

Marla somewhat nervously looked over her shoulder, out the picture window. She took my hand and led me into the privacy of the kitchen where we couldn't be seen from the outside and we kissed. She was a little tentative. The kiss was not long but firm and tender. No tongue but filled with relief and discovery. She gave me a small, warm smile and said softly with a wink, "Very nice."

I kissed her again. Slightly longer, less tentative, her lips softening, her body more relaxed. She closed her eyes more trustingly as our lips met.

There is that remarkable moment during a kiss when we expose ourselves, shut out the light and trust that all will be well. We reach a mutually acceptable level of vulnerability. We were both smiling before our lips parted. I confessed, "That was worth the wait."

Marla said, "You're a good kisser, mister. If I seemed a little stiff, it's not you. My teeth are not the greatest and I'm very aware of them. I'm self-conscious about my mouth."

"It was amazing. Your teeth look fine to me."

We started making a salad. The kitchen was small, but the dining area and the tiny pantry behind a beaded divider gave it the illusion of some depth. Marla quickly showed me where things were in the cupboards. One small overhead was Neil's liquor cabinet containing rum, vodka, gin and bourbon. She said, "I drink wine, but sometimes he would make himself a cocktail or three."

In front of the kitchen window was a plain round butcher block table and three chairs. Next to the table was a bookstand filled with cookbooks and a half dozen of Neil's smaller pieces. It was comfortable, smelled wonderful and appeared to be the center of the house's daytime activity. The aromas of fresh garlic and ginger and herbs added to its invitation. Neil had been a fearless culinary adventurer and it was clear that good things continued to come from this kitchen.

As I sliced a tomato and Marla diced green onions, we spoke of things to come.

She said, "You should take a nap, Johnny. I can tell you're tired. I'll be home from work about 5:30. Then we'll go shopping or maybe have some Thai food delivered. Do you like Thai food?"

"I do. But right now, I want you to give me a list of the things I need to do. I want to get started on them so we'll have more time to play later." I was being honest with her. I was tired, but I knew I would probably not be able to sleep right away. Too much endorphin-adrenalin cocktail sloshing around in my noggin.

She opened the refrigerator to show me my choices of dressings and said, "I already have a list, but you have to promise me you will try to take a nap. Here's the stuff I want to get rid of and a list of some other things I'd like to do while you're here."

I looked at the bottom two shelves of the fridge. "Jesus..." I muttered.

There were at least thirty bottles, bags and boxes of the most high-powered painkillers on the market. In a neighborhood like hers and with the dimwitted goons I believed to be around her, it could be dangerous if anyone got wind of this pharmaceutical buffet.

I grabbed raspberry vinaigrette off the door, looked at her "to-do" list and said, "You've got a deal, Gorgeous."

Standing next to me as I sat at the table, Marla reminded me, "I'm off work except for Thursday. I just know you're going to love San Diego. Maybe we can go to Vital Records Tomorrow and then downtown to the Courthouse. I have to straighten out his taxes and his will. Sometimes I get angry with him for leaving me all this shit.

113

Then I'll take you to the airport early Saturday morning. So we have from tonight until then to play and work. How's your salad?"

"Salad's terrific."

I went over the list with Marla. The hospice people had left her guidelines for the correct way to dispose of the drugs. It wouldn't take long to dilute the liquids, crush and dissolve the pills, obliterate the labels, triple-bag everything, mark it "Toxic" and toss it in the dumpster in the alley.

"The cable's been screwed up for weeks. Would you call them and see if we can get someone to either come here or maybe do it over the phone. Oh...and will you look over Neil's rental contract? It's with the other stuff. I think the landlady may be a problem since I'm not on the lease. She didn't want me here in the first place and I'm afraid she might evict me."

I reassured Marla, "No problem. I should be able to handle most of this by the time you get home."

She sat down heavily in the chair opposite mine. "God...listen to me, giving you all this stuff to do, knowing you're exhausted...and these things aren't even your problem. I'm so sorry. Please...I want you to take a rest before you do any of this stuff."

I said, "They're not problems. They're responsibilities. Don't worry about me. We'll get it done together. This is delicious. I never thought to put green onions on a salad."

She smiled and touched my hand. "You're so sweet. I am so glad to have you here, Johnny. I feel bad about dragging you into this."

I laughed. "Dragging? I couldn't get here fast enough. Don't worry about this stuff. It will all get taken care of. And if we don't clean it all up while I'm here, I'll come back to finish it whenever you need me."

At the same instant that she squeezed my hand and said, "You're the best," I heard a lawn mower starting up, close by. Marla furrowed her brow, looked up quickly and growled, "Well, shit. That didn't take long."

Through the kitchen window I saw a middle-aged woman dressed in tie-dyed coveralls, gray hair in a bun, pushing a mower on the other side of the fence. She snuck a couple furtive glances at the house as she made her first pass over Marla's lawn.

"Problem?" I looked to Marla for clarification.

"Oh, it's Enid."

"She mows your lawn?"

Marla enlightened me. "She mows all these bungalows for the landlady and gets a break on her rent. But that's not why she's out there. She mowed three days ago. She lives in the back on the other side. She must have seen us coming in from the alley. She's trying to figure out who you are and what we're up to...the nosy bitch."

Amused, I said, "So...you and Enid...you're close, I take it."

Not amused in the slightest, Marla sharply countered, "She was a rude, intrusive pain in my ass the last days of Neil's life; always over here, in my way, making a fuss over him, pushing right past me into my house to get close to him. I think she was in love with Neil. She's after the glass, that's all."

That spontaneous, dark indignation again. Bad blood with the woman next door. Terrific.

I replied, "Can't wait to meet her. OK...last chance...no way you can stick around, blow off the rest of the work day and hang out with me?" This while giving her the most licentious, "hubba-hubba", Groucho Marx eyebrow shtick I could muster.

"You are very, very cute. I just can't, Johnny. But after I get home, I'm all yours for four whole days. Please try to take a nap. I have to run." She grabbed her purse and headed for the door. "I always keep this screen door locked, OK? Even if I just run out to the car. So when you take that stuff out to the dumpster, please keep it locked. The key is hanging right here, next to the fridge."

She hesitated, looking up and down the front of the house. "I don't want to run into Enid on the way out." She gave me a warm hug, a kiss on the cheek and out she went. "I'll call you when I'm leaving work," she said and gave me a big grin. "I am so happy you're finally here."

"Me too. Pace yourself."

I didn't waste any time. I changed into sandals and shorts. I was still hungry after the salad so I foraged around and located an English muffin and some orange marmalade. I found the toaster oven and popped in the muffin.

Marla had procured three empty one-gallon plastic jugs for drug disposal. I found duct tape and a big wad of plastic store bags. God only knows why, but she had three coffee grinders and had shown me the one to be sacrificed in the service of grinding up narcotics. I put every box, bottle, carton and syringe from the refrigerator on the kitchen table, spread butter and orange marmalade on my muffin and started pulverizing Oxycontin and various other pharmaceutical weapons of mass destruction.

It made a hell of a racket, but didn't take more than thirty minutes. I put the powdered residue in one of the jugs and filled it with water, far beyond the ten-to-one ratio recommended by the experts. I washed my hands and finished off the English muffin. I moved on to the suppositories, liquids and syringes. With great care, I emptied the syringes into a second gallon jug. I added the liquid drugs and suppositories and then filled it with hot water to more quickly break down the gelatin.

With a black marker, I obliterated the information on all the labels and boxes. I then tore them up and put them into the third jug and filled it with water. I wiped down the kitchen table with a sterilizing wipe and then pushed that wipe into bottle number three.

I duct-taped all three jugs, top to bottom, several times and wrote in large letters on each "TOXIC." After shaking them vigorously, I triple-bagged each jug, tossing the defiled coffee grinder into the third bag. I wrote "TOXIC" on each outer bag.

Locking the door behind me, I took the bags into the alley and threw them into the dumpster. I was done with the chore Marla had most wanted to avoid and which posed the most danger to her. It had taken less than an hour. I had at least another three or four hours until Marla's return from work. The long morning and the short night's sleep were catching up to me. A nap was sounding like a good idea.

I took a more leisurely inspection tour of Marla's bungalow. Cramped, crowded and small, it still had an element of coziness and warmth to it. Like all homes, it had a singular smell.

It would be too easy to call it the smell of death. It was predominantly the pleasant, wholesome and clean smell that a woman fosters in her home. But there was something else. A very subtle, not at all overwhelming yet indistinctly uncommon element. A faint sourness, informing your senses that something bad had happened in this place. It was the smell of unutterable sadness.

As I flopped onto the bed, I was hit by an odd rush of feelings; relief that the bed was the same firmness as mine; anticipation about soon sharing this same bed with the lovely and seductive Marla; a mild sense of discomfort in the realization that no matter where I looked there was Neil looking back; the stark oddity of being back in the belly of the beast - Southern California; how clean this little place was despite the general sense of controlled chaos; the contrast of Neil's fantastic, edgy artwork set against Marla's earthy femininity.

It was sunny and quiet. It felt so good to be warm. Murky, lurid visions of playing with Marla, thoughts of my old comrade Neil, projections of how to handle the rest of my chores - all of these faded.

Rolling onto my stomach, letting exhaustion subdue anticipation, I crashed.

Waves were hitting the side of the ship. Women were calling out. Someone was pounding.

Drool in my mustache, disoriented and sweating, I sat up quickly, looking around frantically for a clock. There was one on an unfamiliar wicker stand next to the place I was lying. It was three o'clock.

So, wherever the hell I was...I wasn't late for anything.

Then, firm knocks on the wall outside the bedroom window.

"Hellooo. Marla?" A woman's call.

I realized that I already had slept through two of these strange interruptions. I had discounted them as dreams and ignored them. I rubbed my raw eyes and tried to get my bearings.

Marla...San Diego...Yes...*that's* where I was.

I slipped out of the bed and galumphed into the kitchen to get a drink, hoping all this pounding was a jet lag-induced hallucination and not the dreaded Enid. I was really in no mood. There was no one at the door.

I went outside and opened the gate. No one there, either. Whoever it was had moved on.

I poured a glass of water and sat down at the kitchen table to take a look at the lease. Standard boilerplate, but Marla's name was nowhere to be found within it. I would contact the wicked old landlady and finesse her into showing some compassion for Marla's loss and grief. I'd clear it with Marla first.

Fifteen minutes had passed and all was quiet. No more pounding or calling out for Marla. I was still hungry. I put another English muffin in the toaster oven and dialed the number for the cable company.

Her television was gigantic and ridiculously complicated compared to my twelve year-old, nineteen-inch GE back in Cleveland. The remote was the size of a cutting board and I was having trouble just getting the goddamn thing to turn on. After several minutes on hold, while spreading marmalade, I finally reached Customer Service Specialist Ronny.

CSS Ronny was an affable wizard. When I explained that he and I were helping a beautiful woman, he became my ally. After half an hour of bewildering long-distance manipulation from his end and frustrated cable switching, button pushing and cursing from mine...we had a beautiful, clear picture for Marla. I thanked CSS Ronny for his yeoman work, inferring that his efforts may have gone a long way toward getting me laid.

"You have a great day, Sir...and good luck with that young lady," was CSS Ronny's measured, and no doubt monitored, reply.

I was making real progress with my list and feeling quite cocky when there came a knock at the front door. Assuming this to be the inevitable Enid encounter, I slowly drank the last of the water in my glass, snatched up my half-eaten muffin and, infusing my voice with exasperation, grumbled, "Yeah...I'm coming."

Obviously not Enid, the woman at the door could not conceal her confusion. Short, mid-sixties and stern, with an impatient look of distaste, she spat out, "Is Miss Stone at home?"

"No. Marla is at work. Is there something I can help you with?"

"I'm Lois Findlay, the owner of the property. And you are....?"

Sensing an opportunity to remove one more source of stress from Marla, I launched the charm offensive. I opened the door and invited her in as I said, "I'm Jack Scanlon...an old friend of Neil's."

She declined to come in, so I went outside into the garden and sat down at the table. Continuing to stand, she said, "I need to talk to Miss Stone about the lease as soon as possible. I can come back another time. Are you staying here?"

Telling her that my sleeping arrangements were none of her fucking business would only hurt the cause. I set to work disarming Lois Findlay.

"I'm here for just a few days. I'll be camped out in the living room and helping Marla pick up the pieces...paperwork, probate, will, etc. Neil and I go back to grade school in Ohio. I promised him before he died that I would help Marla as much as I could. He suffered so much and Marla is an emotional wreck...very fragile. She tries to act tough but she's very shaky right now. I cannot imagine what she must have gone through these last several months. I just talked to EPA and Hospice about their guidelines for disposing of all of Neil's painkillers. Marla is very concerned about having them around."

Staying on point, Lois Findlay replied, "The problem is that Miss Stone was never on the lease." Bobbed gray hair and dressed in brown, she maintained eye contact.

Quickly I said, "She mentioned that. She would probably be upset with me for telling you this, but she's worried she will end up on the street. That would be the last straw for her, I'm afraid. I can imagine that Neil was sometimes a difficult tenant, but as a woman,

I'm sure you can appreciate Marla's situation. She is brokenhearted and exhausted." I was laying it on precariously thick.

We talked about Neil for a few minutes; what a constant pain in the ass he'd been to her and the mad genius comrade he was to the rest of us.

She reached into her purse and pulled out an envelope of papers. She looked at them, looked at me, then again at the papers. She put them back in her purse. "I was going to discuss this with her before giving these papers to her."

Was she going to evict Marla?

"She should be back around five. Can I have her call you? Or I can call her at work for you. I know she's anxious to speak with you about it. Frankly, Ms Findlay, the poor kid is scared to death she's going to end up homeless on top of everything else she's been through."

Lois Findlay looked blankly at me for a few seconds and said, "When my husband passed away six years ago, I was dead from the neck up for months."

"So very sorry for your loss."

"Thank you. He was a philandering nitwit." She studied my face and gave me a long, penetrating look.

She reached into her purse again. She slowly withdrew the envelope and handed it to me. "Will you please give this to Miss Stone?"

"I certainly will."

"It's a new one-year lease with her named as new tenant. Same terms as the old lease. I'm not an ogre, Mr. Scanlon."

With a genuine smile I said, "I made no such assumption, Ms Findlay. Right now, in my eyes you're a saint."

"Nor am I a saint. Have her call me when she's signed them and I'll stop by to pick them up. Or she can just mail them to my office."

I stood to accept Lois's firm, all-business handshake. "I can promise you that Marla will be relieved and thrilled about this. I can't wait to tell her. She needs some good news and this is the best thing that could happen to her. Thank you very much, Lois. You're a good person."

She managed a tiny, pinched smile. "And you are a charming and persuasive man, Mr. Scanlon. I hope she appreciates your friendship. Enjoy your stay in Olinda." She got into her little gray car and drove off.

I went back into the bungalow, a new buoyancy in my step. I was feeling very good about my day so far and said out loud, "Drugs gone. Cable back on. New lease. You are just on *fire*, boyo!"

Right on cue, my phone rang. It was Marla.

"How's it going, Sweetie?"

"I think you'll be pleased with our progress, Miss Stone."

"Tell me, tell me, tell me!" She was like a kid.

"When you get home. How long will you be?"

Marla said, "I should be there soon...about five-fifteen. I can't wait to see you. So, what have you done today? Did you get a nap?"

I teased her. "Been sleeping since you left. Peed the bed and ate all your English muffins."

Laughing, "You are so full of shit. What happened today? Tell me!"

"The drugs are gone, the cable's back on and you had a visitor. And that's all you get until I get another kiss."

"You did all that already, Johnny? What visitor? Enid? Sasha? No...he's out of town. Ben?"

"None of the above. Don't worry, it's all good news that will cost you one earth-rumbling kiss."

"Don't be mean. Tell me who was there. Then you get the kiss."

"I'm not being mean. I am teasing you. I want it to be a surprise. Everything is fine...far better than when you left."

"I'll be there as soon as I can. You really got rid of the drugs? And fixed the TV? You are amazing."

"I'm just getting warmed up. Call me when you're heading home."

"Gotta get back in there. Smooches."

I spent half an hour sitting in the warm and relaxed atmosphere of the garden as the sun went behind the bungalow. I enjoyed the feeling of the dry, warm air on my face and arms and legs and feet. The temperature back in Cleveland would dip into the teens tonight. I daydreamed about what steamy treats Marla might invent to express her appreciation for my diligence.

I went back inside and hopped on the bed, thinking I might doze until Marla got home. I was settling into an aura of mellow smugness when there was another knock at the door.

"Sonofabitch...is it always this busy around here?" I wondered under my breath as I slid off the bed and walked into the living room.

The closeness of a place the size of Marla's tends to compromise privacy. Homes this small frequently engender those weird incidents of turning a corner and scaring the living bejesus out of someone coming from the next room. The distance from the front door, through the living room to the bedroom, was no more than fifteen feet.

Thus it was that the male figure with his back to the door was startled when I said, sharply, a foot from the back of his head, "Can I help you?"

He ducked, executed a rubber-legged sideways hop, made a deep, rumbling "aaack" sound and stumbled to one knee in the middle of the garden, inches shy of flattening Marla's prized yellow snapdragons.

Flushed and glowering, he jerked his head sharply around in my direction. He said nothing as he slowly got to his feet and brushed the dirt from his filthy jeans. He stood still, not coming toward the door, and stared at me with no expression. He seemed to be regulating his breathing.

I gave him a big smile and said, "Sorry. I didn't mean to sneak up on you."

He was about six foot-two, average build, his short black hair poorly cut. He had high cheekbones and a triangular head and face, flat on top and pointed at a clean-shaven chin. Pale blue, bloodshot eyes set far apart and a nose that had been broken at least once. His teeth were small and gray. The effect was reptilian. His jeans and black t-shirt were permanently wrinkled and his work boots splattered with paint, tar and mud. The overall impression was that of an unmade bed. After several more seconds, he took the three steps back to the portico. Looking over my head into the bungalow then back at me, he said, basso profundo, "Is Marla home?"

Putting the pieces together with this bizarre display of questionable motor skills, it seemed I had finally met the all too oft-mentioned Sasha. Marla had said he smoked constantly and this guy absolutely reeked of cigarettes.

"She's not. Can I take a message?" I was giving this guy nothing.

Again he slowly looked over and around me into the house. He said, in a slow, cavernously deep voice, "When will she be back?"

To which I politely replied, "Whom, may I ask, is calling?"

His expression remained largely unchanged, though his jaw set ever so slightly. "I am Sasha…a friend of Neil's. And you are...?"

I'd been here less than six hours and already this smarmy, colloquial interrogative had been thrown at me twice. Who I am, chump, is the guy on the *inside* of Marla's house.

"I'm Jack. I don't know when she'll be home, but I'll tell her you stopped by."

Sasha inquired, "Would it be alright if I called her?"

I remembered that Marla told me Sasha had no cell phone and bummed calls from others... along with cigarettes, weed, meals and cash. She had also told me he was out of town.

"I would assume if you have called her before, you could call her again."

"Can I use her telephone?"

"You mean this phone in here?"

A dim light of cognition flickered on as his eyes narrowed. "Yes. May I use Marla's telephone?"

Locking my stare on his, I answered, "In all honesty, I'm just not comfortable letting anyone into the house without Marla being here. She was pretty specific that I keep this door locked. Maybe you could try your call later." Now I was just being a prick.

Sasha reached to scratch his ear and appeared to be having trouble finding the itch. His bloodshot, metallic eyes stared lazily into mine, and finally he said, "I'll do that."

"Well, it was great meeting you, but I really have a lot to do," I said in a tone civil yet dismissive.

"Yes." He stood in the alcove for a few seconds, seemingly uncertain as to what he should do next. He took one more expressionless look beyond me into the bungalow.

He said "Goodbye", turned very slowly and with a rolling gait, walked out of the garden, down the street and out of sight.

It had been a busy and unusual day. I hadn't even begun the best part of it...the part I would spend with the thorny, enticing Marla. I took a shower to revive myself and my phone rang as I was drying. It was Marla calling from her car to tell me she'd be home in ten minutes.

"How's it going?" she asked. "Any news?'

"I'm getting hungry."

"I'll be there in a few minutes, Cutie, and we'll go to the store and feed you."

"I just want to see you. The food is secondary."

She closed with, "You are so full of it. Hold your horses. I'm on my way."

Ten minutes later, reading the newspaper at the kitchen table, I heard the gate open followed by keys in the door. Marla came around the corner into the kitchen.

She was smiling as she said, "Hi there. How was your day?" Shuffling through a stack of mail, she ran her hand over the back of my neck and said, "Please tell me you took a nice nap."

"I made two aborted attempts. No big deal. Ready for a rundown of my day?" I stood and handed her the TV remote.

She turned on the TV, looked at me with delight and flipped to the country music channel. "I know you're not a big fan, but this is what's on most of the time when I'm here alone." She gave me a hug and said, "Thanks for handling those cable jerks. I have to use the bathroom, and then we'll go to the store and get something to make for dinner. I'll change clothes when we get back. You can tell me all the rest in the car."

On the way to Ralph's, I described my exchange with CSS Ronny and how carefully and safely I had disposed of Neil's pharmacy. Marla patted my leg tenderly, firmly squeezed my knee, and said, "You are really something, Johnny. You have no idea what a relief this is for me."

As we got out of the car in the strip mall parking lot, I stopped her. I would save my odd encounter with Sasha for later. I took the envelope containing her new lease out of my pocket. Deadpan, I said, "A lady came by today and asked me to give this to you."

Leaning against the side of the car, Marla's face went pallid. "Oh, no. The landlady? Oh, no. Was it the landlady?"

"She called herself the 'property owner.' Name's Lois?"

"Oh, god. She's throwing me out. How long can you stay in a property after you've been evicted? Oh, shit, Johnny. Did you see it?"

"No, I haven't seen it," which was true.

Marla opened the envelope. After reading for ten seconds, her eyes got as wide as I'd ever seen them. She said loudly, "Is this what I think it is? I can *stay*?"

She read a little more and then exclaimed, loudly enough to draw attention from several other shoppers, "I get to stay! How did you do this? Did you talk to her? Oh my god... I still have the bungalow!"

Marla's ability to display the purest emotion, the most essential joy and the darkest fiery fury, was enormously energizing for me. She charged me up.

As we practically skipped arm-in-arm toward the grocery store, I told her about my encounter with Lois, ending with her complimentary remarks about my alluring personality. Marla stopped while getting an empty cart and gave me a little kiss. "Oh...I bet you just charmed the pants right off her, didn't you?"

"And hoping to continue that trend."

Marla laughed and said quietly, "You're a patient man, remember?"

As she had in Ohio, Marla shopped deliberately and efficiently. My only contributions were pushing the cart, remarking, "We'll need more English muffins" and picking out a few bottles of wine. A guy should know he's in trouble when the simple act of buying food with a woman is sufficient to make him marvel at her beauty and ability. I was proud and happy in her company and she was enjoying mine.

The sun had nearly set as we put the bags in the trunk and headed back to the bungalow. Marla lit a cigarette. She had smoked one at the bungalow, one on the way to Ralph's and now this one. She was a considerate smoker, careful to ask if the smoke bothered me and she never smoked in her home, always in the garden or on the portico.

It made me wonder what happened to the girl who said she only smoked a couple a day. No matter. I was glowing in the company of a happy woman.

We parked on the street and toted the supplies inside. The plan was salmon with dill sauce and a salad. I poured wine and Marla headed to the bedroom.

"I am going to get out of these clothes and then make dinner."

"Let me know if you need help with either one of those."

"Maybe later," she laughed tantalizingly. Then added, "I cannot believe how much you got done today, Johnny - cable, new lease, your own personal war on drugs. You're my hero. I'll be right back."

Marla returned wearing form-fitting dark blue sweatpants and a pink t-shirt. "I think we should feed ourselves and then I want to work in the garden for a while. Will you water for me?"

"Never water after sundown. It promotes fungus. But I'm up for anything else." I tried with considerable difficulty to not stare at her nipples, which were marvelously accentuated through her top. Predictably Pavlovian, I said, "I love that outfit."

"I'll need a sweatshirt pretty soon."

"Wait as long as possible, will you?"

She glanced quickly at her chest, looked at me, but said nothing. She knew exactly what she was doing. I was prepared to postpone the salmon and go straight to the linoleum.

The fish took no time at all. We refilled our wine glasses and sat down to dinner. After a couple bites and complimenting each other's culinary prowess, I said, "Your friend Sasha also stopped by today."

Marla looked up, eyebrows raised and mouth slightly opened. "What the hell. Why didn't you tell me about this when I called you?"

"Because he showed up about thirty minutes before you came home. It seemed like the least important event of the day."

"You should have told me."

"I just did."

More confused than angry, Marla inquired, "What did he want?"

"He wanted you. He clearly didn't expect to see me coming to the door. We introduced ourselves, I suggested he call you later and he left. He's a real charmer. He seemed preoccupied. Not much of a conversationalist, old Sasha."

"Were you mean to him?"

"Not at all."

"I don't understand what he's doing here. I saw him a couple weeks ago. He told me he was going to be gone for a couple of months doing petition work in Oklahoma and somewhere else… Iowa…Ohio, maybe."

We finished our meal, put the dishes in the sink and took our wine outside to the stone table in the garden. It was dark now, nearly seven thirty. Marla set to pulling weeds. I joined her. Five minutes later, "I'm going inside for a sweatshirt. "

"Do you have to?" I chided.

"You are really something, Scanlon. Yes…as you can plainly see," again glancing down at her breasts, "I have to."

We putzed for a couple hours. The tone, the tenor of our conversation was congenial and playful. The wine flowed, a sliver of moon rose, we found warmth and comfort in each other's nearness. We played in the dirt and talked.

"I thought tomorrow we'd go downtown to the courthouse and to Vital Records to clear up some of the will and probate questions. I need a copy of Neil's death certificate, too."

"I'm at your service." I loved looking at Marla. She was a study in perpetual motion. Whether putting weeds in a bag, pulling dead leaves from a geranium or inspecting for pests, the way she moved was spare in effort yet luxuriously fluid and graceful.

I had to ask, "What do you think Sasha wanted…other than the obvious?"

She lit a cigarette. "Here's a quick Sasha story. The last week before Neil went away, Sasha had been hanging around a lot, for several days. He was getting on Neil's nerves. Neil kept staring at him. I could tell he was angry."

"Sasha wants you. Plain and simple."

"I think that's what Neil thought, too, even though I have no interest whatsoever in Sasha and never will. That day, while Sasha and Enid were outside, Neil motioned me over to the sofa. He glared at me very sternly and whispered…he could barely speak at all at that point… 'Not Sasha. Not Sasha.' He was very serious and very upset."

"Besides your lovely ass, what does Sasha *want*?"

Her mouth suppressed a smile as she answered. "Glass. He wants as much of Neil's glass as he can grab. Over the years, he's acquired a lot of it…probably has more than I do. Whenever Neil was broke, Sasha always found the money to buy glass from him. He sometimes told Neil he would sell them back to him later, but he didn't. Since Neil went away, Sasha's become sort of obsessed with The Seven Deadly Sins pieces."

"Does he have any of them?"

"He claims he doesn't."

"And you?"

"I have five pieces – Gluttony, Pride, Envy, Anger and Sloth. I'll show them to you while you're here. Maybe Tomorrow. They're not here. I have them in storage."

"Afraid someone might steal them?"

"I am now. I've been told there's some buzz about them. Apparently, since Neil left, there's a little more interest in his work. If its value goes up, a set of seven 'theme' pieces would be a valuable collection for somebody." Marla said.

"Where is Greed?"

"I hear things, but I don't really have any idea. Maybe you could help me find it?" She did not mention Lust, the piece in my bathroom back home.

I replied, "Whatever you need. But, isn't it about bed time?"

Marla looked at me with kind eyes and a warm smile. We'd both had a couple glasses of Pinot Grigio and I was feeling warm and funky. She took my hand and said, "I'm sorry, Sweetie. You've had a long day and you must be bushed. I need to scrub this dirt from under my nails and take my shower and then we'll get to bed. And you are *not*, by God, sleeping on any couch tonight. My house…my rules. You sleep with me in my bed."

No sweeter words had ever fallen on my ears. "If you insist."

We washed the few dishes in the sink. After brushing my teeth in the relentlessly yellow funhouse bathroom, I put on sweats, fluffed a pillow and lay down on the bed with a magazine. Hearing her go out the front door, I got up to see if she needed help with anything. She was standing in the glow of the porch light, silently smoking a cigarette. I said nothing and a few minutes later, heard her close and lock the front door.

Marla brought our wine into the bedroom. She set my glass on the nightstand, took a peek into the living room and then closed the bedroom door. I spotted a small, red lace "baby doll" with matching lace panties on a hanger on the back of the door. I offered up a silent, fervent prayer that I would soon be seeing Marla in them…and shortly thereafter be helping her out of them. She sat cross-legged on the chair at the desk, near the foot of the bed. She opened the drawer and reached deep into it.

"I'm going to smoke a little bit of this. I do it almost every night. It helps me relax and sleep. You look like you could stand to relax a little, too. But I do *not* want you to feel pressured."

I have for decades contended that marijuana was a beneficial euphoriant, that the laws regarding its cultivation, sale and use were entirely misguided and counter-productive and that it should be legalized. If I had any misgivings about smoking pot with Marla, they were because I hadn't smoked it in many years. The idea of inhaling hot ashes and then embarrassing myself by coughing for five minutes held little appeal.

As Marla put a piece of a bud into a tiny pipe, I said, "Maybe later."

She replied, "Absolutely. If and when you feel you might want to, I have plenty." She lit the pipe, the weed glowed red-orange and she took a big hit of high-priced smoke. She smiled at me and winked as she held in the smoke and then slowly blew it out. It looked just the way I remembered it looking. She re-lit the pipe and took another toke. Her eyes were shining and her face looked very calm.

"Are you sure, Honey? You look pretty tense."

Nodding toward the lingerie on the back of the door, I asked Marla, "Are you wearing that to bed?"

"I got it out of the closet yesterday. I haven't worn it in years." She actually blushed and her brown eyes smoldered above a slow, intriguing smile. She tapped the ashes into an ashtray and put in a little more herb. I took a swallow of my wine and she took a swallow of hers. Marla said, "I want to be perfectly relaxed when we get into bed together. I want us to be open and easy with each other."

I knew she was right. I was never one to get high and then want to go bowling. I just wanted to listen to music or make love or eat caramel corn...or all three. Smoking marijuana had always been more of a sacramental endeavor than a statement or a tool. I remembered simply enjoying the way it made me feel.

There were people on the Titanic who turned down dessert. I could see the Promised Land and I was not getting any younger.

I moved down to sit cross-legged at the end of the bed, two feet away from Marla. "You know...you're probably right. I am pretty spooled up."

She clapped her hands with a grin that nearly closed her eyes. "Really? Yippee!" She actually said yippee and she meant it. She was elated. She teased me. "Are you sure you remember how to do it?"

"Just hand me the pipe, smartass."

I did not embarrass myself and, after filling and passing the pipe a couple times, it all came back to me. Trying to describe the sensation is like trying to explain what lobster tastes like or how it feels to swim naked. The quality of any experience depends in large part on the people with whom you share it. It was wonderfully liberating and it served to further bond us. It was one more happy shared experience.

I had forgotten how dopey and funny everything seems when you're stoned. One of us called the other a "goofball" and we laughed uproariously. This continued until I had to get up and leave the room because my ribs and stomach began to hurt. Marla actually slipped off her chair and onto the floor at one point. We sipped our wine, smoked a little more. We tried to compose ourselves to talk of weightier things, but each time, we collapsed into helpless laughter. I hadn't laughed that much or that hard in many, many years, stretching facial muscles rarely used. Marla was clearly lifted and gratified by the whole thing. Why had I deprived myself of this for so long?

After an immeasurable time of pure mirth and silliness, I took her face gently between my hands, kissed her soft lips lightly and said, "I think it's time to call it a day, Beautiful Girl."

Marla slowly opened her eyes, stood up and said, "I'm going to go outside for one last cigarette, and then I'll shower and come to bed."

I grabbed the wine glasses and followed her outside for a breath of fresh night air, San Diego-style. As she inspected her garden, sipping the last of her wine, I sat in a lawn chair and watched her. I will forever be fascinated and disarmed by the graceful, natural way Marla's body moved through the world.

"Beautiful night," I said.

"They're all beautiful here, Johnny. You'll see. You're going to love it here."

After several minutes of staring at the night sky, listening to the cosmic hum inside my noggin and leering at Marla, I finally said, "I'm going to brush my nasty teeth and hit the sack." Someone had lined my mouth with dryer lint and modeling clay.

"I'll be right in."

I heard the front door closed and locked as I put my toothbrush in the rack and exited the bathroom. I took my empty glass to the kitchen where Marla was pouring one last splash into hers. I added a bit to mine and we toasted each other.

I followed her into the bedroom, where she closed the door tightly, giving me a smile. She removed the tiny red nightie from the hook on the back of the door and held it up in front of her. "Too cheesy?"

I answered, "Not for me."

She spun toward the bathroom with a look over her shoulder. "I'll be right out."

"I'll be right here." And, for no good reason, we both laughed at that.

As I relaxed on the bed, engrossed by the insides of my eyelids, my brain was a hemp throw pillow, an astral taffy pull, a Magritte DooDah parade, a soft porn musical complete with blimps, Whooping Cranes, surfboards and a tenderly prurient duet with Marla. I was soaring and smiling and life seemed very, very good indeed.

When I heard the shower turn on, I got undressed and under the covers. The only light came from under the bathroom door and from the neighbor's porch light, through the closed blind on the window above the headboard. As my pupils regulated to the darkness, my re-wired, gummy synapses took in the details of the room.

To my left, a blank wall and the sliding closet door. To my right, the nightstand, a file cabinet with a printer and papers on top, the computer desk and the door to the living room. Straight ahead, a small blue dresser, a large mirror and the bathroom door. Beyond that door, a troubled siren, a brunette bombshell and the person most likely to become the primary player in my immediate future.

I sat up on the edge of the bed and looked at the dozen different photos of Neil on the wall next to the desk. Among the many things Neil told me regarding Marla's body and what made her an exceptional lover, I recalled two; her three children had been born Caesarian and she'd never breastfed. I would soon see what he meant.

Less anxious and as stoned as I've ever been, it felt wonderfully odd and rejuvenating. I wondered what Marla looked like right now. It seemed like she'd been in there for hours. Time had stopped and all I could hear was the water running.

As my weightless, elastic mind tossed and turned among explicit thoughts of sex with Marla...the shower stopped. My heart raced. Wanting to get a good look at her in the baby doll, I turned the nightstand lamp on.

After a few long minutes, I thought I heard a buzzing sound. If it wasn't real, then either this was the best weed in America or I was having a stroke. I decided it wasn't my imagination. Remembering her remark that she wasn't a "battery girl", I put aside other considerations and determined it was her toothbrush.

When the buzz stopped and the water in the sink shut off, Marla opened the door a few inches. She was putting her brush in the rack and said, "Honey, do we need that light?" I caught a fleeting glimpse of the lingerie. Her untamable hair was still partially wet. Her face was scrubbed and bright.

"I don't know. What do you think?"

Marla turned off the bathroom light, opened the door and walked around the bed to the nightstand, the whole time looking straight into my eyes. The supple reality of her body through the red lace was breathtaking. She stood there for a second, long enough to smile and say, "You like?" She switched off the lamp.

"Very much. Come to bed." Marla lifted the covers to lie down next to me in what had become our preferred position, her back against my chest, thigh to thigh.

Our eyes adjusted to the darkness as one body warmed and molded to the other. We whispered and giggled and I let my hands delicately slide over her arms and legs, letting my fingers trail against her rump and the edge of her breast. Soon, she reached behind to stroke the backs of my thighs and my butt. I lightly kissed her neck and ears through the wet tangle of her hair. Marla was silent as she let me slip the red baby doll over her head. She wiggled out of the bottoms.

Her form was as pristine as that of a woman half her age. A sculpted balance of muscle and curve, her thighs and loins were all I had envisioned. She directed my hand to her hip. Her stomach and pelvis were trim and welcoming. She was toasty warm and unblemished, lightly bronzed, with tan lines appropriate for the little black bikini she had described to me. Marla's skin was soft and very smooth. Her breasts were lovely – small, but full and firm, proportional to her slight frame, with nipples like gumdrops.

After a bit of girlishly coy resistance, she tightly closed her eyes as I slowly pulled the covers down to admire her amazing body in its fullness. As I drank in the erotic vision that I had waited so long and patiently to see, all I could muster was a reverential, "My god you are beautiful." She had the toned body of a dancer.

Wanting to miss nothing, we explored each other patiently and with tenderness, getting familiar with the newness of our bodies in union. In a brief moment of disbelief, I questioned if I was really there with this sensationally luscious lover. Marla ended any doubt by putting lips against my ear and hotly whispering, "What would you like to do?"

I replied, slowly, into her ear, "I think we should make that dream of yours come true."

She threw her tawny right leg across my hips and sat straight up, straddling my thighs. What I saw in that instant is indelibly burned into my memory. All my favorite things, right there at my fingertips. She was exquisite. Marla said, looking down at me, with husky voice and humid eyes, "I'm pretty small down there...but I won't break", and then slowly, willingly, she gave herself to me.

Without much talk, we allowed ourselves ample time to enjoy every part of this wild thing we were creating. Amidst the rustles and whispers and rhythms of lovemaking - thrust, rest, thrust - we made the mammal sounds of passion: Marla with long guttural purring and short, staccato intakes of breath; me with exhortations, whispers of her beauty and ancient, male noises. I had the sensation we were wrapped in a blanket of electricity. Caution and convention thrown to the winds, invoking deities, we took each other with gusto and joy.

We made love with an ease and abandon that surprised and delighted us both. It seemed endless and new. At one point, I said, "I don't want this to end." Marla breathlessly asked, "We're going to do it again, right?"

It was sex the way sex was meant to be - hot and hard and happy.

Afterwards, in an exhausted state of grace – panting, smiling, and holding onto each other as if our sinews and souls could push away everything unresolved – we breathed in unison a lusty "Wow."

Marla pressed her body even closer and said, "Amazing."

Never at a loss for a snappy retort, I said, "Wow" again.

A moment later I asked her, "Did we make as much noise as I think we did?"

Marla turned her head to kiss me, raised her eyebrows and whispered, "Oh, yeah. I'm afraid there's no way Enid didn't hear *that.*"

I replied, "Honey, people at the airport might have heard *that*." And we started laughing all over again.

She said, "I really have to go to the bathroom, but I'm not sure I can walk."

"Flatterer."

Unwound, we soon settled down for the night. There wasn't room for a bookmark between us. Marla was on her right side, her head on my chest, her pelvic bone pushed firm against my hip, her left thigh across my groin. I cradled her protectively, my left arm tightly around her, my cheek resting on her still damp hair, and my right hand lightly stroking her leg.

"Good night, Beautiful Girl."

"Sleep well, Butterfly."

And the night closed in.

As life-affirming and aerobic as the sex had been, it was another restless night's sleep: getting accustomed to a new partner's shape and rhythms; wanting to touch but wanting to sleep.

But when we got up, there were smug, knowing smiles and no complaints. I felt slightly hung over, but it was manageable. We planned the day over coffee and the morning paper. We spoke of the chance of a nap later, which I instinctively interpreted as more sex and therefore a capital idea. It felt comfortable and right being with Marla. She seemed pleased and relaxed and I was smiling like a simpleton.

We would go to Vital Records and then downtown to the courthouse. It all had something to do with Neil's will and his long-unpaid taxes. This information was promptly lost in my all-encompassing interest in being with her. Where, when or why was immaterial. We would eat lunch in San Diego's version of Little Italy (I was skeptical) and then go visit the five Deadly Sins, stashed at a storage facility in the city.

"I want to get at least that much done today. I have a great place to take you for dinner tonight." Marla was raring to go. "It's only nine. How about brunch?"

We drove a few blocks to a little diner and had pancakes. She had a mimosa. I had orange juice. Mimosa has always seemed another lame Southern California affectation to be avoided. I never blend sparkling wine and maple syrup in the same meal.

Marla drove like a bank robber. I was determined to show no fear, in case this was a test of my mettle. During the twenty-minute drive to Vital Records I blinked twice.

Complicating her demented driving was a ritual for extinguishing cigarettes that was sure to end up killing somebody. She took the ashtray out of the console, held it in one hand, while conscientiously insuring the butt was crushed out with the other hand then returning the ashtray to its rightful place. All of this while alternately stomping on the brakes then the accelerator, steering with her elbows and darting from lane to lane at top speed with no attempt to signal her intentions.

After a safe landing at Vital Records, waiting for an exophthalmic peroxide-blonde bureaucrat to bring Marla's forms, I put my hand on the small of her back and whispered, "I can't wait for naptime. Let's do it in the restroom."

She gave me a sleepy smile and, her hot breath against my ear, murmured "Cameras, silly."

After leaving Vital Records and another sphincter-slamming slalom to the courthouse, Marla signed and initialed one stack of papers in exchange for another stack and we drove uphill to Little Italy. Strolling past a half-dozen laughably hip bistros, every patio littered with the mass-produced Yuppie effluvia that defines cosmopolitan Southern California, we found an authentic Italian place called Fillipi's. They even had baccala in the deli case. We relaxed over a beautiful lunch of lasagna, ravioli and Chianti.

We had found a calm equilibrium and a level of comfort that transformed a simple lunch into a romantic meal. We shared long looks into each other's eyes, conspiratorial smiles and even a little handholding. We talked about the future – hers, mine, and ours. We discussed what might happen after I went home, the tenuous situation at her job, her son, our night together and Neil.

Always about Neil. "Neil used to say…" "Neil and I…" "Whenever Neil…" "Neil would have…" It was impossible for Marla to have a conversation with anyone…about anything…without framing it in the context of what Neil would have said or done or thought. It was perfectly understandable, but it was getting old. Keeping in mind my old friend and Marla's loss and grief, I held my tongue. After lunch, we walked arm in arm back to her car and drove the ten blocks to the storage facility. The neighborhood got seedier with each block.

"*STUFF IT*" suggested the twelve-foot high, red neon sign atop the storage facility. Another three-foot invitation above the entrance flashed; "*Jammed At Home? Shove It Here!*" The building was a dark gray monolith, three stories high and - except for the office entrance - windowless. Nearly a city block in size, it was a fortress.

We parked on the street. Marla shut off the car and turned to me. "I've never shown these to anyone. I don't even have photos of them. I'm sure Neil told somebody about them, but as far as the rest of the world knows, they don't exist. Neil kept them hidden for years and we stashed them here as soon as he got diagnosed. When I saw 'Lust' at your place, I nearly fainted. After he got sick, he couldn't remember who he had given it to. It's good to know it's in safe hands."

"I promise I won't tell anyone about any of this."

She leaned over, gave me a kiss and said, "Thank you."

The guy manning the desk did not inspire confidence or a sense of security. Maybe thirty years old, he had magnificently bloodshot eyes, greasy blonde dreadlocks, and wore a Stormtroopers of Death t-shirt that perfectly complimented the colorful Mighty Mouse tattoo on his neck and the pair of poker chips in his earlobes. His nametag said simply, "Beyond."

He carefully folded the Classifieds, removed his headphones and stood up. After looking Marla up and down, he leered for another second and in a broad Aussie accent asked, "How can I help you, Ma'am?"

We both signed the log and showed our driver's licenses to Beyond who then silently took us to the elevator. He hung back a bit to get a good look at Marla's derriere. Although I did not like it, I'd become accustomed to this behavior on the part of other men. She had the kind of ass you just had to admire.

She slid her card through the security device and punched in her PIN. This opened the elevator door. Nodding a tentative farewell to our grungy host, Marla pushed the button for the third floor and up we rode. The scene as the door opened onto the third level was straight out of a Sixties sci-fi movie.

We stepped out onto a bright white concrete floor. It was all of thirty feet wide. Ten-foot walls of gleaming white fiberglass ran for two hundred feet to the left and right. Brass knobs on bright white doors twenty feet apart were the only interruptions in this flat, sterile landscape. A low, droning hum must have been the temperature control system. *"Always Between 50 and 72 Degrees Fahrenheit!"*

Grabbing my hand and turning left, Marla said, "Spooky, isn't it? Like a mausoleum."

I thought out loud, "Or an android monastery."

We walked to a door halfway down the right corridor. She again swiped her card and entered a code. This door revealed a second hallway about a hundred feet long, fifteen feet wide and with a slightly lower ceiling. These doors were closer together and all secured with large touch pad locks. Still a barren fiberglass theme, but on a less intimidating scale.

At the second door on the left, Marla stopped to fish a piece of paper from her purse. She glanced at it several times as she punched in the numbers. A slight grinding hum as the bolt retracted. She said, "I haven't been in here since right after Neil got sick." And, as if rolling the stone away from a tomb, Marla slowly opened the door.

The room was small – eight by eight with an eight-foot ceiling. It was nearly filled by a kayak and paddles, a stack of folding chairs, three old computer monitors stacked on top of one another and a table. There was barely room to turn around.

Under the table were three cardboard boxes marked "Miscellaneous." On the table were five boxes marked, "Envy", "Gluttony", "Anger", "Pride" and "Sloth." The words had been painted on the boxes with bright oil paint, a one-inch brush and great flourish.

Marla said, "The stuff in these other boxes," indicating the ones under the table, "is mostly books and clothing and old kitchen gadgets. I don't know why Neil wanted to hang onto them. At that point, neither of us was thinking clearly."

"I can only imagine. And these five on top, can we open them?"

"Isn't that why we're here?" she said sharply, with an air of exasperation.

I let it pass. This couldn't be easy for her.

We had a box knife and some packing tape. I cut open the tops of the boxes.

In art glass, size matters. Each piece easily weighed forty pounds and several layers of bubble wrap protected them. We agreed to examine them one at a time, putting the empty boxes in the hall to give us room to move. I took several pictures of each one with my phone.

We both lifted "Envy" from its box and carefully placed it on the table. It was a solid piece in deep emerald green with one solid, blood red stripe running diagonally through its center. It was in the shape of a rough cube, with a funnel-shaped depression at the top. Looking into the depression, one could see the red stripe, but at the same time it seemed to have no bottom.

"Neil said this one was hard to make, but he loved the color and used to remind me that Envy was the nastiest of all the Sins." Marla was speaking very softly.

With great care, we sealed "Envy" and put it back in its box. Opening the next one…I laughed out loud.

"Gluttony" was elemental, unmistakable Neil. It was pus yellow. On the front of the sculpture were three fat, grasping hands with blackened fingernails. On top, a grotesquely wide-open mouth, candy apple red lips peeled back to bare brown, jagged teeth and a large pink tongue.

I said to Marla, "That has Neil written all over it."

She replied, "He knew a little bit about excess." She tried to smile and lightly stroked my arm, but it wasn't working. She was not enjoying this and the walls were starting to close in on me a little, too. We lovingly wrapped and boxed "Gluttony."

Opening "Anger", Marla remarked, "Neil said he could see me in this one. I never really knew what he meant, but it pissed me off." So much for irony.

"Anger" was a black sphere resting on a flat bottom. It was covered with dozens of barbed pieces of clear glass. It was dark and dangerous and unappealing. As much as he must have enjoyed making "Gluttony", I got the impression "Anger" was one piece he had been glad to move away from. I would soon fully appreciate why.

"Sloth" was low and flattish. It was a grotesquely obese nude sitting on a beanbag chair. Her corpulence making it difficult to see where she stopped and the beanbag started. It was a funny, flabby study in orange and white.

As we were opening "Pride", my cell phone rang, loud in the tiny, closed space. It made Marla jump. The caller ID showed Miriam's number. I had given her a key to the house so she could collect my mail and paper and water the plants.

"Hey, Miriam. What's going on? Everything alright?"

Marla shot me a quick dirty look.

"Everything's fine, Jack. Just called to see how the trip is going."

"The flight was fine and Marla was right there to scoop me up. We're having a great time."

"I'm just checking in. All is well here and I'm sure you're enjoying the warmer weather."

"I'm enjoying everything."

"Yes…yes…I'm sure you are, you reprobate."

Not taking the bait, I replied, "I'm right in the middle of something here. How about I give you a call later?"

"Not necessary. Have a ball and soak up all the sun you can."

Marla had taken "Pride" from its box. I helped her remove the bubble wrap. It was a wedge-shaped piece, bright yellow and white with a dozen thin squiggles of purple glass running within it. Maybe sixteen inches high, the lower part was all warm light and sharp angles. A globe of striking cobalt blue the size of a croquet ball sat atop the point of the wedge.

"Not sure what to make of this one, but it's really beautiful isn't it?"

Marla responded with, "Everything alright with Miriam?"

"Everything's alright at the house, if that's what you mean."

Her inquiry basted with sarcasm, "Is she going to be calling you a lot, do you think?" She turned to face me. "How much does she know about us?"

"Only what she needs to know. I'm here to help you out and that we're attracted to each other. I'm not trying to hide you the way you're hiding me. Whatever conclusions she, or anyone else, draws are beyond my control. Frankly, I don't give a shit what anybody thinks about this." I braced myself for impact.

"Is this the first time she's called you here?"

"She left me a message yesterday that I ignored because I was with you."

Loudly, Marla said, "This bitch has a lot of nerve calling you when she knows you're with me. It's rude and completely disrespectful."

My buttons sufficiently pushed, "Are you shitting me? You had fifty calls while you were at my place and you answered every single one of them. When you and I are on the phone, two thousand miles apart, no matter who calls or walks up to your door… you get me off the phone so you can talk to people you see every damn day. And now you're going to bust my balls over *one* call from a friend who's watching my house? Bullshit."

Marla yelled, "Are you screwing her?"

"Jesus Christ, Marla. I don't have to answer that, but…no…I'm *not* screwing her. Never have, don't plan to and she feels the same. I want to enjoy this week, just you and me, and this ridiculous discussion is not helping. What are you really angry about?"

Red-faced, Marla's volume doubled, "She shouldn't be calling you. You know I want to keep this as quiet as possible. I bet you've been bragging to all your buddies, haven't you? You don't have any respect for me at all."

Now matching her tone, "Respect for you is the reason I'm here, Marla. Three people know I'm here; my son, Miriam and my dentist. That's it. There's been no macho locker-room-bragging shit going on. We hadn't even done anything until last night! I'm not getting into a pissing contest with you. If you're so goddamned determined to be angry, have the decency to wait until I do something to deserve it."

"Your dentist? What the hell? *Your dentist*?"

"We were friends long before he became a dentist. You met him at Neil's party. I told him just the facts and I trust him. We need to drop this right now before it ruins our day."

Still fuming, she tersely mumbled, "Let's put 'Pride' away and get out of here," once and for all confirming that irony was wasted on Marla Stone.

After putting everything back in its place and locking up, we took a silent elevator ride to street level, nodded to Beyond, found Marla's car and got in. She turned the key in the ignition. I reached over and turned it off. Marla tilted her head back, sighed deeply and said, "What now?"

"Is this how it's going to be, Marla? I answer a phone call and you explode? I ask simple questions and you give me attitude? I understand this is probably very hard for you, Honey, but if you're looking for someone to be your emotional tampon, I'm not your boy."

After several seconds, she turned her head to me, took off her shades and coolly replied, "If I overreacted, I'm sorry. But she should know better. You should know better. Can we go now?"

"Not if we're going to be sparring with each other the whole time. I came here as a friend and you're not treating me like one."

Marla put her hand on my arm and said, "You know what would help? Some fresh air and a little exercise. A walk around the bay and then some dinner down by the beach with a nice bottle of red. After that we'll go back to the bungalow and relax. Sound alright to you? Please, Johnny...please...I don't want to fight."

The voice, the touch...the immediate tenderness. I could not resist her.

"Alright. We won't fight."

She leaned over to kiss me gently and said, "You're such a sweet man."

She drove, like a lead-footed mental patient, back to the bungalow. We had a glass of wine as she checked her mail. Then we walked three blocks, dashed like teenagers through highway traffic to the long, wide walkway that follows the bay. It was late afternoon and

149

not crowded. Leashed dogs, couples with kids, skaters, people of every age, size and color were all winding down.

The day's strife had fallen away and we were just another couple, strolling and smiling. I was acutely aware of the image we projected and of how comfortable it was. It had been a long time since I'd felt this easy closeness and warm familiarity with a woman. I had never felt stronger or more valued than when Marla put her arm in mine and smiled into my eyes.

We walked for about an hour, occasionally holding hands, finding things to laugh at and talking about everything. I told her I would go over Neil's will with her in the morning. Marla was anxious about ownership of Neil's glass. From her description of it over the phone, it sounded pretty cut and dried; the glass was hers.

Back at her place, we washed up and changed into something a little less casual. In San Diego this meant washing our feet, clean shorts and a Hawaiian shirt for me and a short skirt and sleeveless blouse for Marla. We looked in the mirror, checked each other out, agreed we were "sassy" and headed for dinner.

The place was on the beach, in an adjoining town. There was a large outdoor patio at street level. We went upstairs to the restaurant and got a table with a view of the nearby pier and beach. Perfectly positioned to watch the sun fall into the calm Pacific, I ordered a bottle of Cabernet, oysters and sea bass. Marla ordered a martini and veal osso bucco.

The location was a microcosm of the region. Elevated, we were in relative luxury. But in order to see the beach, the pier and the waning sun, you had to overlook the small park across the street that was populated nightly by a band of young street people. Homeless kids, unwashed and disheveled, dark and defeated, they were in every beach town along the southern coast of California - panhandling, forming alliances, sometimes fighting, and sleeping in shop doorways at night. From inland, they had ended up on the strand like the flotsam washed up by the sea.

150

We shared a quiet dinner, put a long complex day behind us and watched the sun form a small, blazing triangle in the last seconds before disappearing into the Pacific. Marla made short work of the martini. We were hungry and attacked the meal with gusto. I had a pretty good buzz by the time we left the place with a small doggy bag. It was around ten PM and she needed cigarettes, so we walked several unsavory blocks through the town in search of them.

She held my arm tightly as we strolled passed closed businesses and zoned-out transients. A young couple sitting in a doorway asked us for spare change. Marla said, "I never carry cash, but if you're hungry I can give you some osso bucco and rice. It's really good and it's still warm." Clearly with no idea what osso bucco was, they gratefully accepted her offer and thanked us profusely.

As we turned a corner to discover a down-at-the-heels grocery, I said, "That was a nice thing you did there."

Marla said, "You were thinking it, too. That could easily be my kid." We bought cigarettes, strawberry jam, and a bottle of wine and followed the sound of the surf back to the car.

On the drive home, I briefly entertained thoughts I had been pushing to the back of my mind all day. Marla smoked, drank and used more weed than she had led me to believe. It wasn't a few cigarettes, a glass of wine or two at night, or a little pot to help her sleep. This was a small woman of large appetites. I decided to not mention it, partly because we had worked through a dicey episode and salvaged an amazing day. Plus, I hoped to soon be quenching the one appetite we both shared and, selfishly, didn't want to risk spoiling it for either one of us.

I rationalized that we all put on our best faces when first meeting someone interesting and attractive. It's only natural. I also felt concern that possibly Marla really was a little nuts. Maybe her concern about half-truths being tantamount to lies was a way of preparing me for an unpleasant reality check.

But for now, windows down, we were loudly singing "Southern Cross" along with the car radio. On a warm night in a town I was accepting and in this singular, pristine moment, that was good enough for me. I would releive her pain. I would make her happy. I would save her from herself. And in gratitude...she would love me.

At the bungalow, she poured more wine and went into the garden. After an hour of grooming and weeding and planting a few leftover begonias in a clay pot, we sat at the table. Marla lit a cigarette and said, "So, what do you think, Cutie?" It was nearly eleven PM and we spoke in low voices, not wanting to aggravate the neighbors. The tone of her voice seemed to be positive, hopeful.

"About what?"

"Don't tease me. About Olinda. About the bungalow. About the glass. About San Diego."

"About you?"

"Later."

"I haven't felt this good in a very long time. I'm warm and relaxed. You're a sexy and generous and spirited woman. The bungalow is equal parts you and Neil and I love that. Olinda isn't much, but I haven't seen it all yet. I don't hate San Diego like I thought I would. I'm here with you and I wouldn't trade places with any man in the world tonight."

"What about the glass?"

"It's as beautiful and crazy as I knew it would be. Thanks for showing it to me. It makes my piece all that much more important to me."

We drank our wine and she said, "If someone had all seven pieces, what do you think they might be worth?" She was looking sleepily at me, her brown eyes heavy with wine as she tenderly brushed her thumb over the knuckles of my right hand.

"I talked to some friends, called a couple of galleries he dealt with in Ohio and further east. There is a buzz about his work that wasn't there before. They all agree the value of Neil's glass will likely increase now that he's gone. But that usually takes years, if it happens at all. How much? I wouldn't be surprised if the collection of all Seven Deadly Sins was worth twenty-five…maybe thirty grand right now and possibly much more later."

"I wonder where the seventh piece is and if the person who has it even knows what it is."

I broke into a grin. "Sweetheart, I have no real interest in it, but I'll help you find it, if you want. I'm concentrating my attention on you. Being a friend and hoping to have a future of some kind with you." I winked, "And playing with you."

We finished our wine and poured more. I had a warm, mellow buzz and Marla's face was flushed. I gently ran the back of my hand along her cheek and, cat-like, she closed her eyes for a moment. Then she stood up and I thought we were heading for showers and bed. Instead, Marla said, "I want to show you the garage. Maybe someday we can work on straightening it up. Be real quiet. I don't want to deal with Enid and, if she hears us, she'll come out. Her curiosity must be killing her by now."

"Can't we do it in the morning, Honey?"

"Just a few minutes and then we'll take nice hot showers and curl up in bed."

We went quietly through the gate and down the narrow sidewalk between bungalows, passing Enid's place on the left. Her lights and TV were on. Marla unlocked the door to the garage, flipped a wall switch and carefully closed the door behind us.

It was a two-car garage packed to the gunwales with the incredible jumble of Neil's life and times. There was everything from paint cans and brushes to furniture, bicycles and camping equipment. There were blank canvases, ancient framed family photos, dozens of Neil's gaudy shirts on hangers and *more* of Neil's glass. On the floor, on shelves, in the rafters, hanging on nails…stuff was strewn everywhere in boxes and bags and crates. With the exception of some neatly labeled drawers at his workbench -"string and wire", "knives and brushes", "ties and rubber bands", "files", "solder and flux"- the place was a rat's nest. This came as no surprise to me.

On his workbench, among the coffee cans of screws and bolts, were a half-dozen of Neil's signature glass birds, a creation I'd watched him make many times over the years. "Fast cash," he called them. He turned them out quickly during those times when he had to put his "real work" aside and needed living expenses. "Jackie, my boy, it's never a good sign when I find myself making these goddamn birds."

I told Marla, "This might take me two trips."

She nodded and replied, "That would be awesome. I know it's a big job, but you and I could get it done in a day or two. But not this time. I just wanted you to see it and hoped it wouldn't run you off."

"It's going to take more than that to run me off, Beautiful."

A screen door closed nearby. Flip-flop footsteps. Marla hissed, "Aaaw, shit. Here comes Enid."

Enid knocked firmly on the garage door and called, "Hello? Marla?" It was the voice that had called from below the bedroom window. Before Marla could respond, the door was opening and Enid, inviting herself in, stepped from the darkness across the threshold. She glanced briefly at me, looking me up and down with a barely perceptible nod. I nodded back.

The first word that crossed my mind was "Viking." The second was "leather." Descended from people who, once you'd disappointed them, would soon be drinking mead from your hollowed-out skull, Enid wore gray sweatpants, a man's white t-shirt and black flip-flops. She stood flat-footed, arms folded across her chest, vaguely butch. She was five-foot eight, fit for her late fifties, with battleship gray eyes. Her wet, graying blond hair was pulled back severely, rubber banded into a ponytail. She had the smell and the ruddy look of someone just out of a hot shower. Marla had been right; Enid heard our rustlings in the garage and was wasting no time getting her nose into Marla's business.

After her dispassionate assessment of me, Enid turned her steel gray eyes to Marla. "Have you spoken to Sasha?"

"No," Marla answered. "But I guess he stopped by earlier and talked to," nodding in my direction, "Johnny."

As Enid swung her gaze back to me, Marla offered, "Enid, this is Johnny. Johnny...my neighbor, Enid."

We exchanged brief greetings and a handshake as Marla elaborated. "Johnny and Neil grew up together back east and have been friends forever. He's here to help me straighten out this mess Neil left me...paperwork, medications, court and tax things...all this crap in the garage...his will. Johnny's been an awesome friend and he's taken care of an amazing amount of stuff already."

Marla was maintaining a five-foot buffer between us during Enid's visit, an attempt to convey a message to Neil's acolyte that our interaction was purely platonic. As far as I was concerned, it only added to Marla's mystique. But, since Enid's bedroom window was less than twenty feet from Marla's, and since the woman was clearly not deaf...I saw no reason to think Enid was buying any of it.

Enid's voice was assertive. She said that Sasha had talked about buying some of Marla's glass. She talked about Neil, how much she adored him, how strong and beautiful he was and how horrible and

155

sad it was for her when he died. Marla was visibly upset and uncomfortable with the situation. I'd had a lot of wine and it was getting on my nerves, too. Hoping to help Marla extricate herself, I made my move.

"Marla, I need some shut-eye. If you ladies will excuse me, I'm going to get ready for bed. When you're done here, I'd like to take a look at the will before I go to sleep. It was great to meet you, Enid."

Enid issued a cautious "Goodnight."

Marla, following my lead, said, "I'll be right in to find that will for you."

As I went out the door, I heard Enid say to Marla, "Today I made reservations for my trip to Denmark in March." They were gabbing about this latest development as I made my way up the path to the bungalow.

Minutes later, undressing behind the closed bedroom door, I heard the gate close and the two women talking in the garden. I got in the shower.

As I was drying off, I heard the front door close and lock. Marla tapped on the bathroom door and said, "Johnny, I'm sorry about that. She's all excited about going home for the first time in ten years. Do you need some more wine, Sweetie?"

I put on my sweatpants and opened the door. Marla gave me a hug and said, "I just couldn't get rid of her. You're not mad at me, are you? God, you smell good."

"Why would I be mad at you? Of course not." I gave her a small kiss. "I don't really need any more wine, but I'll have a little splash if you are." I could already feel a headache coming on.

"She is just so fucking selfish. She spoiled my last days with Neil and now all she wants to do is keep reliving it. I can't stand her." We walked to the kitchen. She poured two glasses of Beaujolais and we headed to the bedroom, closing the door behind us.

She sat at the desk, opened the stash drawer and put some weed in the pipe. "She wants me to talk to Sasha about selling him some more of Neil's glass. What the hell does she care? And now she tells me she thinks Neil meant to leave *her* some of his pieces. What a witch."

Instantly switching off her seething anger over Enid's interference, she gave me a dazzler of a smile and said. "Will you have a little bit of this with me, Sweetie? Then I'll shower and I'll come to bed, I promise."

There are your fools (and I count myself among them), and then there are your damned fools. Only a damned fool would have said "no" to that deal.

We sipped the wine. We passed the pipe, Marla taking two tokes to every one of mine, and again we were quickly amusing ourselves to the point of abject, stumbling idiocy. It felt so good and so honest to laugh like a loony and let all the day's tension slip away in guffaws and affection.

When I had reached my limit, my lungs aching and my head approaching zero gravity, Marla smoked another bowl by herself. After a moment of just silently staring into her wineglass, she said to me with a wink, "I'm going to go get myself clean for you." We shared a tipsy toast of wine. Marla gave me a long and gentle kiss and disappeared into the bathroom. The red teddy, apparently not part of this evening's plan, hung on the bedroom door.

Among other elastic carnival imaginings, I was aware of just how much wine and marijuana I'd consumed in my first two days in Marla World. Evidently it was like this every day here. Maybe she was going above and beyond to thrill me into staying. Maybe we were both nuts. I wondered how long I could keep up with her.

During this weightless neon reverie, the realization came upon me that the shower had gone off and the tooth brushing had begun. When the buzzing stopped Marla opened the bathroom door a couple of inches to ask, "You still awake out there?"

Before I could form an answer, she opened the door and turned out the bathroom light. She stood, dripping and naked, at the desk, smiling enigmatically at me as if pondering her next move. The sight of her removed all lingering misgivings or questions from my mind.

She smoked what was left in the pipe and dried herself with the towel that had been wrapped around her head. She looked straight at me during the toweling, enjoying the tease. Then, her face flushed, she dropped the towel and bounded over me into the bed, laughing as she scurried under the covers. She put her moist back to my waiting front, pulled my arm around and over her breasts, pushed her body flush against mine and let out a long, low sigh. I buried my face in her wet, chaotic crown of hair.

If the previous night had been introduction, this night was exploration. Finding the buttons, a little dirty talk, tempting each other into new places. Who-liked-what... and how much. Taboos and tipping points. Thresholds and triggers. There was slightly less mirth and significantly more athleticism. We dropped the remaining veils, burned the last bridges of gentility and exposed ferocious appetites.

I made some sounds I had never made before. At one point, Marla, eyes wide open but unseeing, let go a loud expletive, put her nose hard against mine and rasped, "Really?"

Later, she suddenly froze and grunted. Then she slowly rocked me in her arms like a child, murmuring breathlessly, "Easy, Baby. Easy...easy."

We tried…and failed completely… to be quiet. There was no way of telling how much time passed. Sam, the neighbor who worked the day shift and shared a wall with Marla, turned up the volume on his TV.

By the time we finally sank into a drained sleep we were holding each other tight, our feet at the head of the bed. Half-stunned and humming like tuning forks, it was clear that something had shifted. This would be wrenchingly hard to give up, for either of us.

"Sleep well, Butterfly."

"Good night, Beautiful Girl."

Wednesday morning found me moving slowly and feeling a little hung over. Marla seemed fresh as a daisy. As we had our coffee and contemplated breakfast, she asked if I would look over Neil's Last Will and Testament while she went about her morning rounds in her beloved garden. I was relieved to have time to get my sea legs back under me and reflect on the past night's exertions.

As I munched on sourdough toast and oatmeal at the garden table and perused Neil's will, Marla busied herself with the plants. It was a perfect morning and we fell into a thirty-minute bubble of unhurried domesticity. I could hear the sounds of the freeway and neighboring houses waking up; silverware and china, showers, toilets, parents clamoring for their kids to get ready for school, car doors closing as people went to work. I felt at home.

I looked for loopholes in Neil's plan to leave all the glass to Marla. She pruned, patrolled for pests and gently watered. We exchanged smug, conspiratorial glances and she snacked from my plate.

She wound up the hose and sat down with me, pouring more coffee and opening the newspaper. "Thanks for last night," I said.

Marla said, "You know what I really like about you, Scanlon?"

"Can't wait to hear this."

"You don't ask afterwards if you were 'OK'."

"And you, Stone, are a sorceress."

"Are you feeling alright? You sound a little bit down."

I confessed, "I have a small hangover, but the coffee's helping."

"Really? We didn't drink that much yesterday."

This was not posed as a question or a casual observation. This was a statement of absolute fact, delivered with certainty and a whiff of sarcasm.

"Honey, I'm a little out of condition. I'm not used to getting that happy that quickly. I'll be fine, really."

"Neil used to say that any day you're not wasted is a wasted day. Not that I agreed…" she trailed off.

I'd spent enough time with Marla to realize that this might well turn out to be a very long day. She seemed edgy and pre-occupied. Storm clouds were gathering.

Marla broke the ice with, "Since I have to work tomorrow and I want to take you to this wonderful Thai restaurant in Pacific Beach tonight, let's drop off the laundry then go to the nursery. I need your help picking out some plants and a couple of big clay pots for my geraniums."

Soon we were off to the mega-do-it-yourself store. We bought plants, soil, sprays, powders and two twelve-gallon terra cotta pots with trays. In the company of this wise and patient shopper, I was once again surprised that I actually *enjoyed* shopping with Marla. We were back in the groove and life was good.

We dropped our dirty laundry at the strip mall Laundromat which offered a "fluff and fold" service. Since her bungalow had no hook-ups for a washer or dryer, this service was costing Marla easily a hundred a month. I gave her a twenty to help and the girl at the counter said we could pick up our stuff any time after four.

Back home to get dirty in the garden. She had deferred to my judgment on most things plant-related once I told her about my short career in the nursery business. We worked well together. She was quiet, but we were both busy and productive and it was therapy for me.

When we were finished, we put the tools back in the garage and wound up the hose. It was time to wash up and get lunch. We had a glass of wine at the garden table as we dug mud from under our nails and weighed our options.

"I make a mean grilled cheese," I offered.

Marla said, "Sounds good. I'll throw together a quick salad."

We took our quick and easy lunch outside to eat. Marla did not pour any more wine and I was a little relieved. I brought along Neil's will. She was quiet preparing and now eating lunch, taking time only to praise my culinary skills. "You weren't kidding. That is an awesome grilled cheese, Johnny."

I allowed myself to hopefully assume that these times of silence from Marla were not a rejection of me. I could only guess at the whirling mix of emotions going through her mind; insecurity, fear, loss, guilt. I knew she was torn between gratefulness that I had come to fill part of the hole left by Neil's death and an offsetting sense of

161

betrayal. We were fulfilling each other's needs and neither of us knew much more than that. It was a big, fragile endeavor.

As we carried our dishes toward the house, Marla's cell phone rang. I stacked her stuff in the sink so she could talk. It was her son, Ben. Back outside with a glass of iced water, I took another last look at the will. Marla was at the computer looking up something for her kid.

Shortly, from the bedroom, I heard her voice, sharp and staccato, and then she came outside.

"I have to go pay Ben's rent. And, before you say it…yes… I know I'm not helping him by doing this. Neil, Sasha, Ben's father, my boss…every damn man I know…you've all told me that continuing to support him is just making things worse by reinforcing his dependence on me. I get it. Maybe we can pick up the laundry after and then go out for Thai. Sound good?"

With the queasy inkling that I had just heard the sound of one shoe dropping, I replied, "Sure. Dinner's on me."

"You really are a sweetheart." She gave me a small, quizzical smile.

She wrote a check for five hundred dollars, sealed it in a plain envelope, threw her checkbook into her purse and off we went. I had become more tranquil driving with her, resigned to the risk involved and accepting that each ride might well be my last. We drove twenty minutes to a closed real estate office. She asked me to drop the envelope through the mail slot in the door.

Back in the car, Marla said, "Any questions?"

"You pay his rent, his phone bill and give him money for food, right?"

"He's my kid. Yes, he's a mess and he will probably never amount to squat, but I'm the only family he has here and I'm not going to just throw him to the wolves. He can't hold a job, he parties every night and he thinks that, because he can play a little bass, he's bound to become a rock star."

This little jerk-off was peeling her for about ten percent of her gross income every month. He would have friends drop him off at her house at all hours, unannounced, expecting dinner, a shower and a ride across the county back home.

She continued, "I read a study about kids who start smoking weed when they're young, you know…twelve, thirteen…and how it screws up and stunts the development of the part of their brains that handles responsibility and ambition. That's Ben. He only thinks about himself and can't see any farther than the end of his nose."

I asked, "How much longer can you do this?"

Marla responded, "I've put my foot down and told him I'm done. No more. But then he comes back and, what can I do? Put him on the street? Neil used to get so pissed off at me for giving Ben money. 'He'll be at your tit, hanging on your apron strings 'till he's fifty. Do the kid a favor. Cut the cord and make him sink or swim.' And I know he was probably right."

"What if your job disappears like you think it might?"

"I don't know, Johnny. Can we talk about it later? I know what I'm doing is not going to help and that I'm just enabling Ben to continue to act like a bum. But some days he's all I have and I have to protect him. Ya know?" She was getting agitated and I quickly backed off the subject.

"I do. I have kids, too. Let's go grab our laundry, scrub up and go to dinner."

Eschewing courtesy, speed limits and turns signals, and with our clean laundry in the back seat, we returned to the bungalow a little after five. Marla held the door as I carried the huge basket into the bedroom and we put our stuff away.

Quietly, we put clean sheets on her bed, had a little wine and dressed for dinner. She wore a little green dress with just the right amount of cleavage to tastefully showcase her great figure. She was a sight to behold, but obviously unsettled. I trod lightly and dressed to look a little less like Elmer Fudd.

We drove down packed streets, past loud, crowded beach bars and busy sidewalks to our restaurant. It was a nice place, several cuts above the places we had passed. We were seated at a cozy corner table for two.

Marla gave me the quick overview of the menu. She and Neil had, of course, been here many times and, trusting her information, I ordered something spicy and a glass of white wine. She ordered a dish cooked in a clay pot and a Thai Martini.

She seemed tense, looking around the room, fidgeting with her napkin, unsmiling and expressionless. When our drinks came, we toasted clean laundry and sea breezes. We made small talk about kids and the garage. She had to tell me what Neil always ordered when they came here. She asked me about the will.

"Honey, it's all clearly spelled out…all the glass now in your possession and in storage is yours and yours alone. No worries there."

Marla appeared unmoved by this. She made short work of the martini. She offered me a taste. Not being fond of martinis, I said, "Not bad." Marla had a distant look in her eyes and her speech was listless.

When the waitress brought our dinners, I still had a half glass of wine left and temporarily at least, waved off more. Marla polished off her martini and ordered another. "Sure you don't want to try one?"

164

"I think I'll stick with water and wine and concentrate on this beautiful looking meal." This earned me a blank stare. Marla's mouth opened as if she was going to say something and then thought better of it.

The food was delicious. We picked off each other's plates and fed each other. Ten minutes into the meal, she stopped mid-chew and asked, "Why don't you tell me what's bothering you?"

"What do you mean? I'm great. I'm having dinner with a fantastic woman and I'm feeling good."

For the balance of the meal, Marla made no attempt to engage. She drank her martini, picked at her food and made little eye contact. The only conversation was when I asked how her food was and she said, "Not as good as the last time."

We decided to pass on the dessert and while waiting for the check, I asked her, "Did you want to stop at the grocery on the way home?"

She spat, "I just want to get the hell out of here."

Just then our check and our doggy bag came. I handed my credit card to the waitress.

Then, out of left field, Marla said, "I want you to tell me what's going on with you today. You've been sullen and not yourself all day. If there's something you need to ask me, do it now because I'm getting real tired of your pouting." She was sitting straight up in the seat and glaring at me with a look of pure venom.

I was fed up with the attitude and the posturing. "Three times since we met, you've asked me the same question about whether a half-truth is the same as a lie. You said you smoked a few cigarettes a day. You go through a pack a day. You said you had a glass of wine or two in the evenings to unwind. You go through at *least* a bottle a night. You said you smoked a little weed in the evenings to relax and help you sleep. You smoke enough weed at night to immobilize a goddamn mastodon. So you tell me...half-truth or lie...or what?"

Her eyes were slits. Her face had gone granite and I didn't give a shit anymore.

"The truth is, Marla, I don't care about any of that as long as we can be together. But to keep asking me that question just makes no sense. Or do you have another surprise for me? I am crazy about you, but we have to be honest with each other. So, there...that's what's been on my mind."

The waitress brought my receipt and thanked us. Marla had already stood up and marched for the door. I grabbed the leftovers and followed her out. We were parked at a meter about a hundred feet down the bustling street. Twenty feet ahead of me, silent and walking fast, Marla was in a hurry to get somewhere.

As we reached her car, I said, "So that's it? I finally answer your Big Question and now you're not going to talk to me?"

Marla stopped dead in her tracks, turned on her heel and said, loudly, "You think I drink too much?"

Louder, "You think I'm a *LIAR*?"

I finally got my first real look at the full-blown monster. "Should I expect a goddamn *lecture* from you now? Because, believe me...that is not going to fucking happen! If you're here to remake me, you can go home now! I don't need this shit from you! I didn't ask you to come here for some kind of fucking *intervention*!"

Breathing rapidly, her dilated pupils turning black, her complexion turning red, then pale...her voice got louder and her speech cadence quickened. With her contorted face and her small fists clenched, Marla was a study in fury. I could see the people across the street looking at us.

Standing in the street, opening her car door, shouting now, "It's not even two months since my boyfriend died in my arms and if I want to drink a little wine and smoke some weed to ease my pain, I'm not going to let you or *anybody* else judge me for that! *Who are YOU to judge ME?"*

I was startled when two young girls on the sidewalk behind me burst into applause. Marla climbed into the driver's seat and slammed the door. It took me a second to realize that Marla was **not** going to drive off and leave me. I got in and closed the door.

Pulling away from the curb, Marla had opened her window a few inches, lit a cigarette, pulled a CD from the visor and put it in the player. It was the Dixie Chicks and she turned it way up...shy of maximum volume, but sufficient to negate any possibility of conversation.

She smiled as she sang along with the music. This was to be the beginning of my punishment for questioning her lifestyle. Marla was nourishing herself by shutting me out and flexing her control of the situation.

Over the course of the ten-minute drive back to the bungalow, passing the grocery without a glance, she continued to wall me off as I began to seethe at her juvenile display. This was not caprice. This was not righteousness or a tantrum or a measured reaction. This was the assault of the malevolent "woman scorned" that Neil had so often described.

With no space in front of the bungalow, she pulled into the alley. Before she had the keys out of the ignition, I had already grabbed the doggy bag, slammed the car door and walked through the gate, not waiting for her.

She caught up at the front door and unlocked it. She immediately turned the TV to a station broadcasting country music, gave it sufficient volume to annoy me and poured herself a glass of wine, filled to the top.

She went into the bedroom and closed the door. I got a glass of water and sat at the kitchen table for a minute or two, leveling out and wondering what, if anything could be salvaged.

I knocked on the door and slowly opened it. Marla was smoking a full bowl of pot and doing something on the computer. She was studiously ignoring me and I finally spoke the first words since outside the restaurant.

"I'm sorry if I made you angry. I was trying to answer your question. Can we talk about this?"

She tapped the ash from the pipe into an ashtray, took a big gulp of wine, put another bud in the pipe and lit it. She inhaled a big lungful of smoke, held it for a very long time and then slowly exhaled the smoke away from me. Still without making eye contact, she said, "Get away from me."

I sat on the edge of the bed. "You keep insisting I tell what was on my mind. I understand that you're mad, but shutting me out and refusing to talk to me…come on…at least look at me."

Marla took another big drink from her wineglass. One more and it would be empty. The pipe had gone out and she re-lit it. She took another long, deep toke and held it as long as she could before slowly blowing the smoke toward the computer monitor. She would not look at me. She said flatly, as if to a cat, "Go away."

"I'm not going to do that until you at least look at me, Marla."

She got up, sprayed citrus air freshener to mask the smell of the weed, opened the bedroom door and, staring straight ahead, walked out.

It was late and I was tired. Sitting on the bed, trying to figure out how to get through to Marla, I heard her in the kitchen, pouring more wine and talking on the phone. She was talking to a guy, apparently her ex-husband or an old boyfriend. She was cheery and laughed at everything Mr. X was saying. This was a woman who had perfected her own slant on the ancient female art of thrusting in the knife and slowly twisting it. I was surely not the first man to be in this unenviable position.

Fifteen minutes later, as she was saying goodbye and getting off the phone, I walked out of the bedroom and toward the kitchen. The country music was still blaring and Marla was dialing another number on her phone. I poured myself a half glass of wine, hoping this might help. I said, "We need to talk about this."

Her party answered and Marla brightly said, "Hey, Sweetie. Whatcha doin?"

I was blocking her exit from the kitchen. She held the phone away from her face just long enough to glare at me with flat, black eyes and hiss through tight lips, "Move."

She went out into the garden and sat at the table. From the exchange I gathered she was talking to one of her daughters. When I walked outside a few minutes later and sat in one of the lawn chairs, Marla stood up and went back into the bedroom, closing the door without acknowledging me.

She laughed heartily and made light chat for ten minutes before I decided to make one last effort to reason before she got too wasted. She was ending the call and lighting the pipe when I came in to sit on the corner of the bed.

"Marla, if you're not going to talk to me or look at me, at least turn down the TV so I can get some sleep."

Staring at the computer screen, she released a cloud of smoke. In a slurred, sneering monotone, she said, "Stop following me around." She sprayed more citrus, stood up and went into the living room, leaving me sitting on the bed. She was unsteady on her feet.

I watched as she went to the kitchen. A moment later she walked out the front door with a bottle of wine. I heard the gate open and close. I heard her knock on Enid's door and be welcomed inside. Within minutes I could hear them laughing.

Tired and my patience worn away, I brushed my teeth and got into bed. I was frustrated and pissed off…worried things were ruined between Marla and me. I had given her chances to do the reasonable thing and she had opted instead to be an asshole.

I occasionally heard bursts of women's laughter from Enid's. After about an hour of tossing, I heard Marla come back. She rushed into the bedroom and got the baggie out of the stash drawer. Without a word or any recognition that I was there, out she went again. More gaiety from next door and then, blessedly about one AM, I fell asleep. She was supposed to be up for work at six-thirty.

When Marla finally came home, I heard her bump into something in the kitchen and say, "shit." She spent a few minutes in the bathroom and got into the bed. She quickly, wordlessly, fell into a snoring sleep. We remained in our neutral corners the rest of the night. Twice we both rolled to the middle of the bed, but as soon as we touched, instantly retreated to the edges. I dozed and tossed until five-thirty, when I gave up, put on some clothes and made coffee.

At the kitchen table that last hour before I woke her for work, I decided I'd had enough of the deteriorating situation. This claustrophobic, pressure cooker atmosphere, the mood swings, the disrespect and the incessant Neil references had worn me down. I had to get out of there. The bungalow seemed to be airless and shrinking. There was nowhere to run and the entire mood had gone venomous.

I had compromised my pride as far as I was willing to. I would miss the astonishing sex and the thrill I felt when Marla touched or kissed me. Her smile was pure electricity. Her laughter was a balm. But this unreasoning anger and bile…I deserved better. I knew I had to get out before things got any uglier. I needed to fall back, regroup and give Marla time to decide if this thing was worth salvaging.

I called the airline and jumped through the hoops necessary to change flights. The next available flight was at six forty-five the following morning. I had a whole day to kill. I'd get a room near the airport and take a cab over there after Marla left for work.

At six-thirty, I opened the bedroom door, walked to the side of the bed and said, softly, "Marla. It's time to get up and go to work. Marla, wake up."

She stirred, gave me a puzzled one-eyed glance, looked at the clock and rolled onto her back with an annoyed wheeze. I went back to the kitchen. Shortly, I heard the rustle of sheets and the bathroom door closing. I poured a little more coffee, making sure to leave a full cup for Marla.

She stumbled silently into the kitchen wearing panties and a bra. She looked like she'd slept under the bed…and still managed to be remarkably sexy. I said, "There's coffee."

Without comment she poured a cup and started toward the bathroom.

"I'm leaving," I said.

"What?" She stopped and turned her head halfway but did not face me.

I spoke to her sleepy profile. "If you're going to ignore me there's no reason to be here. I have a flight out tomorrow morning. I'll get a room near the airport as soon as I can check-in today."

Marla's head bent very slightly, her small shoulders lax, and she took a slow breath. Then she said, "Whatever" and shaking her head, continued to the bathroom.

When I heard the shower start, I made the bed, trying to get it to look the way I had helped her do it. I put my travel case on the bed and began packing my clothes from the dresser.

I could have waited to do this until after Marla had gone, but I wanted to make certain that when she came out of the bathroom, there would be no doubt I was really leaving. It was petty, but I was tired and bewildered. I was starting to feel wounded and angry. But she would see none of that today.

I got on the computer, found a cheap motel right outside the airport fence and reserved a room. I went to the airline's Internet site and printed out my boarding passes. Eager to remove myself from the suffocating corner into which I had painted myself, I called the motel to ask how early I could check in. The disinterested desk clerk said two PM.

I had no transportation and nowhere to go. I hoped Marla would let me hang around the place until I got a cab to the motel. I would settle for sitting in the garden with a book for six hours if it came to that. I had no plan of action if she bounced me, which I fully expected her to do. I sat at the kitchen table and tried to concentrate on the newspaper. It was impossible.

When Marla finally emerged from the bathroom, I heard her mutter as she passed the loveseat and saw my bag, "Oh, boy."

Dressed in a charcoal business suit, she came into the kitchen, poured hot coffee into her car mug and said, "So… that's it, huh? You're just leaving."

"I can't check into my room until two. I'd be grateful if you'd let me hang out here until then. I'll sit out in the garden."

"I don't want you sitting in my garden for six hours. Make sure you lock the door and the deadbolt behind you. Leave the key under the big geranium."

"I'll make sure the place is locked up."

"I didn't figure you for a quitter, Johnny."

"I didn't figure you for a sadist."

"Oh, please..." And on that note, Marla took a sip of her coffee, grabbed her purse, checked herself quickly in the mirror and walked out the door.

I finished packing, poured the last of the coffee into my cup and went to the garden table to try again to read the paper. I would have to arrange for someone to pick me up at the airport in Cleveland. Miriam would likely ask the fewest questions.

I called to have a taxi pick me up at one-thirty.

It was too early to call Ohio, so I had time to reflect on just what the hell had happened. I came up with nothing, other than that I should have given more weight to Neil's warnings about Marla's split personality. I was completely sapped and just wanted to sleep. I felt sick to my stomach and oddly agitated. My head was as thick as lard.

I went back inside to shower and shave. After, I lie down on Marla's bed and fell quickly into a fitful sleep. When I awoke, I jumped up and experienced that cartoonish "Oh-shit-what-time-is-it?" thing. It was nearly noon. I had slept over three hours and my cab would arrive in ninety minutes.

I called Miriam. Seeing my name on her caller ID, she answered with a cheery, "So, how's the tan coming along, Scanlon? Had your fill of surf, sex and sea bass yet?"

"Listen, I need you to pick me up at the airport tomorrow. I arrive in Cleveland about six PM. Can you swing that?"

A moment of awkward silence and then, "Are you OK? What the hell happened?"

"I will tell you the gory details later. Can you pick me up?"

"Sure...of course. How bad is it?"

"I haven't had a chance to figure that out yet, but right now it's not good and I need to get out of here." I gave her my flight information and told her I'd call during the layover in Minneapolis.

At one twenty-five I took my bag out to the garden, locked up the bungalow and dutifully put Marla's key under the geranium. I looked at the beautiful pot filled with geraniums and alyssum that we had planted together. A voice in my head said, "What the hell happened here, Jack?"

I mumbled under my breath, "Goddamned if I know" just as the cabby pulled up and blew his horn.

A thirteen-minute drive from Marla's, the motel was the closest one to the airport, a cheap national chain. I paid the cabby and walked into the small office. A middle-aged woman wearing what appeared to be a diaper on her head took time from her personal phone call with "Ralphie" to book me in and give me my key. I asked if there was anywhere nearby to eat.

She said, "Hold on, Baby" to Ralphie and pressing the phone to her ample bosom, pointed down the street. "There's a Denny's down that-away about a block. Anything beyond there gets real spendy."

I thanked her and headed to my room, second floor in the corner. I opened the door and then the drapes. The view from the window was an area directly behind the building filled with old stuff from the motel--furniture, sinks and toilets. Beyond that was an open area extending about one hundred feet to the rapid rail tracks, where at that very instant a train loudly clattered past. It sounded like it was in the room. This would continue, every twenty minutes, all night. I told myself it was only one night.

I turned on the TV to make sure it worked, and was somehow oddly relieved it was not black and white. At that instant, a huge commercial airliner flew directly over, close enough to see the rivets on the wings. The entire building shook. I could not hear the TV, no matter how much I raised the volume.

174

I turned on the ceiling light to look at the room and quickly turned it back off. The theme was "1980's Massage Parlor". It was big enough for a chipped dresser/entertainment center, a desk, a chair, a pair of mismatched nightstands with mismatched lamps and a queen bed. The "carpet" was dark blue turf, better suited to a football field.

Even in the dim light of the cheap lamp on the peeling wooden nightstand, I could tell the floor was irredeemably filthy, crushed and stained by years of accumulated grime and god-knows-what. I determined to make sure my feet remained covered at all times during my stay.

The lamp on the second nightstand had no bulb in it, the shade leaning crookedly. I put it straight.

No pictures on the walls. No paper or pen or phone book or ice bucket or plastic cups on the desk. No clock. No coffee maker. No newspaper. No Gideon Bible.

The bathroom was equally grim; a rust-stained sink and shower stall and an ice-cold pinkish-gray linoleum floor. All edges of the sink bore a dozen orange-brown nicotine stripes, indelible glyphs from decades of men and women of meager fortunes, not-so-carefully balancing their cigarettes as they shaved and made-up. I was glad I had already showered. Two stiff, gray towels and two washcloths complimented the pair of domino-sized soaps. I did not take anything out of my shaving kit to put on the sink.

"It's only one night," I again reassured myself.

I was staring at my shoes and trying to cement two coherent thoughts together when another jet, this time a smaller commuter, shrieked overhead, within what seemed like inches of my roof. The door handle and desk drawer rattled as the lampshade tipped over again. The stark fact dawned on me…I was directly under the flight path into San Diego International Airport.

175

I considered packing up my stuff and getting a better room. But something in my Irish Catholic background prevented me from interpreting my situation as bad luck or poor timing.

This had the metallic taste of penance.

I pulled back the bedcover. Rough sheets and hard foam pillows. The inescapable smell of that shitty antiseptic found only in the cheapest and least reputable of fleabags like this one. Nostrils irritated, I walked out onto the breezeway, locked the door and headed down the street to Denny's for a hot meal and a small serving of human contact.

It was a rough-looking block and a half, but the Denny's looked safe. Pancakes and eggs sounded like the ideal comfort food for my sudden predicament. As I sat down in a booth, I realized I was the only customer in the restaurant.

I confirmed this with the waitress as I ordered a short stack, two eggs over easy, bacon and home fries. "Yep. Just you and me and the cook." Then, as if to reassure me I hadn't stepped into an episode of The Twilight Zone, she added, "But we were very busy just an hour ago and the dinner crowd will start coming in soon."

While I waited for my solitary meal, I tried to make sense of how I had gone from Eros and joy to skid row. I was shocked that Marla had turned so viciously cold-blooded. I had done everything asked of me and done it right. Yet here I was, tail between my legs, alone in a strange town, staying in a rat hole motel and eating a three PM breakfast at the Denny's of The Damned. My life had turned to shit.

I had little appetite. I left half the food on my plate, gave my waitress a nice tip, and walked out. The place was still empty when I left. The sun's angle was low in the sky, the flat light making the mean, littered street even more vague.

On heavy feet, I made the slow march back to my room.

4

Shooting beer from his nose, Painless coughed, spluttered, and then composed himself.

"You are not seriously considering going *back* there! You're as crazy as she is. What the hell for? Never mind…never mind. I know what for. But…come on, Jack!"

It was a Monday evening. An hour earlier, he'd replaced a filling for me. I was his last patient of the day. We closed up his office and drove to Brennan's Colony for a pitcher of Dead Guy Ale. The left half of my face still numb from the Novocain, I was having trouble keeping the beer off my shirt. It had been nearly three weeks since my premature evacuation from Marla's Olinda love shack and I had just given him the lowdown on everything that had transpired.

Back at the airport motel, I requested a five AM wake-up call. Having no faith in the desk clerk, I set the alarm clock feature on my phone, which requires leaving the cell phone turned on. All through that miserable night, Marla left dozens of voicemails and text messages. It rang and buzzed and chimed all night. Finally around two AM, the battery nearly dead, I turned the phone off. I decided to stay awake the last three hours before the shuttle arrived to take me to the terminal. This was made simpler by the ceaseless cacophony of trains and planes shaking the structure.

During a three-hour layover in Minneapolis, I listened to her messages and read her texts. She seemed surprised, upon arriving home from work, to find me really gone. Each attempt to contact me was more disjointed and angry than the last as Marla drank and smoked more. She accused me of lying to her. She said she didn't think I'd ever known Neil at all. She raged that I was only interested in sex, that she hated me, that I had never really been a friend to her and that nothing I'd done for her mattered.

She tried to call while I was cooling my heels, waiting to board my flight home. I did not answer. In a new voicemail left while she was getting ready for work, she shrieked because I hadn't returned her calls. She pronounced me a coward, a false friend, a lousy lay and an insensitive, chauvinistic bastard.

By the time Miriam deposited me at the front door of my house (which seemed cavernous after Marla's tiny place), I'd gone two days with no real sleep. Sore and terrifically tired, I turned off the phone. I had a hot shower, a bowl of split pea soup, washed down two nighttime pain relievers with Maker's Mark and went to bed at nine PM. I fell asleep quickly with an old rhyme in my head;

"There once was a girl who had a little curl, right in the middle of her forehead. And when she was good, she was very, very good. But when she was bad…she was horrid."

I slept for nearly ten hours. I still felt like hell. My confidence was shaky, my joints ached and my eyes looked like two piss holes in a snowdrift. But my back had loosened up and, once again in front of my fireplace, the sofa felt like a throne as I sipped my coffee.

I poured a second cup and grabbed the paper from the sidewalk. I poured a bowl of raisin bran and moved to the dining room. I spent the next hour trying to read the news, but my concentration was shot. I put a load of laundry in and opened some mail.

Around ten thirty I took a deep breath and turned on the phone. Only two new messages, both from Marla. The first was from the previous night, judging by its manic incoherence. She was incensed that I hadn't left the phone turned on all night. There was a bizarre new twist; she was howling that I send back two of Neil's old

Hawaiian shirts she had given me. "He would have wanted you to have these," she had said.

She raved for five minutes and then began to cry, saying, "I'm a good person. People like me. I have no idea what I did to make you abandon me this way, Johnny. You're a mean, hateful person. Neil should have warned me about you."

The second message was only an hour old, left while she was getting ready for work. Like Marla, it was short and a little scary. "So, is this how it's going to be, Johnny? My life is falling apart and now you're not talking to me? If you're going to say 'goodbye', be man enough to say it to me in person, not by running away. I swear to God, Johnny, if I had your parents' phone number I'd call them right now and have them contact you for me. I need you to call me."

Taking a few minutes to control my anger, I dialed her work number.

"Bay Synthetics. This is Marla. How can I assist you today?"

"You can knock off this horseshit about calling my parents."

Five seconds of dead air. Then, "Yes, sir. I'm sure I can help you with that."

Another five seconds. Under her breath, "Johnny, I would never have really…"

"Shut up and listen closely, Marla. Under no circumstances is it acceptable for you to phone my mother and father about our difficulties. Am I making myself clear?"

In a hushed, subdued tone, "Completely. Can I call you right back? I'll go outside and call on my cell. Please, Johnny? We need to talk."

"Talk about what? What an asshole I am? How all of your problems are my fault? How I'm to blame that you haven't grieved for Neil yet? I don't want to talk to you."

Whispering, "Johnny, honey, give me five minutes, OK? I'll call you right back."

"I'm busy. Call me tonight when you get home."

"Will you answer your phone?"

"I'll answer my phone."

"Promise me."

"Call early, before you get too wasted to talk."

Another delay and then, a barely audible, "Bye."

All I could think about was how I had missed hearing her calling me "Honey."

She phoned as soon as she got home from work. Her son, Ben, was waiting in the garden when she got there, Sasha was on his way over and she had a headache. I told her to call me the next day.

She said, "No, no, Johnny. I'm going to get rid of these people because I want to talk to you." When the phone rang again, two hours later, I was tired and in no mood to chat.

Ben needed to be fed and showered and driven home. Sasha was pressing her harder to sell him some of Neil's larger pieces. Enid had come over for a glass of wine. Marla finally dispatched all of them and seemed eager to talk. I was jet-lagged and bent out of shape.

"Johnny, they've laid-off six people in the last two days; three under me and three above me. I have a real bad feeling about this. It's only a matter of time now."

"I thought you could hang on 'till the end of the year."

"Nobody's safe. The word is that the company who bought us will cut ninety percent of this staff, offer jobs in New York to the survivors and close this office. It could be any day now."

"So, what do you do?"

"I'm not moving to New York, that's for sure. They're giving all these people a hefty severance package, a couple months' salary and extending their health insurance for a year. So it could be worse, I guess."

"So, you'd stay in San Diego?"

"I don't know, Johnny. I'm so screwed up right now. All of this with you and Neil and work and family...I don't know which end is up any more."

"Don't worry about me. Concentrate on your future and your welfare and don't make me a part of it anymore."

Her voice registered hurt and indignation. "What do you mean you're not a part of this anymore? I need your help. I miss you, Johnny."

I told her the truth. "Marla, I am dead tired. With the travel and the drama and you kicking me in the nuts every time I pick up the phone...I'm worn out. Call me tomorrow. I need some sleep."

"Johnny... don't hang up. Please just talk to me for a few more minutes. I've missed your voice. Are we ever going to patch things up?"

"I can't think about that now. You've said a lot of hurtful and cruel shit."

"The things you said to me were hurtful and cruel, too."

"The things I said were honest answers to your incessant questions. As a reward for my honesty, you treated me like garbage. I am not going to re-hash this, Marla. Once was enough."

Softly now, "Do you want to see me again? I haven't had a decent night's sleep since you left."

"Not if it's going to be like the last time. I'm addicted to you, Marla, and you know it. But based on what I've heard lately, there's no reason to think you really want to see me."

"Oh, hell...here comes Enid again."

"I'm going to bed."

"Will you call and wake me up tomorrow about six?"

"Is your clock broken?"

"No. It would be nice to hear your voice first thing in the morning."

"Six o'clock sharp."

"Sleep well, Butterfly."

"Goodnight."

For once the three-hour time difference worked to my advantage. By the time Marla's wake-up call rolled around the next day, I'd done my laundry, eaten breakfast and paid all the bills. At nine AM, my time, I put my anger aside and called her.

Three rings and a tiny, soft "Hello."

Equally softly, "Good morning, Beautiful Girl."

"Morning."

"Time to get that magnificent tush of yours out of bed."

"Baby? Will you give me fifteen more minutes? Please?"

"You won't be late for work?"

"I promise. Pretty please, Johnny?"

"Fifteen minutes, but then you have to rise and shine."

With warmth in her voice, "You're sweet."

We repeated this ritual every weekday thereafter.

Over the course of the next several evenings, we spoke openly about the things uppermost in our minds. It was clear that during all these conversations she had been drinking. For the first time, she mentioned that her drinking might have been a factor in our falling out. I knew it was a difficult thing for her to admit, so I didn't dwell on it. Instead, I applauded her honesty.

She did her best to be open-minded and tender. I was empathetic. I was sympathetic. I was every shade of pathetic. I was forced to consider that I was nothing more than the ultimate "rebound" for this woman.

I wondered briefly if she might be Leonard Cohen's "Suzanne." I knew she was half-crazy but that was why I wanted to be there.

She talked a lot about not having time to grieve for Neil and how much that troubled her. She revealed that she felt pressured to commit to something long-term. She confessed a "special kind of love" for me, but she just wasn't able to make the great leap so soon after Neil's death.

I told her how exasperating it was walking on eggshells, constantly on alert that something in my tone or expression might

184

spark her incendiary ire. I reminded her of how she castigated me for mentioning old lovers and that sometimes I got weary of hearing about Neil all day, every day.

Predictably, she shot back, "I loved him, Johnny, and now he's dead. Can't you understand that?"

"I loved him, too. I'm going to miss my old friend for the rest of my life. I can't even imagine what you're trying to overcome right now. I just wish that, when we're together, we could occasionally talk about us."

We talked about her anger. It was the only fully developed emotion Marla had. It was her default reaction. Everything she showed to the world required the sublimation of that anger. She had trained herself to mitigate her hair-trigger rage into more appropriate displays. It was understandable given her history and background, but being the person in the line of fire was exhausting and required a level of patience I wasn't sure I could sustain. It must have been a constant wrestling match for her.

After a week, things were mellow again. We could laugh and play with each other, though the situation at her job was getting critical. She was pretty well into the bottle, some nights downright drunk on the phone. I told her that she was killing herself with alcohol and nicotine and THC and that I worried for her safety and health.

A couple of nights, she'd smoked so much that I could hear her wheezing.

I strongly made the point that I had already been through that part of my life and was not going back to it. I quoted Crosby, Stills, Nash and Young to her;

"You are living a reality I left years ago. It quite nearly killed me.

In the long run it will make you cry, make you crazy and old before your time."

"I don't want to watch you die, Marla. Don't make me go through what you went through with Neil. Please be good to yourself."

On the brighter side, I had just landed a twenty thousand dollar advance on a two-book deal and that part of my life was looking good.

Late one night Marla said, "Maybe we could try another visit sometime? I never got to take you to Balboa Park or Torrey Pines or Old Town. We could finally clean up that giant mess in the garage. There's still a lot to do here. I really miss you."

I had been thinking of her constantly and I missed her more than I would have thought possible. She was two thousand miles away. The sense memory of her touch pushed me to convince myself that I had nothing to lose.

I asked, "If you had to describe our relationship, what would you say? Just what am I to you, Marla? "

With no hesitation, she responded, "You're my friend and my lover."

To expect or demand more would have been unreasonable. This was what she was able to offer and more than I could resist. I had felt the bitchslap of Marla's vicious pettiness. I knew her capricious fury and unpredictability. And though seven minutes of every hour spent with Marla was a jalapeno enema, the other fifty-three delivered a sublime joy against which my quixotic heart had no defense.

"I have an idea. You interested in hearing my idea?" I asked her.

Perking up a little, she said, "I'd love to hear your idea, Sweetie."

"I want very much to come see you again. I'll help you clean out the garage. We can go to all the places you wanted to take me. But we have to change things so it doesn't lead to another meltdown."

"Can't we do that?"

"Only if I stop living in the future and you stop living in the past. I won't keep talking about where our relationship is going if you can spend a little more time being fully with me."

"I think they call it 'living in the moment'…and you're right."

I admitted, "It might not be easy, but we're smart people and if we can put aside those things that aren't positive…my god, there's no telling how happy we might make each other. It would be a shame to give up on it."

"How soon were you thinking about doing this?"

"I won't push you into anything and you won't drag me back into anything."

Marla paused and then said, "Of course. I have a few sick days left. I might as well take them now, since I may not have a job when you get here."

"This is Sunday—how about Friday?"

"*This* Friday?" Her voice rose an octave.

"Too soon?"

"No, no, no. I want you here…in my garden…in my bed…as soon as possible."

"Hell, between your son's friends, all the guys at work and that Marine down the block whose girl friend just dumped him--you'll have no trouble finding someone to share your bed."

187

"They're boys, Johnny. That would just be creepy. I've told you before, I like older men. You guys don't require as much training." She laughed.

"Oh, please. That Marine's been working you--bringing cookies, asking for advice, telling you war stories—since I left. You give that young buck a tumble and you'll throw rocks at me."

"Johnny? Please listen to me very closely, because I am only going to say this one time."

"I'm ready."

"Do I have your undivided attention?"

"You do."

In a deep mahogany whisper, Marla reminded me of unfinished business. She took three minutes to describe, in detail, the carnal cornucopia awaiting me upon my arrival at her boudoir.

With blood flow redirected and face breaking into an idiot grin, I reaffirmed, "No fighting and no pressure, right?"

"I can do it if you can."

"I'll get on the computer and call you in half an hour. I'm going to rent a car this time. A convertible."

"Why?"

"Because your driving gives me angina, and it will be more fun for you."

In her wonderfully childlike way, "Are we really doing this again? This is so cool! Call me right back."

"So you're leaving this Friday?" Painless asked, incredulous.

"Six AM. Coming home the following Wednesday."

"I think you've finally stepped off the curb, buddy. But I wish you luck."

"I know the odds of a lasting relationship with her are one-in-a-million...not even that. But, I have to play this hand I've been dealt. Being with Marla has re-defined 'happiness' for me. I didn't know I could feel the way she makes me feel. She has also given new meaning to 'misery'. But I won't walk away without giving it every opportunity to succeed."

Painless observed, "She has really gotten into your head. I mean, I can fully understand it: she's sexy and dangerous. But you're really putting yourself out there to get hurt again...big time."

"I shit you not, when this woman throws her leg across my belly, lays her head on my chest and calls me "Baby'...I'd rob a bank for her."

"I wish you luck."

"This is no dress rehearsal, Doc. I don't want to spend a minute of my future wondering what might have happened. If she burns me down, she burns me down. This late in the game, even a long shot chance at contentment is worth the gamble."

"I want to hear all about it when you get back." Then Painless took his cell phone out and said, "On a similar note...I think I might have some good news for you. A few months back you told me about a piece of Neil's that you were interested in."

I'd never discussed the significance of "Greed" or the seven pieces with him, only that there was some missing glass that Marla and I were curious about. I felt my gut tighten. "You found it?"

"Could be. My daughter in Chicago saw this in a gallery and thought it was one of Neil's. She took a couple pictures and sent them to me. I've got some of Neil's stuff and she thought I might want to buy it."

Handing me the phone, he said, "The piece is untitled, but it's got Neil's name on the bottom. I thought you might be interested. They want nine hundred for it."

There were four small pictures. One was blurred, but the other three were sharp enough to raise my heart rate. The object was the right size and unmistakably Neil's work. On a two inch-thick base, fifteen inches square, I saw a gaping, blood red mouth and a grotesque purple tongue. The teeth were gold and the mouth was filled with gold coins and bars. There was no doubt. This was "Greed."

"It's hard to be sure without seeing it up close. Where is this place?" I was trying not to betray my excitement.

Painless slid a piece of paper to me and said, "I wrote down the name and number of the gallery, if you want to call them."

"It sure looks like Neil's. I'll give them a ring before I go to San Diego. It could be some rare good news for Marla. That's very exciting. Thanks buddy." We finished off the pitcher and headed home.

Out in the parking lot, Painless called across a row of cars, "You sure have one hell of a life, Jack."

All I could think to say was, "So far."

As soon as I arrived home, I printed out driving directions. The gallery was called "Visible From Earth." On Chicago's North Side, it was a six-hour drive. I went to bed at ten, and by six AM Tuesday, I was headed in the general direction of Wrigley Field. It was a pleasant day; sunny and cold with herds of dark, Great Lakes clouds scudding across the brilliant blue sky.

Always feeling comfortable in Chicago, I found the address with no trouble. I parked about a block away and strolled in around noon. It was a bright, small space and I was their only patron. I found the glass I was looking for straightaway. A skeletal young woman in a long denim dress offered to help me.

"It's quite an interesting work, isn't it? My name is Janice. Do you collect?"

"Hello, Janice. Tom Bolton. Oh, no…not a collector. I have an hour to kill before a lunch date and just sort of wandered in."

"We don't know too much about the piece. The artist passed away recently in California and has done some very unique pieces over the years."

"It caught my eye. I'm working on a book about the cult of consumption in the Nineties and its effects on our current cultural and economic landscape. This piece could be viewed as a vivid representation of those times."

"I think it's playful." Neil hated that word.

Janice gasped and put a hand to her bony neck when I lifted the heavy, crazy thing. Assuring myself that Neil's name was on the underside, there was no doubt what I was holding.

"How did you folks come into possession of it?"

"The gallery owner acquired it at an estate sale, if I remember correctly."

This was probably pure horseshit. More likely Sasha had wheedled it, dirt cheap, during one of Neil's hard times and somewhere along his slimy path, sold it for quick cash.

"I'm sure it's beyond my decorating budget. Very intriguing, though. A friend is looking for some things for a new home near here. I'll have to tell her about this place."

"Let me ask the owner, Carol, about the price. Can you stay a moment?"

Turning toward a large metal sculpture and looking at my watch, I said, "Sure."

Janice was back in two minutes with Carol, a zaftig diva in a chartreuse caftan, turquoise tiara and dozens of bracelets. We shook hands and exchanged introductions.

"Janice tells me you've expressed an interest in this astonishing piece. Isn't it just wild?" Another word Neil hated.

"It certainly is unlike anything I've ever seen. But, now that I really look at it, I don't know if my friend would like it as much as I do." It was starting to get deep.

"Do you live here in Chicago, Mr. Bolton?"

"Bolingbrook."

Carol quickly said, "We've had this piece priced at nine hundred for a couple of months, but I think we could go as low as…seven-fifty, for the right buyer. Janice tells me you're an author. It might go nicely in your den or study. Something to provide you a little creative ammunition, perhaps."

"If I could tell my wife I got it for five hundred, she might not shoot me." We all chuckled, nervously. "Tell you what--she's meeting me for lunch shortly. I'll run it by her and get back to you."

I needed to close the deal. I was starting to make myself nauseous.

Carol, recognizing a bird heading back into the bush, offered, "Do you think you might escape the firing squad at six-fifty?"

I wasn't sure how much longer I could play footsy with these two. It was a fair price. I knew I wasn't leaving without it, and I was still looking at a six-hour drive back to Cleveland.

"I really do like it." I dithered for effect. Then, hopefully putting an end to the armaments references, I gushed, "Oh, damn the torpedoes! Wrap it up and I'll take it with me. This will certainly cause a stir at lunch."

I paid cash. They wrapped it like it was the Holy Grail. Ten minutes later I was carrying "Greed" down the street to my car.

Now I had two and Marla had five. Neil's Seven Deadly Sins were closer than ever to being united for the first time. No one, not even their creator, had ever seen them together. With "Greed" in the backseat, it seemed I was driving more defensively than usual on the trip home.

It was dark when I got back to Cleveland. I put the car in the garage and toted the heavy box upstairs to the bedroom. I didn't open it, but set "Greed" on the bathroom floor near the shelf holding its companion, "Lust". With a smile, I shook my head and thought about Neil. I wondered what he would have made of this whole lunatic pageant.

As I stepped from the shower, the phone rang. I let it go to voicemail. It was Marla, calling on the way home from work. As if her driving wasn't spastic enough, it made me uncomfortable picturing her with a cigarette in one hand and her phone in the other, jousting with thousands of cars for rush hour position.

"Hi, Handsome. I have some errands to run before I get home. I'll call you in a couple of hours. Can't wait to see you. I miss you." She sounded good...energetic.

After cold pizza and a Popsicle, I returned her call.

"Where are you?" I asked.

"At the grocery store. Then to pick up some more potting soil for some of the planters out front. Where are you?"

"Settling in for the night. I'll be there in three days."

"I know! Are you excited?"

"I am very excited."

She was in the checkout line at Ralph's, trying to talk to me and the cashier. I said, "I'll let you go. Call me if it's not too late."

"I will, Sweetie. Bye."

I decided to not say anything about "Greed" until I had a chance to see how things went in Olinda. It was less about leverage or secrecy than it was about keeping things as simple and drama-free as possible.

Marla called while I was watching the eleven o'clock news. I had dozed off in the Big Chair and the phone startled me awake.

"Hey. What's going on out there?"

In a low voice, "Sasha's here. He called after I talked to you. He's leaving in a couple days to do some kind of survey stuff back in your part of the country...Ohio or Michigan...and wanted to borrow some money."

"That story again? And why would you loan him money?"

"I'm only giving him twenty bucks."

"Where is he?"

"He's out in the garden. I'm in the bathroom."

"Let me talk to him."

"No…that won't help. He's also asking me about the glass in storage and the piece you have."

"The piece I have? How the hell does he know about the piece I have?"

"It just slipped out. I'm sorry, Johnny. Please don't be angry with me. Please don't."

"Goddammit, Marla! What the hell were you thinking?"

"I wasn't, Honey. I'm so sorry."

It wasn't bad enough that she was worried about her glass. Now I began to question the safety and security of mine.

"Do you have a gun?"

"Do you want me to shoot myself?"

"Do you have a gun? Simple question."

"Neil had a revolver somewhere. It's in a bag of junk under the bed, I think."

"Do you know how to use it?"

"Come on, Johnny," still in a whisper. "I hardly think I need a gun to handle Sasha."

195

"Marla…do you know how to use the fucking gun or not?"

"I'm sure I do."

"Put this scumbag on the phone."

"I'm not going to do that."

"I don't like him hanging around there."

"He will be gone in a few minutes and then I'll call you right back."

"Are you getting high with him?"

"I'm giving him a little to take with him. Saving the good stuff for us."

"I'm really starting to hate this guy. Call back soon or I'll be in bed."

"I will. Bye, Sweetie. Don't be mean to me."

"Ask that asshole if he can hang around for a few days. I need to talk to him."

She called back about a half hour later. Neither of us mentioned Sasha. We chatted around for a few minutes. I knew she was high. There was no way she had opened that drawer and taken out that baggie without smoking some of it.

I'd had my fill of Marla for the day and wanted to get off the phone. "I'm beat. I had a long day in the car."

"Where did you go?"

"To see an old friend in Chicago."

"Oh…"

"I need some sleep, kiddo. I have laundry to do before my trip." I was pissed off about Sasha, she knew it, and our customary "goodnights" were muted.

I made my wake-up call to Marla the next morning. Once she had poured her first cup of coffee and was reassured that I was not angry with her, I hung up and forced myself to do some work on the new book. My literary output had suffered as a result of my romantic adventures. Barring another disaster during my upcoming visit, I would be away for six days and a deadline was looming.

I spent enough time at my desk to crank out about eight hundred words and developed some ideas for a better ending to the novel. It was close to one o'clock and I needed a break. I poured a beer and started to make a BLT. As I put the bacon on a paper towel to drain, the phone rang.

Marla was crying. "I just got fired, Johnny."

"Shit." I took a breath. "Where are you?"

"I'm sitting in my car…down the street from the office…trying to compose myself to drive home."

"Are you OK?"

"Did you not hear what I just told you? I got *fired*, Johnny! I don't have a job! No, I'm not OK. What a stupid question. That's not helping at all. What the hell am I going to do now?"

"Do you want my help?"

"Yes, of course I want your help. That's why I called you. Asking me if I'm OK isn't helping. Oh my God, Johnny…I'm shaking all over, my heart's pounding and my hands feel like they're frozen."

She needed to talk it out. I continued to speak soothingly while turning her toward the details of the event. It had all been very civil; they hated to see her go, she had been a great asset, her release was in no way related to her impeccable performance, they would be happy to compose a letter of reference…they felt just awful about the whole thing. Routine HR crap.

Through the process of describing it, Marla's voice grew more controlled, less panicky. She stopped crying.

I had her take a few deep breaths and visualize the drive home.

"Do you have any savings?"

"I have a little less than five thousand in the bank. They gave me a bunch of paperwork explaining the severance package and some forms to sign and return."

"That's a good start. Here's what we're going to do; take another deep breath and close your eyes."

"OK…I'm doing it."

"Visualize the two of us taking a slow walk by the bay at sunset and then carefully drive back to the bungalow. Call me when you get there, so I don't worry. We'll go over the severance thing together. Sound good?"

"I wish you were here right now."

"So do I, Sweetheart. But it's Wednesday already. I'll be there in forty-eight hours. We'll get it all figured out, I promise."

Marla let out a very big sigh and said, "I'm starting the car. I'll call you in a few minutes. I'm sorry I yelled at you, but you do sometimes ask dumb questions."

"And you sometimes give dumb answers, but we can talk about all that later. Drive safely and call me."

"This is going to be OK, isn't it? We can handle this, right?"

"Of course we can handle this."

She called a half-hour later, after changing into her garden clothes. She read to me from the "Separation Package." It was generous; she would get an eleven thousand dollar severance payment at the end of the month. In addition, she would receive two-month's salary and her medical and dental insurance would be extended for ninety days.

"That sounds pretty decent, kid. You make what…four grand a month?"

"Forty-two fifty." Her voice was flat.

"Eleven thousand plus eighty-five hundred…Honey, that's close to twenty grand. Add the five in the bank and you've got six-month's income as a cushion."

"That's pretty good, right?"

"That's more than I made all last year. Plus, now you have the time and the means to get your dental work done. I'd say you're in damn good shape."

"I'm still shaking. I've never had this happen to me before. What if I can't find a job? The economy is in the shitter and I'm not a kid anymore."

"Marla, I've seen your resume. You won't have any trouble finding work." I wasn't stroking her. Her resume was impressive. Hoping to inject some levity, "You're smart, you're industrious, you're garrulous, you're affable…you're pulchritudinous."

Marla groaned, "And you're a goofball…but I love it when you talk dirty."

And for a minute, things were good again.

She decided, "I'm going to play in the dirt until I feel better. Can I call you later this evening?'

"Sure. Day after tomorrow I'll be there and we'll figure this all out. I was thinking we might go over it together in the bathtub."

"I'd like that." Then, a voice, talking to her in the background. "Johnny, Enid's here. She's leaving for Denmark right after you get here and she wants to show me what to do in her garden while she's gone. I'll call in a little while."

I didn't know where Sasha was headed or exactly how driven he was. But if he showed up in my geographical area with a yen for Neil's glass--he wasn't getting mine.

That afternoon, in an uncharacteristic act of paranoia, I took "Lust" from its space in the master bath and carefully wrapped and boxed it. I then drove it and "Greed" to Miriam's place and asked if I could store them in her basement for a while.

"Should I even ask, Scanlon?"

"Probably not."

Ten hours later, with no word from Marla, I finally called her. I was tired and aggravated that she'd left me hanging. I assumed she'd gotten drunk with Enid. She had two good excuses; getting sacked and an early 'bon voyage' party. Not that she needed an excuse.

I called the house phone twice and her cell twice with no luck. I tried again around midnight and finally went to bed angry. Maybe I'd just show her once and for all and cancel the trip to California. Fat chance of that.

There was a message from her in the morning, left around midnight, her time. She apologized for not calling earlier. Sasha and Enid had been at the bungalow when Marla's idiot son stopped by with a couple friends. Marla's explanation; "the time just got away from me."

It was Thursday. I was to fly out early the next morning. Dragging out my suitcase and selecting clothes, I let her first two calls go to voicemail. With her customary hint of hostility, she seemed to be launching a pre-emptive strike, getting upset at me before I could be upset with her. This was the kind of convoluted logic and misplaced malevolence I was learning to expect from her. I twice stopped while packing to ask out loud, "Does this thing have a chance in hell of working?"

The answer was self-evident; yes, there was a chance in hell. There had to be.

I called her back. She asked if I was mad at her. I told her I thought she'd been thoughtless and that her excuse was pitiful. "Why would you make me wait ten or twelve hours when you say you'll call 'in a little while'? I wouldn't do that to you."

She said, "Johnny, if this 'living in the moment' thing is going to work, we should probably start now and not wait until you get here."

She had me. The calm and assured tone of her voice made me smile.

"I'll call you when I pick up the rental in San Diego and see you tomorrow morning around eleven."

"I'll pack a picnic lunch. We'll eat at that little park you like, down by the bay."

"That may be the most beautiful thing anyone has ever said to me."

201

"Fly fast, Johnny. I need you."

After a brief layover in Cincinnati, at eight-twenty Friday morning I was buckled into a westbound bulkhead window seat, wrestling gravity to thirty-six thousand feet, four and a half tedious hours from embracing my dark star.

I tried to convince myself that Marla and I had a chance at being nice to each other for six days, that we might be adult enough to leave the vicissitudes of past and future to follow their natural courses. I was left to wonder if her scornful animosity was the residue of grief over Neil's loss, or whether she'd always been filled with bilious fury and I had become the latest in a parade of horny, bewildered nebbishes to be caught in the snare.

My emotions during this flight were different from those of the previous journey. I allowed myself lofty hopes, but they were mitigated by my first-hand exposure to Marla's instability.

It nagged me that she was the only one of Neil's women not involved in the arts. Indeed, there was not an artistic bone in her delectable body. She didn't read, write, paint, sculpt, draw or sing and, beyond Neil's glass, exhibited no interest in the creative process. It became increasingly plausible that his attraction to her really had been purely physical. This was certainly understandable, but I resisted the notion that my attraction to Marla was no deeper than skin.

Maybe I had assumed too much based on her four-year involvement with Neil. Maybe in my lust for Marla, I had granted her esteem-by-association. It seemed the only shot at notoriety in her prosaic little life had been her meteoric connection to a flamboyant, outrageous artist. Her stock had certainly enjoyed a significant rise as a result of that chaotic connection. She had felt the quick, hot rush of minor celebrity. With Neil she had been lifted above her white trash background into the liberating eclecticism of the artist's realm.

That was all over. Now she was looking down the barrel of middle age—addled, unemployed and descending into a lifestyle of permanent self-medication and all-consuming discontent. She was offering little resistance to her precipitous decline and it was killing me to watch it. I couldn't expect a miracle or some soul-shifting epiphany that would cause her to anoint me as "The Chosen One." That would always be Neil. But I hoped that this visit might reveal and clarify our needs and expectations.

I saw no chance that Marla would sell the glass to make ends meet. She would starve before committing that kind of betrayal to Neil's memory.

I had not yet decided if I would tell her I had acquired "Greed." There was no telling what would unfold if she knew. It could be anything; cold fury, attempts to charm it out of me, offers to buy it, recriminations the likes of which I'd never seen.

Off the plane in San Diego, I walked to the car rental desk. Ten minutes later I was on the freeway, top down, calling Marla.

"Where are you?"

"I'm in a sweet little convertible, ten minutes from you."

"Awesome! Please tell me it's not some hideous color."

"Baby, this thing is 'Come-Fuck-Me' red."

Laughing, "You're a nut case. I'll start putting our picnic together."

"I'll be right there."

Minutes later, I parked in the back alley and walked up to the bungalow.

"Anybody home?"

With a giggle, Marla unlocked the door. I was greeted with something new; she immediately gave me a very long hug and a firm, full kiss. I put my bag on the same closet shelf as last time and went back to the kitchen to help with lunch.

We made small talk about the perfect weather, my flight and the changes she had made to the place. It was now a full-blown shrine and museum. It was overwhelming; new shelves filled with Neil's glass, several more of his paintings hung and more photos of Neil and Marla. The only room that looked the same was the bedroom.

There was a new photo in the kitchen, taken at the party in New York. Neil was holding a drink and grinning. Marla had both arms around his waist and was smiling as she planted a big kiss on his cheek. These were two people clearly in love. I wanted a picture like that of Marla and me. I tried to imagine how it would feel. It seemed possible but unlikely.

As we moved around the kitchen and made ready to leave for the park, I picked up on something else new. Whereas before I had been the one to initiate physical contact, Marla was touching me. In the half hour before we left, she several times looked me in the eye, gently stroked my arm or bushed against my shoulder, almost as if to reassure herself that I was really there. We laughingly bumped hips at the chopping board and exchanged a couple gentle hugs and small kisses. There was no sense of barriers.

The car delighted her. She walked all around it and immediately dubbed it "The Floozy-Mobile." She said, "I never would have taken you for a red convertible kinda guy, Johnny."

I said, "Honey, *you* are the red convertible. I'm just your driver."

With an enormous smile and laugh, she said, "You really are a goofball."

"You're the goofball." We did that all the way to the park, as the wind tossed her hair and she kept her hand on my knee in what seemed an act of tender confirmation.

We spent a quiet afternoon together with bread and cheese, chocolate and wine and light conversation. It was warm and sunny and we tuned-in to how good we made each other feel. After we ate, I put my head back in the grass and she put her head on my stomach. We talked a little about work and money, but agreed to hash out those things later.

"I decided to take advantage of the insurance extension to get my teeth fixed, like you said. I have an appointment with an oral surgeon in El Centro the day you leave, eleven AM."

"El Centro's a two-hour drive, Honey."

"I know, but he's supposed to be the best and he came highly recommended by a friend of Neil's. My insurance won't cover it all and I know it's expensive…but I might as well get it done while I have the opportunity."

Leaving the park, she asked if she could drive the convertible. She enjoyed styling through town, to the grocery and the post office, then back to her place. Marla drove conservatively, by her standards. To my great relief, when we got to the bungalow she said, "I'm so afraid I'll scratch it. You should do the driving. I'll sit back and enjoy the scenery."

She talked more about the changes to the bungalow and we worked in the garden. Later, we made egg salad and a simple dinner of fish and rice. We poured Zinfandel and ate at the garden table as dusk settled. I was dog-tired but it had been a day free of conflict and I felt good about the prospects.

We would set aside one day to clean the garage and stick with it until it was done. As she handed me her separation papers to look over, she said, "I'd like your ideas about cutting expenses until I find a job. Neil told me a dozen times after he got sick that I should find a rich guy to marry."

"Do you know any rich guys?"

"A couple. My old boss, Barry, is loaded and has been after me for a year to come and work as his personal assistant. I think he wants more than just an employee, though."

"Marla, speaking for men everywhere, there are many things we may need from you, but there is one thing every man you will ever meet *wants* from you. You are irresistible."

"So, I should marry a rich guy?"

"If that's what will make you happy and give you the things you want, then…yeah, what the hell…marry money."

"So, what do you think of my situation?"

"From what I'm reading here, you're in good shape for the next five, maybe six months. With the severance and extended salary, you can pay all your bills and eat. How honest do you want me to be?"

"As honest as my friend and lover should be." She winked at me and squeezed my hand across the table.

"You spend a lot of money on weed." I left out wine. "You might consider a less expensive storage facility. You could stop supporting a kid who refuses to work. Maybe a less expensive way to do laundry. These alone could save you maybe a thousand a month. Not enough to live on, but it would buy you more time."

Expecting a stony-eyed reproach or worse, I was relieved to watch Marla's face take on a look of introspection. Instead of blowing up, she nodded as she considered my advice.

"I know you don't approve of the weed. But it's a part of my life. Maybe I could cut back."

I replied, "It's not a question of my approval, Marla. I love getting high with you. It's expensive and cutting back might save you a surprising amount of money. I think it's a good place to start."

"There's no way to hook up a washer or dryer in this old place, so I don't know what else I can do about laundry."

"Maybe, while you're looking for work, you could do it in the machines and fold it yourself."

"Seems like a big hassle and boring as hell. And I know you're right about Ben. I made a promise to myself that I am not paying his phone bill anymore. He's going to have to take whatever shitty job he can find to pay his own rent."

"He will only follow through if you are strong enough to resist him when he ignores your threats and tells you he's about to be evicted."

"All that stuff about THC stunting the growth of young kids' brains and how that leads to poor intellectual and social and job skills. That's Ben. He's lazy and clueless and has no regard for other people."

"He's a narcissist."

"Whatever he is, I feel guilty for not preventing it and it drives me crazy. But he's my kid...ya know?"

"Then prepare to have him living here with you. If you can't say 'no' to him, you'll wake up someday, up to your ass in dirty laundry with a forty year-old teenager throwing non-stop parties in your living room and stealing your weed."

"I'll try to be stronger. I think I like your idea about the storage space, though." She had slowly let go of my hand and her voice had taken on a thin edge. It was time to stop talking and follow her as she changed the subject.

"That won't make a big difference. But if you find a cheaper place, maybe closer to home, you could probably save a few bucks."

"Why not bring it all back here?"

"Jesus, Marla…I thought we were going to clean out the garage, not put more stuff in it."

"We can do both. A third of that stuff in the garage I'm going to toss out or give away. His family didn't have any interest in it. If there's something you want, you can have it. We can hide Neil's 'Deadly Sins' up in the rafters for now. They'd be safe there."

"Anything we leave in that alley overnight will disappear."

"Exactly."

"I'm here to help out and have some fun. If that's what you want to do, then we'll do it."

"But not tomorrow. This weekend I want to take you to Balboa Park and Torrey Pines and a winery I think you'll like. We'll work on the storage and garage stuff Monday."

"Fine with me."

"I've had a beautiful day with you. Thank you." She kissed the tip of my index finger and smiled. "I like being in the moment."

It was around nine. As I poured more wine, Enid came through the gate, failing ridiculously to look surprised at seeing us.

We exchanged greetings, more cordially than our initial meeting, but contained. I did not want to share Marla with anyone tonight.

I went inside to fetch a wineglass for Enid. Back at the table as I poured for her, I asked, "So, when do you leave for Denmark, Enid?" hoping she would say, "In about five minutes."

"I leave in a couple of days. I am excited about going to see my family."

We chatted about her family, Denmark, how long since she had last seen them...Marla and I taking every opportunity to roll our eyes and mug when Enid was looking at the other. It was clear that Enid was prepared to spend the whole night drinking with Marla and whoever else happened to be around.

Enid asked, "Johnny, how long will you be here visiting Marla?"

"I'm going home early next Wednesday."

"We should all have dinner together before I go to Denmark."

"Sure. That would be great. I really need a shower. I'll be right back."

I was not saying anything to encourage her to stay. Marla seemed indifferent.

I was finishing my shower when Marla came into the bathroom to say, "She's gone."

"Oh, damn. I was so looking forward to a long evening with her."

"I told her you and I had a lot of stuff to discuss. She really wants this dinner tomorrow night or the next."

"She's your neighbor, kid. You have to get along with her. I can stand one dinner with her if it helps."

"You're a sweetheart. I'll be outside."

We had a little more wine. Marla did her thing with the plants. From my garden chair I watched the moon rise. The day had been one of laughter and kindness. Never had I wished more strongly that I could stop time. Right then, right in that garden was everything I had ever wanted. She was glowing. I was content. It was a crystalline moment, full of grace.

Marla looked at me and said, "You ready to call it a day, Handsome? You must be tired."

"I'm ready for anything."

Marla closed the bedroom door behind us. We finished our wine and smoked a little before she took her shower and brushed her teeth. Damp and naked, she floated through the few feet of darkness between the bathroom and the bed. She undulated into my arms, making sure every point of contact was perfect, and for ten minutes we silently held each other.

She said, "This is a very, very good day, Johnny."

We roamed over each other bravely, without haste or restraint. In heated communion, riding rough whispers, we loved in the moment. Resonating…we dissolved into sleep.

In the years since moving back East, I had splashed my contempt for Southern California around with a broad brush. Saturday brought another pristine morning and I was starting to like San Diego. Not far inland from Marla's bungalow was the desert, hideously hot. To the South was Mexico, a place that had never held any appeal for me. To the north, the toothy cynicism of Orange County, and north of that…the cannibalistic bedlam of Los Angeles. But this was a sweet spot…temperate, with a pace that seemed manageable in comparison to the rest.

At the kitchen table, over coffee and blueberry-mango pancakes, Marla and I made a rough schedule for our remaining time together.

"How does this sound for your weekend? We'll go to Torrey Pines today. I want to show you a winery not far from there. They might have some of Neil's glass. We can eat lunch there. Tomorrow, we'll go to Balboa Park. That's two pretty full days. And there's Old Town…so many things I want you to see, Johnny."

"Honey, I'm up for anything. I'd like to spend five minutes in the garage before we leave today to get some idea what we're up against."

"Why don't we plan to clean out the storage space early Monday, bring the Deadly Sins back here and try to get the garage done sometime Tuesday? Whatever I don't have room for we'll drag to the dumpster and leave for the scavengers."

I told her, "If you're sure that's how you want to do it. There won't be room in the convertible for everything that's in the storage space. We'll need both cars. Maybe there's a dumpster there we can use."

"I don't want to spend all of your time here cleaning. I want us to have some fun, too."

"We will. Let's finish breakfast, take a peek in the garage and head out."

On the drive to Torrey Pines, Marla continued to touch me lightly, to look at me quietly. Several times that day, I would catch her and ask "What?"

"Just looking at you."

I've been sized up before. She was trying to make a decision. So far she had been on her best behavior. She would get all the things she wanted from me over the course of this visit. I wondered if I would make the cut or if she'd administer the coup de grace. I reminded myself that I was breaking the rules about "living in the moment" and returned to the immediate joy of being with Marla.

We parked in the State Parking lot, put the top up, slathered ourselves with sun block and hit the beach. We walked along the water, then close to the cliffs. Marla had never heard of sea glass. I found a piece and showed it to her. With childlike enthusiasm, off she went to gather white, brown, green and even a few of the rare and coveted blue gems from the sand.

At one point, as I was busy looking down for glass, she walked on a hundred feet ahead of me, never looking back to see where I was. When I reached her, she was sitting on a rock outcropping, looking out to sea. I sat next to her and handed her a few tiny shells. With a smile, she put them in her pocket and kissed me.

Putting her arm through mine, she offered, "One time last year, Neil wanted to take nude photos of me on these rocks. He started to undo the top of my bikini, and I nearly let him. I saw the parents with their kids and said, 'No'. He was very angry with me…said I was chickenshit."

She shook her head and said, "Sorry. Just thinking out loud. Ready to do some hiking?"

We took the longer trail in the mid-day sun, joking about how many days it might be until someone found our bleached bones in the scrub brush. I took pictures with a throwaway camera. Marla alternately vamped and demurred.

The trail was a challenge in sandals and we'd forgotten to bring water. By the time we reached the trail's end an hour later, we were toasted and parched. We located restrooms where we tossed cold water on our faces, drank deeply from the water fountains, and headed back down the hill to the beach and the convertible. The mood was good, but we were sweaty and hungry.

Near the parking lot, we washed our feet. Marla asked, "Do you want to see the winery? They have sort of an artist's village where Neil used to blow glass and teach classes. There's a nice little bistro and they have wine tastings every weekend."

"Let's do it."

I was not so deluded as to believe that Marla would not bring up Neil during this visit. I had mentioned him a couple times myself. The pattern unfolding was one of honest reflections on their past together. But I knew she was comparing me to him. I would never win a contest with the memory of a larger-than-life, dead lover.

I was enjoying Marla's company and the generous nature of her attention to me. I was determined I would not add to her burden. I was seeing the Marla I loved and wanted. In the back hallways of my mind, a small voice nagged, "Wait for it. Wait for it." I was honestly and fully taking it one minute at a time, pushing those thoughts away.

The winery was not crowded. Marla wasted no time finding the space where Neil had worked. The guy who owned it was introduced to me as "Robert." Of course, I asked, "Can I call you Bob?" I recalled Neil referring to him as a thief and a condescending swine.

As Bob leered and slobbered over Marla (she was wearing a short denim skirt and suede boots and looked unbelievably sexy), she put her arm in mine and introduced me as her "awesome new friend and Neil's oldest buddy."

Bob observed, "I guess I don't remember Neil mentioning you."

I rejoined, "He spoke frequently of you, Bob."

Bob's face fell a little once he sensed the vibe. He pasted on the "you lucky prick" smile that men wear when they realize they're holding no cards. I showed him every tooth as he reached to shake my hand. That's when another piece of this puzzle was revealed to me. I understood how Marla made me feel.

Preferred. This was the uniquely electrifying feeling that only this complicated woman had ever given me. Preferred.

I feigned interest in Bob as he tried every trick in the book to get Marla to commit to a barbecue with him and his "gal." The smarmy fraud actually had the stones to tell her he'd had a dream about Neil "just last night." I groaned audibly and said, "Sweetie, what do you say we grab a bite to eat? We can come back and talk more to Bob later."

We stopped at several other kiosks and exhibits on the way to the restaurant, Marla dropping Neil's name all along the route.

We sat outside at a table for two in a shady corner, surrounded by banana trees, brilliant red geraniums, Bird-of-Paradise and bromeliads. We had wine and iced water and salad and chili rellenos.

She said, "Neil always hated that guy, Robert. Did you hear him invite me over to his place, knowing his girlfriend is gone for a month? Do you think he really had a dream about Neil?"

"Yeah, right. On the night before you show up here. No, Marla. Bob wants to get into your pants. Nothing more, nothing less."

"How can you be so sure of that?" she asked with a sly look.

"Because I'm a man."

"Stop it. Sometimes you embarrass me. By the way…" looking furtively from side to side, summoning me with her curling index finger.

I leaned in.

"I got a little turned-on back there by the way you called me 'Sweetie', at exactly the perfect moment …exerting your dominance and all." Under the table, one sandal off, her bare foot brushing my leg, Marla blushed slightly and whispered, "I have a little something special in mind for you…later."

"I'll try to pace myself."

After lunch we strolled around for a while. We asked another couple to take a photo of us. I took a couple pictures of Marla alone. As I took one of her sitting on the seat of an old stagecoach, an uncomfortable feeling hit me. The look on her face was beatific. I knew in the second I snapped it that it would be on the wall in the room where I died. The photo about which people would inquire, "Who is *that*?"

In the wine shop the tasting was soon to begin and we signed up. Over the course of an hour we tried six wines. We bought a bottle of Merlot and a bottle of Zinfandel and decided to head home. It had been a full day. We were dirty and ready for some down time. We agreed to skip farewells with Bob.

It was nearly six o'clock as we got out of the car in front of her place. Marla asked, "Do you want to have dinner with Enid tonight or tomorrow night?"

"Between you and me and the Floozy-Mobile…I never want to have dinner with Enid."

"I know, but we promised."

"*You* promised."

"I'll go tell her we'll do it tomorrow."

Marla walked ahead of me as we approached the bungalow. I saw someone moving in the garden and then she excitedly said, "Ben! What are you doing here?" I was finally going to meet the wastrel son.

He was five-eight, pale and gaunt, with his Mother's murky brown eyes. Under a crushed porkpie hat, his hair was fashionably disheveled and dyed Goth black. Below his lip was a wispy "soul patch." Wearing orange flip-flops, black jeans and brown t-shirt, Ben unfolded from his chair like a rusty pocketknife. He gave his mother a quick hug. "I just came from my yoga class and I'm hungry and I need to use your shower."

Marla's kid seemed to struggle to keep his eyes open. As a friend of mine once observed about Ben's generation, "They have trouble concentrating when they're awake." He had delicate features and a thin voice. Not effeminate, but untested and weak. A Momma's Boy.

"Who brought you here? I wish you would call first. I hope you arranged a ride home."

He looked lazily at me. "I guess you must be Johnny."

"It's nice to finally meet you." I extended my hand. His grip was tapioca in a mitten.

"Mom says you're Neil's oldest friend."

"One of them."

With a wry smile, "So, you gonna sweep Mom off her feet and take her back to Ohio with you?"

"I'm sure your Mom doesn't want that. I'm here to help out, that's all."

Marla quickly piped up. "Ben, go ahead and shower. What do you want to eat? Can you call someone to pick you up?"

"Dinky dropped me off, but he wasn't sure if he'd be back this way or not."

"Then you better get your ass on the phone because I do not intend to drive you all the way back to your place tonight. You have to stop doing this shit, Ben." Turning to me, "It's a half-hour drive each way."

It was agreed we'd all have a salad after Ben showered. She dug out a change of clothes for him. "He forgets to bring them, so I keep some here."

I said nothing.

Over what turned out to be a remarkable Waldorf salad, I listened to Ben update Marla, ad nauseum, about his "band" (they played for free at their own parties), his many sexual conquests ("bitches and hoes"), his perennial poverty ("I just can't find anything worth taking time away from the band") and how wasted he got the night before, ("I thought I was gonna hurl a couple times at yoga class.")

His movements and speech were affected. He accentuated his discourse with slow-motion martial arts-type movements and movie dialogue. Marla's diagnosis seemed to be accurate. This was a young man who had smoked himself stupid.

As far as Marla was concerned, I had disappeared. The only recognition I was granted was a swift, embarrassed glance when Ben said, "Can you cover my phone bill again this month?"

Finished eating, Marla went to Enid's to discuss the following evening's dinner plans. I took the dishes to the sink. My hands in the warm water, rinsing plates, I again wondered what the hell I was doing there. I suddenly understood that I had become part of a cast of characters that only Neil could have assembled, and I let my mind wander through several bizarre endings to the story.

Ben made one half-hearted call to find a ride home. Back in the garden, sipping the new Merlot, I was grateful he had sense enough to not ask to sleep at Mom's.

Waiting for Marla to get back from Enid's, Ben broke the uncomfortable silence. "Have you met Sasha yet?"

"For a couple minutes, last time I was here."

"Yeah. Dude's really after my Mom. Or at least he was. I don't know if anything ever happened between them, but Neil got real mad at her just before he died. Jealousy, I think. Sasha followed her around like a horny little puppy…for weeks. I stay out of my Mom's business, but he was starting to piss me off. Like, I know he was a big help to her, taking care of Neil and all, but he couldn't hide what he was really after."

"Your mother is a very beautiful woman."

He smiled at me and said, "She really likes you. She says you're really smart and you make her laugh."

"I made a promise to Neil that I'd do all I could to help her. I've become very fond of your Mom. I'll be her friend for as long as she wants."

"Neil was awesome. He didn't act like an old dude. No offense. He and Mom used to have some massive, wild fights. Not, like, physical fights, but it got loud enough a couple times that the cops came. He had a nasty temper, but he would get high with my friends and me. He was nutty, but he really listened to us. Too bad he died. It was real ugly and it crushed Mom."

"I miss him. We had a lot of great times together."

Just then, Marla came through the gate. "Are you guys talking about me? My ears were burning."

"As a matter of fact, we were. So, what's the verdict with Enid?" I asked.

"She's coming for dinner tomorrow, whenever we get back. She might stop over in a bit for a glass of wine."

Ben said, "For real, Mom…what's up with you and Enid? You're always talking trash about how much you hate her and what a heartless bitch she is…but she's always over here, drinking and eating with you. I don't get it."

She furrowed her brow, turned to me and asked, "What was that you said today about enemies, Johnny?"

"Vito Corleone said it before I did; 'Keep your friends close and your enemies closer.'"

"Exactly" said Marla. To Ben, "Who's picking you up?"

"Nobody's available. Can you take me?"

"Goddamn it, Ben, you have to stop doing this. Don't drop by until you've made arrangements for transportation home. This is the last time I'm doing it. I'm not your personal taxi service. Get your stuff and let's go, then."

This was pure theater, solely for my benefit, to bolster the idea that she was finally taking a tough stand with her shiftless kid.

I stood up. "We'll take the convertible."

"Johnny, no…you stay put and take it easy. You've been driving all day. I'll be back in about an hour."

"What do you think, Ben?" I asked.

"Top up or top down?"

"Down, of course."

"Convertible all the way, Dude."

She gave Ben a filthy look, to which he responded with a vacant smile.

To me, "You don't have to do this. It's not your responsibility."

"It's OK. It's a beautiful evening for a drive."

"You're awesome."

"I thought I was a goofball."

"That, too."

With her son sprawled across the back seat and the dusky coastal sky beginning to display a few faint stars, we cruised on the cooling night air.

Driving back to the bungalow after dropping Ben off, Marla sat close to me, her head on my shoulder, hand on my leg. The irony of my situation rolled over me gently. I smiled and shook my head in amusement. The ultimate skeptic, luxuriating in the iconic Southern California postcard; Saturday night, palm trees silhouetted against the last of the Pacific sunset, beautiful girl at my side, cool car, top down. This was living large.

"What do you think of Ben?"

"I like him more than I thought I would. He seems like a gentle kid…harmless enough. I see what you mean about him being twenty-two going on fourteen. You'll be supporting him until the day you die, but he's not so bad."

It was past eight when we rolled up to the bungalow and, to my disappointment, Enid was waiting for us in the garden, sitting at the table with a bottle of something.

I was eager to relax and get to bed, primed and ready for Marla's "something special", and now here was this strange Dane again, messing with my nookie plans. I sullenly put the top up on the car while Marla headed to the garden to greet Enid.

I quietly called, "Marla?"

She stopped, looked back. Twenty-five feet of vine-covered fence separated me from Enid. I drew my finger slowly across my throat, held my thumb and index finger an inch apart, mouthing the words, "Can we cut this short?"

With a look of impatience, she took a few steps back in my direction. Sternly, Marla said, "I am not going to encourage her to stay, but I'm not going to be rude to her either. Don't be so selfish. I'm not going to forget you're here." Then, off to engage Enid in their warped charade.

We sat at the garden table for a while, drinking Enid's Chianti, and then adjourned to the kitchen table. I learned that Enid had a daughter in high school and was still legally married to a guy in Los Angeles. We opened a bottle of Beaujolais and I excused myself for a quick shower.

Heading toward the bedroom, Marla said, "I'm going to let Enid try some of this new stuff before she heads home…if you want to join us."

"I'll wait."

"Well, peek before you come bursting out of the bathroom."

While I showered, Enid and Marla smoked in the bedroom. They were in there the entire length of my shower, so they would be baked by the time I got out. I smelled the smoke and the sweet citrus spray. They were laughing as they went to the kitchen.

By ten-thirty, I was tired of drinking wine and had long since run out of things to say to Enid. For two hours, they sat in the kitchen and talked about Neil; Enid embellishing the myth of his saintliness and Marla growing morose. They'd had enough to smoke and drink that they were primed to party all night. I went to the loveseat to watch TV for a little while, yawned frequently enough to earn a couple dirty glances from Marla and dropped other hints that I was done with socializing and needed to recline.

This was tricky since, as far as I knew, Marla was still maintaining the ludicrous façade that our friendship was platonic and that I was sleeping on the sofa...twelve feet from the kitchen table.

Finally, Enid stretched and said, "I have to go start packing and I know you two have things to discuss. We will see each other at dinner tomorrow night, right?"

They walked out to the gate and I went to brush my teeth. It was another twenty minutes before Marla finally came back inside to say, "Don't you think you were a little rude?"

"Who was I rude to, Marla?"

"You couldn't have been more obvious that you were waiting for her to leave."

"She's been here for three goddamn hours. I thought we were spending tomorrow evening with her and tonight was for us."

"She's my neighbor and I have to get along with her. I've already explained that. Don't you think she knows why you want her to leave? She's not stupid."

"So...we're no longer pretending I'm sleeping out here?"

"Enid knows we're sleeping together. I know she has mixed feelings about it, but she understands. It makes me a little uncomfortable…not so much that we're knocking the bottom out of it every night, but that she's right over there," pointing towards Enid's bungalow, "being judgmental."

"I'll do whatever you ask. That includes leaving you alone, if that's what you decide you want. Again…I don't give a shit what Enid or anyone else thinks about what we are doing."

"But when you go back to Ohio, I'm still here to deal with it. Don't you get that?"

"Why waste time living in *that* moment if we can live in *this*, much better, moment?"

She hugged me and rested her head heavily on my shoulder. "Sometimes I wonder if this isn't just all about the sex for you. Even Neil and I didn't do it every night." She pulled her head back and smiled broadly, "Don't get me wrong…it's breathtaking and I love it all. But, it seems like, once the sun goes down, you want the world to go away so you can have me all to yourself."

"It's not just the sex and you know that. But you're right about the rest of it. I do want you all to myself. You see and talk to these people every day. You will see and talk to them every day after I leave. I'm with you for five days and I don't know when I'll see you again. It's only for another few days. Let me be selfish."

"Selfish is not the same as possessive but, sometimes you come close to that line, Honey. I was ready to be very mad at you."

I had one more glass of wine with her and we smoked a sample of a different weed before her shower. The new stuff hit me like a ton of feathers. My brain was a smooth jazz circus with Dali flourishes. I was a Power Ranger in The Sixth Dimension.

Later, Marla's fine, freshly scrubbed body on mine, she sighed into my ear, "And now…something very special."

If it's Sunday in SoCal, it's brunch. At a small beach diner, Marla, (one Mimosa ahead of me), winked salaciously over our Denver omelets and said, "You look pretty pleased with yourself there, Mister."

I had to smile. "I had a very special evening." Then it was on to Balboa Park.

My unfamiliarity with the terrain and her insistence on always trying to find "a good place to park" led to twenty grim minutes of driving around and arguing. Out of futility and tedium, I finally said, "This is insane. We could do this all day," and parked in the next available space.

Unhappy with my choice, Marla said, "We could have done better than this."

"So, I'll carry you in."

Balboa Park is a fine place to spend a Sunday. Of course, Marla first wanted to visit the Art Center. Open and colorfully tiled courtyards are home to dozens of studios and galleries displaying the work of hundreds of regional artists.

"Neil had some things in a few of the shops here and knew some of the folks who display here." It was yet another installment of "Places I Went With Neil" and she missed no opportunity to drop Neil's name, inquire if the artists had known Neil, and otherwise try to connect the dots.

I began to feel embarrassed for her. After more than an hour, only one of the many people she approached even recognized Neil's name and none of his glass was anywhere to be seen. She bought a

224

couple small prints that we later hung in her kitchen, but she seemed a little distant as we made our way to the giant pipe organ.

We spent half an hour in the huge amphitheater in the sunshine, listening to the mighty Spreckels. I thanked her for bringing me. "The architecture is unbelievable. And so are you."

"I knew you'd like it here. You'll love the Botanical Building…thousands of plants indoors."

We strolled through dozens of cottages, each one displaying cultural and historical exhibits from a different country. Dancing and music from every corner of the planet moved through the space around us. Marla was quiet, with a detached, determined expression. We finally agreed we'd had enough culture.

She declared, "I'm thirsty and I have to pee. How about a little lunch?"

"Sure. Where?"

"There's a pretty upscale place here Neil and I went to a couple times. Or we could drive somewhere else."

"I'm feeling upscale today. Lead me to it."

The Prado is one of those toney places that make me self-consciously reach around and pat my left rear pocket, as if, through fabric and leather, my touch might magically replenish my wallet.

We were quickly seated. Marla excused herself and asked me to order her a Mojito. I watched her walk away in her leather skirt and bright yellow blouse, and again observed how she commanded the attention of every man she passed. Her form and raw sexuality trumped not being the most economically advantaged couple in the place.

The waitress brought menus. I ordered Marla's Mojito and a Guinness for me and asked her to give us another few minutes.

Marla and the drinks arrived at the same time. We toasted Balboa and consulted our menus. She drained half of her Mojito in two sips and said, "Will you get mad if I ask you a question?"

"You just did and I'm not mad yet."

"Seriously. I need your word."

"I won't get mad if you ask me a question."

"Do you have any plans for that piece of Neil's glass, the one in your bathroom?"

"Lust? I plan to enjoy it with pride and fond memories."

"Would you consider giving it to me?"

"I've never thought about it. Giving it to you or selling it to you?"

Our waitress was back to take our orders. Marla's expression seemed to have sharpened. We ordered panko-crusted crab cakes as an appetizer. Marla settled on the grilled fish tacos for lunch. I chose the goat cheese ravioli and sipped my Guinness.

"It's funny. A part of me believes that Neil meant for me to have the whole set of seven. He left everything else to me, so it seems logical, doesn't it?"

"Are you asking me to just give it to you?"

Marla sat stiffly upright in her chair, one hand in her lap, one gripping her drink. She looked at me with a mix of distaste and surprise, as if I had just asked her to smell my feet.

"Well, I'd pay you for it, if that's the way you'd prefer to handle it. You're the one who said his will gave me everything." The tone of her voice had gone flat.

"Not other people's things, Marla. He gave that piece to me and it means a lot to me. I wish you had told me this was going to be a business lunch."

She drained her drink and began looking for a waitress. "It's not a business lunch, Johnny. You said you'd help me put the pieces together, remember? It was all part of you being friend and lover, remember? Will you please flag down that waitress?"

Marla was nervously rearranging her silverware and poking at the ice in her water. I motioned our waitress over and Marla ordered a Mango Martini. We were assured our crab cakes were moments away.

"Do we have to talk about this right now? Do you even know for sure that there are seven pieces?" I wanted to know what she knew, but I didn't want to go through another hysterical drama in another nice restaurant.

"I don't think anyone's seen all of them together. But Neil told me more than once that he'd made seven pieces--The Deadly Sins-- and that one of them was with a friend and one was unaccounted for. MIA, he called it."

The Martini arrived with the crab cakes and we were informed that our entrees would be out soon. I declined a second beer, eliciting a peeved look from Marla. She was silent through the appetizers. The tacos and ravioli came and we lost ourselves in the excellent food.

Near the end of the meal, Marla asked, in her mock-playful voice, "Is it really asking so much, after all I've done for you...plane tickets, room and board, Neil's shirts, sex, weed...that you let me have what is rightfully mine?"

Feeling my neck getting warm, I polished off the last inch of Guinness. I fixed my eyes on Marla's and replied with quiet restraint, "I have repeatedly offered to pay you for the tickets and you've assured me I shouldn't worry about it. You *insisted* I take those shirts. I didn't realize you were running a tab on the rest. Total up what I owe you and I'll pay you when I get home."

I took a fifty and a twenty from my wallet, carefully put them in the middle of the table, stood slowly and neatly laid my napkin on the last ravioli. "I'm going out for some air." I needed to get away from Marla and the cookie-cutter Barbies and Kens around us.

There was a cash machine near the exit. I withdrew three hundred bucks and walked outside. Unsure of my location, I saw signs for the Botanical Building and walked slowly in that direction. After five minutes, I found a long bench with room at the end. As I took a deep breath and sat to ponder my predicament, my cell phone rang. It was Miriam.

"I'm at your place and something odd is going on." Years before, I'd given her a key so she could pick up my mail and newspapers and water the plants when I was away.

"'Odd' as in a family of anteaters has moved in or 'odd' like the sink is leaking?"

"Somebody's been in here."

"You mean broken in? Don't go wandering around in there, Miriam. They might still be there."

"The door from the kitchen to the deck has been jimmied open. I was here yesterday about four and everything was fine, so it happened overnight or very recently."

"Shit. Any damage? Anything missing?"

"The door isn't busted up. They just pushed back the latch. I can fix it. You *have* to put a deadbolt on this damn door, Jack. Everything downstairs looks alright. Haven't been upstairs yet. I called you as soon as I noticed the door."

"Did you see anyone around the house?"

"Not really. Some guy walking down the street, four, five houses away."

Out of the corner of my eye, I saw Marla a hundred feet to my left. Her jaw set, one arm tightly across her chest, she held a cigarette with the other hand. She had come out the front door and hadn't spotted me. She was tapping her foot and scanning the terrain through her sunglasses. She looked so tiny. I made no attempt to attract her attention.

"Go upstairs and see if you notice anything obvious. Be careful."

As Miriam climbed the squeaky stairs, she said, "They were smoking."

"What?"

"Oh...strong smell of cigarettes. I smelled it as soon as I opened the door."

Synapses sparked. "Tell me again about the guy walking down the street."

"Tall, dark black hair...dirty-looking guy, dirty clothes...walked kind of funny."

Sasha. Sasha was in Cleveland and he had been inside my home.

After a few more seconds, "None of the drawers in your room are open. Closets look good. Let me check the other bedrooms."

"No, there's nothing in there to steal. Miriam…check the bathroom."

"The bathroom?"

Marla had spotted me and was closing fast.

"Yes. See if everything seems to be in place."

A moment later, "Huh…that's weird."

"What's weird?"

Marla was now standing six feet from me, finishing her cigarette and trying to not make eye contact. Her shoulders thrown back, her expression a rickety attempt at bravado…she was ready to fight but I could tell her heart wasn't in it.

Miriam said, "The linen closet's been tossed…towels all over the floor. I think possibly some doodads and baubles on the shelf…the shelf where your big piece used to be…are gone. But I can't be sure, Jack."

Marla sat down, carefully allowing two feet between us.

Miriam asked, "Jack, do you want me to call the cops?"

"No. Sounds like you've got it under control. I'll be home in a couple days. Thanks for the call."

Miriam asked, "Things going OK out there?"

"Ducky. Everything here is just ducky. Talk to you soon."

I put the phone in my front pocket, reached around back for my wallet.

Turning to me, Marla probed, "Everything alright?"

"Like you heard...ducky."

"Just for the record, Johnny, if you ever get up and leave me at a table like that again, we're through."

I firmly pressed fifteen twenty-dollar bills, folded, into her hand. "For the plane ticket. Let me know the balance for the rest and I'll send you a check when I get home."

Trying to push it back to me, "Don't do this, Johnny."

"Put it in your purse and don't mention plane tickets to me again."

"I wasn't trying to make you mad, I was just..."

"Send me a bill for the rest, Marla. I'm done talking about this shit. Let's go look at plants."

As I stood up to go, she grabbed my hand. "I'm sorry I made you angry. I was just trying to be honest. Isn't that what you want?"

I sat back down. "You just reduced our relationship to dollars and cents and some half-assed idea that you have a right to my property. That's about all the fucking honesty I can handle for one day. Tell you what...lie to me for the rest of the day. If I don't get up and move right now I'm going to say something I'll regret."

We started in the direction of the Botanical Building. We walked, not touching or addressing each other, through the lush foliage and exotic blooms. It was a magnificent place...one that I bookmarked for another visit, preferably on a day when my resources were not being diverted to anger management.

231

After, we walked outside to a bench in the sun. Marla lit a cigarette. We had not exchanged a word in an hour.

Finally, she said, "I didn't mean it the way it came out. Thank you for the money, but it's not about money. I never meant to say I had a right to your property. I was trying to express myself and I did it badly. I'm not as good at it as you are. What do we do now?"

"That's a really good question, Marla."

"I meant, have you seen enough here? Would you like to go somewhere else?"

"I need to do something physical…and, no…I don't mean sex, Marla. I'm not going to hound you for sex anymore."

She looked at me with a mix of surprise and hurt. She opened her mouth to protest, managed to sputter, "That's not fair…"

I talked over her. "I don't want to spend all day tomorrow at the storage place and then in the garage. Let's go back to your place, change into some grubbies and do the storage thing today. We can have it taken care of in time for the dreaded 'Dinner with Enid' portion of our day."

"Are you sure you want to do it today?"

"I sure as hell don't want to spend all day Monday at it."

The tension partially broken, Marla said, "I think it's a good idea."

An hour later, in shorts and t-shirts, we pulled the convertible up to **STUFF IT** and walked in the front door. A new face at the desk; an effervescent, stocky young woman with deep blue hair, a tattoo of Bullwinkle on her neck and a two-pound wooden crucifix around her neck. Her nametag said "Kahliani." I let Marla do the talking.

Kahliani fixed us up with a low, flat cart. She told Marla that they provided a dumpster around back for customers to use and also recommended donating unwanted items to the Salvation Army Store a block away.

"They're only open 'till two on Sundays, so you'd have to come back another time. Lots of our folks take stuff there and they'll give you a receipt so it's a 'write-off' on your taxes."

We pushed the cart to the elevator. Marla swiped and punched and we rode to the third floor. After another swipe and the key pad, we were back in the musty little treasure house of Neil's left-behinds.

That it was untouched, undisturbed from the last time was oddly unsettling to me. These things were as dead as Neil.

Marla had already consumed two mimosas, a Mojito and a martini and was in no mood to trifle over the finer points of disposal versus sentimentality.

"These computer monitors can go. I don't think they work. Those three boxes on the floor I don't even want to open. Crap that we just stashed here. At that point, we still had hope. The folding chairs are no use to me at all."

I suggested, "So…Goodwill or dumpster?"

"Salvation Army. Neil's family has no interest in the kayak or paddles, but I can't bring myself to throw them out. He always looked so happy in that kayak. Little guy, little boat. He was so cute."

A couple of empty seconds passed before she turned to me with the face of a shattered little girl—a little girl who had just realized that her bicycle, with her dolly and her teddy in the basket, had been stolen and were never, ever coming back.

Her mouth opened in a silent wail. I saw the lights go out behind her wide open eyes. I wrapped my arms around her at the instant she dissolved into rattling sobs. I held her up, swaying, as she surrendered to a paralyzing finality. She did not try to squelch the choking pain passing through her, finally out there for the whole world to see.

Gently easing her down as her legs gave way, I went to my knees on the white concrete floor with her--my shirtfront wet, her face a picture of agony. Marla wept and keened and cursed. I became concerned that she would hyperventilate and faint. Marla Stone was nowhere near finished grieving for Neil. She was nowhere.

I ended up sitting on the floor, my back against the wall, legs straight out in front of me. After ten minutes, Marla settled, lying on her side, curled up with her head in my lap. I murmured, over and over, "It's OK Honey...it's OK." I continued to gently stroke her hair, her small shoulders. For a moment I thought she had fallen asleep.

A young couple appeared at the door. The girl quietly asked, "Are you guys alright?"

Marla turned her head slightly, away from the voice, into my hip.

I said, "We're fine, thanks. A little overwhelmed. Thank you for asking."

"Can we get you anything?"

Giving Marla a second to respond and getting nothing, I said, "It's very kind of you. Really, we're fine."

The girl pulled a small package of tissues from her purse and handed it to me. I started to pull one out.

"Keep them," she said as they started to walk away.

"Thanks."

After two or three very quiet minutes, Marla slowly sat up next to me and said, in a hushed voice, "That was nice of her."

She took a few tissues to blow her nose and wipe her face. "I'm sorry. I don't know what happened. It just hit me...out of nowhere. I must look awful."

"You look beautiful. Nothing to be sorry about."

"I'm so glad you were here. Wow. That was scary. We should get to work and get out of here."

"No hurry. Whenever you're ready."

"No...I'm fine." We stood up. She took a deep breath, flashed a weak smile and said, "Let's take the monitors to the dumpster and then take the glass down to the car. We can come back for the kayak later, when I decide what I want to do with it. We can't use The Floozy Mobile for it and I really don't want to mess around with putting the roof rack on my car."

"The chairs and the three boxes to Goodwill tomorrow?"

"Salvation Army. That's what I was thinking. And maybe the kayak."

"They're only a block away. We can rest it in the back seat."

"And I get my deposit back from these people."

We loaded the monitors on the cart, padlocked the door and went behind the building. I chucked them into the big green box, enjoying three satisfying crashes as the glass screens exploded.

Back upstairs, we carefully put the five heavy cartons on the cart. The garishly painted names on the boxes made us chuckle. "Envy", "Gluttony", "Anger", "Pride" and "Sloth" in bright, lemon yellow with Neil's squiggles and cubes and faces around them.

With the top down, we easily put two on the back seat. The remaining three went into the trunk with no room to spare.

When we returned the cart, Kahliani told us that the couple we met upstairs had expressed an interest in the kayak. She handed Marla a business card with their contact information. We thanked her, told her we'd return on Monday.

At five thirty we pulled into the alley. Marla wanted to start dinner. I wanted to get the glass into the rafters of the garage immediately. I would be spending a lot of time there tomorrow and I wanted this heavy stuff out of the way.

Marla went inside the bungalow while I got a ladder and started dragging things down from up above. She was back in five minutes with the good news that Enid was not home yet. Enid didn't need to know about this.

She opened the overhead door to let some air into the place. I handed down to Marla two bicycles, an inflatable raft, two boxes of old wooden picture frames and two Styrofoam coolers. Now there was room for her Sins. I had seen a stack of two-by-fours standing on end in the corner and asked Marla to hand them to me, one at a time.

"What are you going to do?"

"I'm going to reinforce the rafters with two-by-fours. We're putting a few hundred pounds of fragile stuff up here and I don't want anything to come crashing down on that lovely concrete skull of yours. We'll put a tarp over the boxes so no one will see them. Nobody will ever know they're here unless you tell them."

"You're pretty smart, Scanlon."

"Yeah, yeah...more boards, less talk."

After I'd made a solid base for them, she struggled to lift the first of the heavy boxes up to me as I stood on the ladder.

"If you just hold the ladder steady for me, I can get the rest of them."

In forty-five minutes, the collection was sturdily supported, safely stashed and completely out of sight from ground level. We were dusty and hot, but feeling good about not putting it off.

"It's nice to have them safe at home. You're an animal and even though you were mean to me today…I'm grateful you're here." She grabbed a handful of my ass and, with a sound from deep down in her chest, kissed me.

"If you want to thank me, ditch Enid and take me to dinner." I pressed her against the workbench, put my hand on the back of her head and kissed her hard.

Her lips a half-inch from mine, Marla said, "You know I can't do that, Baby. She's leaving for Denmark in the morning and I promised."

Locked in a rough, hungry grope, we were seconds from going to the filthy garage floor when a car pulled in close by. Breaking away, Marla peered through one of the dirty windows. Once again, I was treated to, "Shit. It's Enid."

Smoothing her hair while I zipped up and cursed all things Danish, she silently locked the door. I gave her a look of surprise and raised my hands in the "What-the-hell" gesture. Stifling laughter and grinning like a pair of imbeciles, we stood stock-still in a cartoonish attempt to conceal our depravity from the neighbors.

Enid walked straight past the garage and into her bungalow. I teased Marla; "Why did you lock the door?"

She laughed, "No idea…instinct, I guess."

It was six o'clock, the sky losing its light, and we still had to clean up and prepare dinner for three. I would try hard to not be jealous or covetous of my time with Marla and to let her do whatever it was she did with Enid.

We weren't in the house five minutes when Enid knocked. She had two bottles in one hand and a bag in the other. I opened the door, welcomed her in and took the bottles to the kitchen. Enid had brought three nice swordfish steaks and some dill. I opened a bottle of Merlot, poured three generous glasses and went outside to sit down heavily at the garden table. Marla and Enid chatted and decided on a menu.

Ten minutes and half a glass of wine later, Enid called from the kitchen window, "Johnny, will you make a marinade for the fish? Marla says you're good at it."

"Sure."

Enid looked happy and talked with excitement about her trip. With a glass of Merlot in me, she didn't seem such an evil piece of work after all.

I made a marinade with dill, a little white Zinfandel, a bit of strawberry balsamic vinegar and a few drops of sesame seed oil.

"You got me hooked on this stuff, Marla."

Behind me, her chin resting on my shoulder as she looked over, "What stuff?"

"Sesame seed oil. Ever since that dish you made at my place, I'm a fiend for it. Every time I make rice, it gets sesame seed oil…and I make a lot of rice." I put the fish in the marinade and put the whole thing in the fridge. "Thirty minutes should be enough."

As Marla reigned over her tiny kitchen, Enid and I sat at the table, getting up only to help when needed. We talked and drank wine and the mood was comfortable. Marla stayed busy and I could not take my eyes from her. Every time our eyes met, we shared a conspiratorial smile.

238

"Enid and I are going to go back to the bedroom for an attitude adjustment. Wanna come?"

"I think I'll wait until I shower. I'll go back outside and enjoy the night air and the wine. I'll catch up."

After fifteen minutes, I went in to fill my glass. Finishing the bottle of Merlot, I locked the front door and went into the bedroom. It was smoky and I had obviously interrupted a conversation that switched tracks when I entered the room.

"Did you lock the door?"

"Of course."

"Want a little of this?"

Enid's eyes were glassy and red. Marla's were wide and inviting.

I took a couple tokes on the little pipe and soon felt my groin tingling and the interior of my skull draped with purple velour.

After Marla sprayed her crappy citrus air freshener, we all adjourned to the kitchen again. Enid wasted no time opening and pouring more wine, Cabernet this time. Marla and I made rice with ginger and saffron oil and a salad topped with croutons she'd baked in the oven.

Between bites of salad, she seared the swordfish in an iron skillet. When it was done to perfection, she rested the steaks on three beds of her rice. We topped off our wineglasses, toasted Enid's safe travels and shared a delicious, convivial dinner. After the table was cleared, Marla washed the dishes.

Marla's capacity for alcohol was a given and Enid, no mean tippler herself, kept pouring. She opened a third bottle of wine. I was warm and mellow and didn't really need any more. Enid was ready to

239

let it all hang out before spending most of the next day on a plane. Marla was following Enid's lead. She was less inclined now to hold eye contact with me and she got a little louder and more demonstrative as she drank.

She and Enid went back to the bedroom again. I went back to the garden and settled into a comfortable chair with my wine. During lulls in the freeway's low drone, I could hear them talking quietly and laughing. They came out to fill their glasses and joined me.

Marla did not look at me. I'd seen this stage before. She was at the point where she would now continue to smoke and drink until she collapsed. I had to be prepared for anything.

A tipsy Enid said, "Johnny, what will you do after you leave here?"

Marla's phone rang. "Hello?"

I went on to tell Enid I would just get back to writing and my part-time job.

Enid asked, "Do you think you will come back here again?"

I answered truthfully, nodding toward Marla, "That depends on her."

Marla switched the phone to her other ear and quickly walked into the house, saying in a loud whisper, "What the hell?" She went into the bedroom and closed the door, hard.

Enid guessed, "Probably that derelict son of hers. He will be the death of her. She can't continue to support him if she's out of work."

"I am not going to get caught up in that mess. She asked my opinion and I gave it to her. She says she'll change."

"Neil didn't like him. Neil was such a beautiful and kind soul. How did you come to be friends with him?"

I gave Enid a synopsis of the uniquely debauched and hearty kinship I had shared with Neil. I was distracted by Marla's absence.

"Excuse me a minute. I want to see if she's OK."

"More wine?"

"Sure."

I tapped on the bedroom door, then pushed it open a foot and stuck my head in. Marla's eyes flashed angrily as she waved me back, out of the room. She was smoking the pipe and holding the phone to her ear.

I mouthed, "Are you OK?"

Marla got up, took my arm and, gently but firmly, guided me out the door and closed it. I went back to the garden.

"Is Marla alright?"

"She was not glad to see me."

"Do you love her?"

Ambushed by Enid's lack of politesse, I chose my words with care.

"She's an amazing, beautiful woman. I have strong feelings for her, but I know she will always belong to Neil. I'm trying hard not to fall in love with her. It's complicated."

"I see the way you look at her. It is easy to see you care for her very much."

"I want her to know that, no matter what she decides, I will do all I can for her. I made a promise to Neil, but Marla sometimes makes it very difficult."

The bedroom door opened. Marla went into the kitchen to refill her glass.

When she sat down at the table with Enid, Marla's eyes were slits and her hands were trembling. She took a long swallow of wine, her foot tapping nervously on the ground.

Enid asked her, "Is everything alright, dear?"

"I wish I'd never met that asshole, Sasha. That stupid, stupid, clumsy bastard."

The wine made it easy for me to ask, "What happened?"

Marla looked at me with blank eyes. They betrayed nothing, but her voice was more fearful than angry. She lit a cigarette and stared at a huge red geranium.

"All he cares about is Neil's glass. My glass. That's the only thing he has ever cared about. And he's just stupid enough to do anything to get it. He never gave a shit about Neil or me. It's all about doing whatever it takes to get his hands on the glass." She took another long drink of wine.

"So…what happened?" I ventured.

I got a glower of pure indignation.

"Why would I talk to you about it? For all I know, that's what you're really after, too."

Sharply, Enid said, "Marla! That's a terrible thing to say."

I stood up. "I'm going to take a shower."

"Sure, walk away again, Johnny." And I did.

They came into the bedroom to smoke more weed while I took a long, thoughtful shower. I could hear their voices, but not their words. They were laughing, so maybe there remained some hope of salvaging the night. I came out of the bath to an empty bedroom, smacked by the smell of fake citrus.

I found Marla and Enid at the kitchen table, engaged in the disjointed honking of intoxicated women. They were feeling no pain and opening a bottle of grappa.

Grappa is Italian liquor. It is made from what is left after the pressing of grapes for winemaking; skins, seeds, leaves, stems…the occasional dog turd, fallen from someone's boot heel. After crushing, fermentation and distillation, the noxious residue still clinging to the bottom and sides of the vat is grappa. It is also used to make charcoal lighter fluid, industrial drain cleaner and hair straighteners.

Historical anthropologists concur that grappa has been the primary cause of madness and domestic violence in Europe since the Crusades…syphilis running a distant second. Two drops of grappa will burn through a slate pool table in six minutes. The experience of drinking grappa is akin to being rhythmically kicked in the kidneys while having ammonia poured into your nostrils. Roughly half of regular grappa drinkers eventually lose peripheral vision, sense of smell and all regard for rudimentary personal hygiene.

Those fortunate enough to survive a night of grappa-drinking frequently report an unfamiliar funk that lingers in the mouth for days, sometimes weeks, immune to the most liberal and energetic applications of mouthwash or brushing. This is dog turd.

They were talking about Neil again. Marla briefly glanced at me with empty eyes and pursed lips.

From the cupboard, she took three of Neil's shot glasses, clear with red glass dripping down the sides like wax. She filled them with grappa. We tossed them back in unison. My ears got hot and my eyes watered. Marla closed her eyes and gasped, "Damn". Enid took a small sip of water chaser and smiled.

I'd had all the grappa I would ever want, but Marla was already pouring three more shots as Enid grinned.

And that is when the true dynamic of this love/hate relationship between Marla and Enid landed full on me--they were drinking buddies. Nothing more than that.

They weren't required to like each other or have much in common. Marla and Neil had certainly been enormous consumers, individually and together. With Neil gone, Enid was a willing substitute with a similar capacity. They had gotten drunk and high with Neil hundreds of times. This ritual, in his absence, was a link between these two women and their shared homage to him. Alone and in middle age, they'd bonded over the only things they shared…a fascination with the growing legend of Neil and a history of drunkenness.

As it became more apparent to Marla that I could not drink that way anymore, my luster dimmed in her eyes. I couldn't hang and my stock was plunging.

"What time is your flight tomorrow?" I asked Enid.

"We take off at ten fifteen. So I should get there around eight thirty."

Marla, molding her words thickly, "She was going to take a cab, but I told her we'd take her." Eyebrows cocked, chin out…a look of defiance in her eyes as she awaited my reaction.

This was news to me, but I calmly turned from Marla to Enid. "No problem. We'll take the convertible and save you the cab fare."

"That would be great, Johnny. I should go home. It's getting late and I still have a few things to pack."

Marla lifted her grappa in toast and said, "Don't run off. You can sleep on the plane. Cheers!" She drank hers in two gulps. Enid tossed hers back.

I took a sip and said, "I can't drink any more of this shit. It's taking the enamel off my teeth."

Marla stood and took Enid by the arm. "I have to take a shower. Come have a few puffs with me before you go." As they closed the bedroom door behind them, I poured my grappa down the kitchen drain and went to sit in the garden. I was as buzzed as I'd been in a while, and could only imagine how wrecked Marla would get before she finally collapsed. I sipped iced water and enjoyed the quiet.

I could see the clock in the kitchen from where I sat. It was ten thirty when they emerged from the bedroom. They poured wine for themselves and came outside. Marla announced, "I'm going to take a shower", to no one in particular and went back inside.

Evidently Enid was not leaving as planned and sat at the garden table. We spoke softly, as the neighbor's next door, never fans of Neil's or Marla's, were probably in bed.

"I promise I'll leave as soon as Marla comes out. She asked me to stay."

"Of course. Don't worry about it."

"She's mad at everybody right now; Neil, Sasha, her kid…you."

"And did she tell you why she's mad at me?"

"Not really. I know she has guilt about getting into a relationship with you so soon after Neil died. I told her you seemed

245

like a very sweet and honest man. When you're here, you're too close and when you're not here, she misses you. I think she cares more for you than she's able to handle."

"I don't know how this will turn out. She will probably push me away. I worry what will happen to her, but it's her life. What was all that about Sasha?"

Enid hesitated. "I guess he did something foolish, trying to get some of Neil's glass while he was back East. Marla didn't say what exactly, but she is pretty shaken up about it."

I said nothing.

Enid continued, "She said she might go to work for that millionaire she's been talking to. He calls her frequently and has offered her a job. I met him once and he seemed intense. Very handsome."

"She says Neil told her to marry a rich guy. Maybe he will be the one."

Enid said, "I'd rather see her with you."

We talked more about glass, Denmark and Marla. I was getting some interesting insights from Enid when Marla came out of the bedroom. Resplendent in her short green après shower attire and hair piled high in a black towel, she poured a glass of wine in the kitchen. Coming outside to light a cigarette, she ignored me and sat next to Enid.

"Did you finish packing already?" she asked Enid.

"No, I've been talking with Johnny."

"Anything juicy?"

"Not really. Boring Danish stuff, mostly."

Marla took a big sip of wine and turned to look at me. Her eye movements were about an inch behind the movement of her head. Surely having made a smoke stop on the way from the bathroom, eyes blazing--she was wrecked. Revived by her shower, she showed no signs of slowing down.

She said to Enid, "Have one more glass with me."

"Marla, I have to get at least a little sleep. Do you want to help me finish packing? Just take a few minutes."

Marla quickly said, "Go on and I'll be there in one minute." She jumped up from the garden table, wobbled slightly, regained her balance and went inside.

Enid looked at me with what seemed to be sympathy and said, "I will see you about eight o'clock, Johnny."

"Count on it. Sleep well."

As Enid went through the gate, Marla came from the bedroom to pour some more wine. She showed me the top edge of a baggie in her pocket as she came out the front door. She grabbed the wine bottle by the neck and headed for Enid's. "I'm gonna get her high one more time."

Knowing I was wasting my breath, but hoping to avoid trouble later, "I'll probably be in bed when you get back. We've got a lot to do tomorrow."

She shot me a quick look of dismissive impatience. "Whatever."

The front edge of her flip-flop caught the corner of the brick planter. Marla stumbled and pitched forward, her wineglass flying into the next yard. She caught herself just as I reached her. The palm of her hand had a slight scrape from the brick, and her wine glass had landed, unbroken, on the neighbor's lawn.

I looked at her hand. "Honey, let's wash this off."

"It's fine," as she twisted away from me.

I handed the wine glass to her. "Well, at least it didn't break."

Walking through the gate, she said with a hollow laugh, "Drunky luck."

Eleven PM and I was done for the day. I brushed my teeth, threw some water on my face and climbed into bed. I intended to read for a while, but fell asleep almost immediately.

Something woke me about an hour later. Without speaking, Marla came in, went straight to the bathroom and closed the door. After a few minutes, I asked, "What's up?"

"I'm fine. Go to sleep." She was wheezing.

She came out shortly and left the bedroom, saying nothing and closing the door. Concerned that with no one to drink with, she might decide to get in her car and go somewhere, I warily went to the kitchen.

Marla was standing in front of the stove and facing the window. The towel had shifted on her head and a mad tangle of wet hair hung partially over her right eye. Her facial muscles were slack. Her shoulders were slumped and her eyes were voids. Her bare feet were spread a little, as if to steady herself. She held a glass of wine that looked all wrong. It was a bright candy-apple red, not like wine. She displayed absolutely no reaction to my entry.

I sat at the table and once again asked, gentle and low, "You alright, Sweetie?"

Her lifeless eyes finally focused on me. "Go to bed."

Before I responded, I noticed that the upper cabinet behind her was half open. That's where the hard stuff lived. Disguising liquor with red wine and stationing her body between the cabinet and me. Damn, damn, damn.

"I just want to make sure you're alright, that's all."

Staring back out the window, "Leave me alone and go back to bed."

I went to the bedroom and opened a book. After a very quiet hour passed, I went back to the kitchen. Marla was in the exact same spot, same pose, glass full.

I tried again, calmly, "Marla, please come to bed. It's late and we have a long day tomorrow."

After several seconds, she said, "Leave me alone and go to bed. I do not want to talk to you anymore. No more talking." She was thick-tongued and slurring. She looked down at her glass as if she'd just seen it for the first time, and took a long swallow. "Just go away. Go. You worried you won't get your sex? Get away from me, Johnny."

"Forget about sex. You need some sleep."

"I need you to stop telling me what I need." Raising her voice, "You're making me fucking angry. Go to bed. I'll be in when I'm ready."

I retreated to the bedroom. An hour later, past one thirty now, I heard breaking glass and Marla saying, "Shit!"

I hurried to the kitchen. She'd dropped her wine glass in the sink and was standing, staring at it.

"Stand still... there might be glass on the floor. Are you cut?" I turned on the overhead lights and looked at the floor. The glass was confined to the sink. Marla was looking at her hands but not speaking. I gently took her hands in mine and assured myself she wasn't bleeding.

I said, "I'll get all the glass from the sink and put it in the trash."

"I'll do it."

"No. I'm going to clean this up and then we're both going to get some sleep. Why don't you get ready for bed and I'll take care of this." Instead, she silently staggered outside for a cigarette.

After I dabbed up the last slivers of glass with a wet paper towel, I went to the living room and sat heavily on the sofa.

Marla was just outside the door, dimly lit by the porch light. One small foot crossed behind the other ankle, leaning her hip against the pillar, she was a portrait of excess and defeat. She stared off into space, mechanically smoking a cigarette, her hair still piled up inside a towel and her lovely body barely hidden.

I knew that this exact tableau had been re-enacted a million times under the porch lights of trailer parks and housing projects and cheap duplexes all over the country. This low-rent still life was being duplicated in thousands of places this very night; where people drank and smoked and fought too much; where sadness and desperation and anger ruled the night.

I felt a new, colder sadness. I had spent all of this time in a mad crucible, suspended between hate and honeymoon, only to reluctantly conclude that this beautiful woman was every bit as crazy as Neil had warned me she would be. Nothing I could say was going to change that. Given enough chances, she would ruin my life…one long, ugly night at a time.

But, right now, I wanted to embrace her, take her pain away and get her safely to another morning.

Marla finished her smoke, locked the door and walked silently past me to the bathroom. I got into bed and turned out the light. She brushed her teeth and minutes later I heard the toilet flush. Marla climbed in from the bottom of the bed, rolled to the far edge with her back to me, and without speaking a word, was asleep in minutes.

This was Marla's broken, smothered way of saying goodbye to me.

On five hours of fitful sleep, I got up at seven thirty and put on the coffee. Marla had not stirred. I felt a little shaky and she was going to be a mess when she woke up. I decided to take Enid to the airport by myself and let Marla sleep. I sipped coffee for ten minutes, steeled my nerves and went back to the bedroom.

Sitting gently on the edge of the bed, I put my hand on the small of Marla's bare back and whispered her name. She rolled half-way over with eyes still shut and mumbled, "What?"

I looked at her perfect body and said, "I'm going to take Enid to the airport so you can sleep."

"Is it time to go?" She opened one eye to look at the alarm clock.

"In half an hour. You go ahead and sleep and I'll be back a little after nine."

Up on one arm and trying to focus on the clock, "You sure?"

"I'm sure. Then we'll have breakfast and head to the storage place whenever you're ready. Sound good?"

In her smallest voice, "I want to sleep, Johnny. Just a little longer."

"I'll clean up, get dressed and be back in an hour or so."

"Sometimes you're good to me. Lock the door, Sweetie." Then, a barely audible, "Bye-bye, Enid." She rolled over and was snoring by the time I had my sandals on.

Dressing, flushing my aching eyes with drops and finishing my coffee, I marveled at how she could possibly call me "Sweetie" after the night before. I shrugged, locked the door and shuffled the thirty feet to Enid's.

She was waiting inside her door with one very large bag and one carry-on. With a knowing smile she said, "Good morning, Johnny. Marla's not coming?"

"No. She's going to sleep in. She sends her rest."

I took the bags to the car as Enid locked up her bungalow. I put them in the trunk and we pulled out of the alley. It was a Monday rush hour and slow going. We were no sooner on the freeway than Enid handed me a piece of paper.

"Keep this. It's my name and phone number. In case things don't go the way you hope and you want to keep tabs on her."

Pushing the paper into my pocket, I said, "That's very thoughtful. Thanks."

We talked a little about the weather as traffic crept along I-5. I began to ask about her childhood in Denmark when Enid suddenly put her hand on my arm and said, "I have to tell you this thing. Don't be mad at me."

Assuming it was about Marla, I was grateful that, even at this snail's pace, I'd be dropping her off in a few minutes. "I won't be mad."

"At dinner last night I saw the way you looked at Marla and talked to her. You are in love with her and I think you should know these things."

"So, tell me."

"She was with that soldier after you left…that young Marine…twice."

Already queasy from too much alcohol and no breakfast, I felt my stomach do a funny kind of flop. "After I left?"

"The last time you were in Olinda and you had a big fight with her and went home early. Marla had a party two nights later. Probably twenty people. Food, wine, pot, music…lots of fun. Great party. He was there and after everyone left, I heard him come back to Marla's place and they had sex."

"She said he was too young for her…like a child."

"He was no child that night…or the next night."

It felt like being told of a death in the family. Not a distant great-aunt passing peacefully beneath her ancient quilt. More like a cool, favored cousin, raped and stabbed in an alley.

"Does he still come by?"

"No. I don't think so. I have not seen him since that second night. They fought and he left…like you. I'm sure this is hard to hear. But, last night when you said she would probably push you away, I decided you deserved to know what you are really dealing with. If you have a good life in Ohio, go back to it."

I had to ask, "What about Sasha?"

She gave me a quizzical look and, nose upturned, said, "Marla and Sasha? No way. Except for Neil's glass, there is nothing Sasha wants more than Marla. It's sickening, the way he lusts for her. But, he's grotesque…and I heard Neil tell her not to trust him. Marla and Sasha? Never."

"That phone call last night really set her off. Any idea what made her so angry?"

"Only that Sasha did something dangerous and foolish. Something about trying to get a piece of Neil's glass while he's in Iowa or Ohio or Idaho…wherever he is. She did say 'This will ruin everything', but when I asked her what she meant, she didn't answer."

Coming down the off ramp for the airport and moments away from probably never seeing Enid again, I decided to ask her the question that plagued Marla.

"You and Neil?"

Enid smiled and replied, "I know Marla thinks we did. But, no. If the situation had been different, maybe. It was clear that sooner or later they would destroy each other. There was as much anger and fighting as there was love and kindness. Before he got sick, she treated him the way she treats you, Johnny. It changed him…weakened him. I hated her for that."

We were at the airport. I maneuvered the car to the doors nearest the KLM desk and jumped out. We quickly got Enid's bags from the trunk and exchanged a hug. I handed her my business card.

"You never know. Have a great visit and thanks for everything."

Enid waved. "Thanks, Johnny. Good luck!" she shouted.

As I eased the Floozy-Mobile back into the sun-drenched crush of the freeway, I said out loud, "Yeah. I'm going to need some luck."

Back in the alley, I shut off the car and sat there for a few minutes. My brain was not finding room for these new pieces. It was probably safe to assume Marla had slept with the "rich guy" at some point. I tried to rationalize that she was a lonely female with a strong libido, but it just didn't fly.

I took a deep breath, opened the car door and girded my loins for the unknown awaiting me in the bungalow. I understood how routinely I was repeating this behavior with Marla—striking postures of combat and defense--and by how uncomfortable it felt.

Marla was making the bed when I knocked on the door. She gave me a weak smile as she unlocked it and asked if everything went all right with Enid.

"Not much to it, really."

"Can I change the plan today?"

"My plan was the airport and then storage. I'm half done with my plan. What do you want to do?"

"Let's go down to the bay and lie on the sand. I don't want to send you back to Ohio all 'fish-belly' white. Some sunshine would do us both good. You wanted to see me in my little black bikini. Here's your chance."

She looked green around the gills. Marla had no doubt learned that a good long sweat is therapeutic after a night of over-indulgence. I just wanted to get through the day without a fight. That's what it had come down to. And sex. I had two more nights. I went along, fully realizing that we were now just playing each other for our own selfish purposes.

"Fine with me. No storage, then?"

"Let's do that tomorrow and play today. Do this for me and I'll buy you dinner tonight. Then we can go down and walk along the bay after dinner."

"You had me at 'little black bikini'."

"Are you going to pout today?"

"I'm not going to pretend that nothing happened last night. I'm sure you don't want to talk about it. But it was fucked up and ugly and I didn't deserve it. The sick thing is that I'm to a point where I don't even expect an apology anymore."

"I'll get you one of Neil's bathing suits and put some snacks in a basket with some cold drinks. Let me get the blanket, a couple towels and some sun block and we'll go and have a good time. Or would you rather stay here and feel sorry for yourself? I'm going to the beach either way."

"That's it?"

Marla sat down at the kitchen table and looked up at me with weary, bloodshot eyes. "Whatever I said last night should have made it clear just how messed up I am right now. I am sorry if I made you sad, because I don't like doing that. But I feel like a rat in a maze sometimes...like I can't catch my breath or relax."

"I don't want to stay here alone. I came here to be with you. Let's go to the beach. I haven't been in salt water in a long time."

Still sitting, she took my hand and pulled me toward her. She put her head against my stomach and her arms around my waist. "Please don't pout and be angry today, Honey. Pretty please? We can make this a good day. 'In the moment', right? We'll take a shower together when we get home. How does that sound?"

"You don't have that basket packed yet?"

She hugged me hard, looked up with a tired smile. "You are so easy."

"I know. And you love it."

"I kinda do, actually."

She went into the bedroom to get the gear and sat down to smoke the pipe. "Do you want a little, Honey?"

If she had been doing this all along, I had not seen it. Either way, Marla no longer felt the need to conceal any aspect of her indulgences from me.

"It's nine-thirty in the morning."

"So what?"

"Thanks...I'm fine."

We gobbled down English muffins and scrambled eggs. Eschewing anything that fell into the "work" column, we dropped the top and went to the beach.

Once the blanket and towels were spread and basket placed, we stripped down to our bathing suits. The sight of Marla in the little black bikini excited every hedonistic molecule in my body. It was not some tacky attempt to reveal as much as possible. It was a proper bikini, crow black and tasteful, and she filled it perfectly. It was the first time we'd seen this much of the other's bodies in the full light of day and I was certainly getting the better of the exchange.

"Is the bikini alright?"

"Oh, god yes. And everything in it."

In about five minutes...the time it took for us to put lotion on each other's backs...I had spotted the rubberneckers who show up solely for the eye candy. Lame, lone wolves, clumsily attempting nonchalance as they leered, they were a pitiful lot.

Far from the youngest woman on the beach, Marla was clearly attracting her fair share of attention. Her small, youthful body molded into that simple arrangement of fabric magnified her raw appeal. The evidence was in the long looks from the other people around us. My ego stroked, I felt "preferred" again.

Lying on her stomach, she undid her top and settled in. I put lotion on the exposed area and she fell asleep almost immediately, content to sizzle in the Southern California sun. I went into the water a couple times to cool down, but generally left Marla to herself.

After an hour, we drank icy lemonade and munched cool avocado and bean sprout sandwiches. We took a quick dip in the cold water. Very few words had been exchanged and I no longer automatically took that as a danger sign. I was ready to leave, but Marla went right back to the blanket to cook out more poison.

Maybe an hour later, Marla said, "Wow…it is hot. Will you fasten my top?"

Both dripping with sweat and thirsty, we grabbed two more lemonades and waded out to where the water was chest-high. I went under several times to cool off, holding the drink over my head. Marla, not wanting to get her hair wet, gently tossed water on her face and the back of her neck.

"So…no hitches getting Enid on her way?"

"Nope. Your routine stop and drop."

"Did you guys get a chance to talk at all?"

"A little."

"About what?"

"Scandinavian agriculture, primarily. We talked about you, goofball. What else do we have in common?" Then a gentle probe. "She thinks you should marry the millionaire."

"Really. His name is Barry, by the way, and I already told you about him. He used to be my boss. What else did Enid tell you?"

"Nothing." Changing the subject, "Since we're not going downtown today, we should call that young couple who wanted the kayak."

Walking out of the water to dry off and pack up, she said, "So, you'd like to see me with Barry? He asked me to marry him. I told him no."

"I'd like to see you happy. I don't care who you marry, Honey. It would solve your immediate situation and fulfill one of Neil's wishes."

"You don't care?"

"Jesus, Marla…let's not go down that road. This moment…right here, right now…you're with me, I'm with you, we're not fighting and that should be good enough."

Putting the stuff in the trunk of the Floozy-Mobile, she goaded, "You really don't care who I marry, Johnny? That's pretty cold."

"It's not cold at all. I do care, but there's not a damn thing I can do to sway that decision. If marrying this guy will afford you some happiness at this point in your life, then…why not?"

"That shocks me."

"Because the dopey romantic hick can be practical? I want you to be happy!"

"Is that really how you think I see you? As a dopey romantic hick?"

"I sometimes think so. Hey, we have less than forty-eight hours and I don't want any of it to be like last night."

Nothing was said for several minutes. I could tell Marla was rolling something around inside that crowded skull of hers. This, as always, could go either way.

On the ride home, stopped at a light two blocks from the bungalow, Marla looked straight at me and put her hand heavily on my leg. In a clear, full voice she directed me. "When we get inside the house...I want you to just take me. I don't want you to think of me as Marla. I don't want you to think about me or my feelings or my comfort or my orgasm. I don't want you to *think* at all. I want you to have me the way you want to have me. Just for you. All for you. Will you do that for me?"

"I will."

Marla moved her hand a little higher on my thigh. I overcame the impulse to crash the light and take the next turn on two wheels. As we approached the bungalow, Marla said, "Unbelievable." Her son and another young guy were just getting out of an old car parked in front.

I strung together a few choice expletives. She winked. "Not to worry, Sweetie. I won't forget about you."

We parked in the alley and, as we unloaded our sandy cargo, her phone rang. She looked at the phone and again said, "Unbelievable!" She did not answer, letting it go to her voicemail.

"Who's that?'

"Barry."

"Hey, great! Maybe he'll stop by and I'll finally get to meet him."

"Let's just deal with what's going on now, shall we? Shit…"

Marla poured me a glass of wine as she greeted Ben and his sullen, pimply friend, Josh. I exchanged pleasantries and excused myself to go shower. After receiving Ben's assurances that she didn't need to provide transportation for anyone, she came into the bathroom to tell me she was going to feed them and send them packing. She pulled back the shower curtain and whispered, "Make sure you wash all that sand off. It gets into everything."

They were all eating in the garden. I grabbed a few shrimp and a little cocktail sauce, refreshed my Pinot Grigio and joined them. The boys were polishing off leftover Thai food and tossed salad when Marla's phone rang again.

Her son said, "Betcha it's 'Big Bucks' Barry. You better watch this one, Johnny. He's serious."

Marla leveled a withering skunk-eye at Ben and slapped the back of his head. She stood up and headed to the house as she answered. "Hello? Yes, I got your voicemail. This is really not a good time, Barry." The rest went unheard as she went into the bedroom.

"So, Ben…what's the story on this guy?"

"He's got a shitload of money. House here, one in Laguna, another one in Aspen. He's asked my Mom to marry him a couple times, but he's a real pushy kind of guy and she's not into it."

Ben's buddy piped up, "Once when I was here, the dude picked up Ben's Mom in a Maserati."

"They've been out together?"

"Just once, I think. I don't keep track. She said he was a real dick to work for, but always paid her very well. He wants her bad. He's kinda like Sasha, but with lots of money…and smart…and he doesn't smell bad."

Ben walked into the living room to call, "Hey, Mom…I'm going now."

Marla was out the door in seconds. "Did you boys get enough to eat?" She poured herself a little more wine and started bringing in dirty dishes.

Ben was soon on his way to a party in Escondido, surprising me as he left by giving my hand a spongy waggle. "It was real nice to meet you, man. Good luck in Ohio."

"Keep playing that bass. I'll buy your first album."

After the boys drove off, Marla lit a cigarette and watered plants for fifteen minutes. She abruptly said, "Yuck…I have to get out of this sweaty, sandy bathing suit. Time for a shower." She walked to me and kissed me lightly. "Thanks for being so nice to Ben. More wine?"

"I'm fine. If you want, I'll call those folks who want the kayak. Have you decided what you want to do with it?"

On the portico, she took off her blouse and shorts to shake the sand out, standing oiled and gritty in her little black bikini. She went inside and said through the door, "Let's give it to the Salvation Army. Someone can benefit from it."

"I'll tell them it's not for sale. We'll talk about dinner when you come out?"

Shaking her butt at me, "Or something."

I had not forgotten her instructions at the traffic light. I allowed Marla the normal fifteen minutes for her shower, during which I left a message for the kayak couple.

Quietly entering the bedroom, I smelled weed. I tossed my clothes on the bed and, without a knock, opened the bathroom door. Marla was brushing her teeth; her flat, bare stomach pressed against the sink, mouth full of foam, naked but for the white towel wound high in her hair. Her immediate expression of startled embarrassment turned serious as she understood why I was there. Not giving her time to finish brushing or rinse, without speaking, I took her to the cool floor.

It was primal. It was fast and unformed. It was noisy with few words. In cramped quarters--it was a rut. The caring part of my brain switched off in a flushed blur of tile and porcelain and terrycloth and Marla's sweet flesh.

Twice she clearly indicated she was uncomfortable. When I hesitated the first time, she snarled, "Take it", and moved her body hard and rough against mine. The second time I ignored her.

After, on the floor halfway between the bathroom and bedroom, she held onto me tightly, speechless for ten minutes. When we eventually caught our collective breath, we slowly, reluctantly disentangled from each other. She thought that the top of her head had been flattened as a result of repeated sharp contact with the bathtub. On rubbery legs, we shared a shower, during which we laughed about the unusual places we were discovering toothpaste.

The rest of the day bobbed along in a mellow haze, measured and tranquil. It seemed important to both of us that we stay in physical contact. I kept putting my arm around her waist or kissing her hand. Depending whether we were walking or riding, she kept touching my arm or my leg. Even facing away from me, she had a hand extended back in my direction.

We held hands as we walked into the grocery. Waiting for her at the bank, I read the paper. She winked at me while a young male representative fell all over himself trying to please her. Back at the bungalow, we put the groceries away, and had our second glass of wine of the day in the garden. It was about three.

Marla had hurt herself the day before and she knew it. The alcohol and weed and anger had taken their toll. Sweating it out at the beach had helped, but she was weak and tired and pacing herself.

We agreed on a nap and then an early dinner. We kicked off our sandals and jumped on the bed. Marla pushed her back to my front as she pulled my arms around her and made cat noises. Fighting to keep the thought at bay, I knew this might be the last of the sweet times with Marla...those times that made the callous darkness and the cold madness I'd seen the previous night...and on other nights in other places...worth the pain.

Nearly asleep, she turned and said softly, "You're strong."

We slept deeply for an hour and a half and awoke still holding each other. We talked about dinner as I shaved and Marla smoked a small bit of "herb."

We had reached an unspoken agreement that she need no longer pretend her pot smoking was not an everyday, all-day thing. I was welcome to partake if and when I wished. I shared some each evening with her before bedtime.

There was a knock at the front door. Marla scurried to put on her robe and sprayed to hide the smoke with fake orange. I asked, "Who would be here at four-thirty on a Monday?"

"I don't know, but I'll get rid of them." She closed the bedroom door on her way out.

I heard the opening and closing of the front door, then a man's voice. Whoever was with Marla, they were talking outside in the garden. I took my time shaving, put on shorts and a shirt and walked into the living room.

I saw the red Maserati at the curb. The mailman and two young girls were already circling it, murmuring reverentially.

Marla was sitting across the table from a man whose back was to me. As she shot me a crooked smile, he quickly stood to greet me with a firm handshake and a thorough once-over.

In a clipped tenor voice out of the side of his mouth, "Barry Battaglia. You must be the famous Johnny I've heard so much about. Nice to finally meet you. Marla's had an awful lot of good things to say about you." He might have been calling a dog race or selling onion slicers at a flea market.

Barry was the guy who always got the girls that guys like me never got. He was five-eleven and in his late forties. Blue-eyed with a full head of light brown hair and blinding white teeth, his aquiline profile was perfectly tanned, his complexion flawless, his nails meticulously manicured. Trim, fit and filthy rich, Barry was everything I was not.

He wore (I discovered later, after a little research), Berluti shoes, razor-creased APO denims, Gucci leather belt and an Alexander McQueen t-shirt. On the lanyard round his neck (yellow to match his shirt) hung a pair of Prada sunglasses. Barry's outfit was worth more than everything in my closet.

The pairing of these two people was inconceivable to me. If there was any truth to Marla's claims that money, age and looks were less prized than caring, wisdom and affection…then Barry was all hat and no cattle. Clearly, she might be facing devastating times and a rich husband would be a sure fix for what ailed her. Still…from Neil's world to this pretty boy? I just couldn't see it.

"Call me Jack. Pleasure to meet you."

"Just in the neighborhood, as they say. I'm still hoping to convince Marla to come back to work for me."

Ignoring his interest in Marla, "That's a beautiful automobile. Ben was just telling me about it yesterday."

"Ben?"

"Yes. Marla's son? Ben?"

"Oh...of course. Ben. Ever driven one?"

"I can't say that I have."

"Would you like to take it up on the freeway?"

"As tempting as that is Barry, Marla and I are running a little late and we have dinner reservations. Maybe next time."

"You bet. Whenever you'd like...Jack."

Marla's face was frozen in a crooked smile. She looked uncomfortable, self-consciously rubbing her right forearm with her left hand and looking back and forth between Barry and me. She finally recovered and asked, "Barry, would you like a glass of wine?"

"Sorry, but I really have to run. I just stopped by to say hello. I've got friends coming over later tonight." Looking now at me, "You two should definitely stop by for a drink. Marla knows where I live."

Surprising me, Marla stood up and said, "Well, thanks for dropping by. Good to see you. I'm glad you two guys got to meet." She was giving him the brush-off and none too delicately.

Barry didn't smile so much as he squinted and grimaced. He did his best as he once again shook my hand and said, "Enjoy the rest of your visit, Jack."

"Oh, I will, Barry. I will."

He and Marla exchanged the most awkward, arms-length "hug" I'd ever witnessed; like lepers on opposite sides of an electric fence. Barry said, "Call me sometime, Marla." The Maserati made its rich, throaty music pulling away.

Marla waved weakly and said, "That was a surprise."

"Didn't you talk to him earlier?"

"I told him we were busy. I think he wanted to get a look at you."

"Nice car."

"We should get dressed and go eat. I'm starved."

"I'm with you."

She smiled a lopsided smile. She put her arms around my waist, her cheek on my shoulder. "And I'm so glad you are."

Her words had the same reassurance I'd given my decrepit twelve year-old Cocker Spaniel when I put him in the car for that final drive to the vet's office.

We drove up to a place in La Jolla with the unlikely name of "Herschel's Crab Palace." Early on a Monday, we got a great ocean-view table with no reservation. Marla looked smashing; a Carolina gypsy princess in a low-cut, short yellow dress, long dangly earrings and a gold ankle bracelet.

I ordered half a dozen oysters on the half shell as an appetizer, tossed greens and a glass of Zinfandel. Marla got a shrimp cocktail, tossed greens and a Margarita. As I looked at her across the table, she appeared to be fully recovered from the night before.

She asked, "What did you think of Barry?"

"I think you could do worse. But, I can't imagine what you two could possibly have in common. All I know about the relationship is that you worked for him and now he wants you to marry him."

She stopped mid-shrimp. "Did Ben tell you that?"

Our drinks arrived. "He said you'd gone out with him and that he had asked you to marry him... more than once." We toasted our libidos, sipped our drinks and watched the waves roll in.

The oysters were superb. Marla made the obligatory joke about "re-charging." I winked and made a sophomoric comment about lightning striking twice. I chose Sea Bass for dinner and Marla wanted to try the Cioppino. As dinner progressed, we talked about our futures and about tomorrow being my last full day in California. In keeping with the prevailing mood of the day, we kept it light and grown-up.

"Maybe you'll invite me back sometime. I'm starting to like it here."

Marla took two good slugs of her enormous Margarita. She said, "Johnny, I have to tell you something. Something unpleasant."

She seemed stuck, like she was having a hard time forming a thought. It was the perfect setting and time for the kiss-off I figured had to come sooner or later. I had always assumed that it would take more booze for her to do it. Cue the cellos.

"Just say what is on your mind." I held up my glass and said, "It will hurt less if you do it fast." We each took a drink.

She put her bare ankle to mine and took my hand across the table. "You are the most charming man I have ever known…but it's just too much, Johnny. I still haven't grieved for Neil and with you coming into my life and my idiot kid and losing my job and my drinking," she paused and squeezed my hand, hard "…I'm just overwhelmed all the time. I feel like I'm drowning and being with you is both pulling me down and keeping me afloat. I try to disguise it so you're not hurt, but then it just comes bursting out and I hurt you even worse. I need to put a lot of space between us, Johnny. It's just too much, too soon. I'm going crazy."

I felt equal parts heartache and pride. I was proud of her for her honesty. While I felt a sickening kind of vacuum in the pit of my stomach, I knew she was right. It would be healthier for me to be away from her, too.

"I'm so sorry, Johnny."

I kissed the back of her hand and smiled at her. "I love your honesty and your huge heart. Let's enjoy the dinner and then take a long walk by the bay. We can talk about it then. Honey, I understand. Honestly, I do."

Then, like six months before--on the day we first met—a tear rolled down her cheek and I caught it with the back of my index finger. With a look of surprised recall she grasped my hand and held it tightly to her face. A few more drops followed. And once again, she tenderly dried her tears from my finger with her napkin.

"Please don't hate me, Johnny. I couldn't deal with that."

"I don't hate you. Don't worry about me."

"I must look awful. Excuse me a minute." She went to the ladies room.

When Marla returned, eyes a bit puffy but with a game smile, we had one more drink and finished our dinner. We shared a

269

tangerine-colored sunset drive to the bay. It was a quiet ride, but not tense. For my part, it was more a sense of somber resignation.

It would soon be dark and there were lots of folks out enjoying the warm evening. Marla held my hand briefly, but for most of the hour-long stroll, we walked apart, the backs of our hands brushing occasionally. There were many long looks and longer silences. I asked her what had happened with Sasha.

"Sasha is an imbecile. He did something dangerous and foolish and I'm done with Sasha. He is one screwed-up man. Selfish and careless."

Minutes later, "Isn't it nice tonight? Oh, I meant to tell you...remember Robert...from the winery?"

"You mean 'Bob'?"

She smiled, "Yes...'Bob'. He called while you were in the shower yesterday to tell me about an article in Time magazine about glass. There were two paragraphs about Neil...complimentary things about his art...how experimental and unique it was. Pretty good, huh?"

"That's great. The more buzz, the more your stuff will be worth, kiddo."

"So...we're OK?"

My heart was breaking, but I knew if I tried to talk her out of her decision or showed weakness, I would murder whatever infinitesimally small chance there might be for us later.

Secure in my belief that straightening out Marla was a very long shot, I said, "We're fine. We still have work to do tomorrow, and then I need to get ready to go back home. I will miss you very, very much."

After a few quiet minutes, she said, "Enough about that for now. Let's get some ice cream on the way home. I'm sore all over and think I might turn in early." She kissed me hard on the cheek.

We grabbed two soft ice cream cones at a shop by Sea World and drove the long way back to the bungalow. She opened a bottle of Merlot and poured two glasses. We changed into scrubs pants and t-shirts, smoked enough to get the giggles, and then sat on the loveseat to watch some TV.

By ten-fifteen, after a second glass and all the shitty programming we could bear, we were both falling asleep. I followed Marla outside for her last cigarette of the day.

She said, "What a weird day this has been."

"They don't come much weirder. Very busy, lots of different players and very much 'in the moment'. How's your head feeling?"

With mock concern, "I'm not kidding you, the damn thing is flat on top."

"I should check to see if you dented the tub. Hey... I was only following your instructions."

"I'm not complaining." She gave me a long, forlorn look.

I smiled at her. She crushed out her cigarette and smiled back. "Ready for bed? I'm beat." For the first time since I'd met Marla, we left wine in the bottle. After a little smoke, we undressed and crawled into bed.

As frantic and mindless as the afternoon's encounter had been, that night Marla and I made love unhurriedly. She softly apologized for hurting me. I reminded her that this would be a great time to take my mind off of it. Going slowly to accentuate the care we felt for one another...long kisses and soothing touches...it was perfect.

"Sleep well, Butterfly."

"Good night, Beautiful Girl."

Tuesday dawned on a quiet and brooding Marla. She silently got out of bed before I did and put on the coffee. When I came into the kitchen, she was sitting at the table, chin resting on both fists, staring out the window into her garden.

"Good morning."

"It doesn't feel right giving away his kayak."

"Let me get some coffee." I poured two mugs, grabbed the cream and sugar and sat across from her.

She still hadn't looked my way. "I know it's just sentimental crap. I'll never use it. Nobody wants it. It won't fit in your car."

"Would you feel better about selling it to someone? I mean, if you donate it to Goodwill..."

"Salvation Army."

"Right, Salvation Army. If you donate it to them, you don't have to put a price on it. Maybe somebody who's always wanted a kayak but can't afford a new one will find it. It could change their whole life. You could make somebody you'll never know very happy."

Marla took her chin off its perch, finally looking at me, and said, "Are you ever wrong about anything? I mean...I know you're absolutely right about the kayak, but it gets pretty goddamn irritating sometimes."

"I'm wrong a lot. Mostly about the really big matters…marriages…stuff like that."

"So…you never choose the right women, is that it?"

Having seen this face, heard this tone and felt this cold stare before, I chose my words carefully. "I've never had the right woman choose me."

"Jesus. You have an answer ready for every question, don't you?"

"What are you angry about already today, Marla? I've been up for five minutes and you're already digging into me. Let's get ready and head for the storage place. You can think about what you want to do with the kayak on the way there."

"No…you're right. Neil would want someone to enjoy it as much as he did." She took her coffee into the bedroom. She closed the door and I heard her open the desk drawer. She was getting high at seven forty-five in the morning.

Within an hour we were en route to STUFF IT. We had exchanged very few words since coffee and, with only one day and one night remaining, I was determined to not further aggravate her by being right about anything.

Quickly, we emptied the storage cube and had the boxes of clothes and the folding chairs in the trunk of the convertible. It was a little dicey positioning the kayak in the back seat so it wouldn't damage the car during the short ride. Marla signed the paperwork, turned in her card and got her deposit back in cash.

The people at the store saw us pulling in and excitedly came out to meet us before we even got out of the car. "We don't get many kayaks," a gentleman said with an enormous grin as he gently helped me carry it inside the store. Two women helped Marla remove the chairs and boxes from the trunk. We had made their day and Marla seemed very pleased, smiling and chatting with people.

While she told one of the women the whole story of Neil and the kayak--without crying--I looked around at some of the doodads, second-hand masterpieces and clothing. I concluded that Barry Battaglia did not get his apparel here.

As we walked out, she offered me a small. "Thank you."

"For what it's worth, I think you did a good thing. Anywhere around here we can get brunch?"

We found a place that looked decent and decided on omelets. Marla had her usual two Mimosas. Near the end of the meal, she said, "Sasha broke into your house, Johnny."

Finishing the last sip of coffee, setting my cup on the table and suppressing a belch, I said, "Sunday morning. Yeah…I know all about it."

She sat sharply back in her chair. She looked more frightened than surprised, and her face reddened. Her mouth hung open for a good three seconds before she said, "You *knew*?"

"I knew within ten minutes."

"You knew and you didn't say anything to me?"

"Why say anything to you? You found out too, right? Well, of course you did…you just told me about it."

"But…how?"

"Miriam went over to get my mail and called me. Are you going to take me to Old Town? Sounds like fun." I gave her a smile, stood up and reached for my wallet.

As soon as we were outside, Marla yelped, "You kept that from me?"

I stared her down. "And you kept it from me. Don't make an issue of this, Marla. It's no big thing; no damage, nobody hurt and he didn't get my glass. End of story."

We got in the car and she directed me to Old Town San Diego. It was an unusually warm day, but we had a good time looking around, trying on bad hats, splitting a huge churro, taking pictures and talking about anything but glass. Marla bought me a woven bracelet and tied it to my wrist, but was generally reserved...a little pensive.

I knew her instincts were to be angry, but I guessed she couldn't decide where to direct her anger. She wore a look of confused resignation throughout the sunny afternoon. Hot and hungry, we chose a Mexican place and sat down for lunch.

Marla immediately ordered the "Mucho Mojito" and kept looking up at me over the top of her menu. I settled on a Modelo and when the drinks came, ordered chiles rellenos. She distractedly chose carne asada and went immediately to work on her drink.

Looking at my wrist, I offered, "I like the bracelet. Thanks."

"You looked cute in that black cowboy hat."

"We got a lot done today. If you want to tackle the garage when we get back, I'll help you. Use me...I'm gone in the morning."

"Not today. But I do need to drop off laundry. I'll get Enid to help me with the garage when she gets back. I am not looking forward to driving two hours to the dentist tomorrow and then driving two hours home in pain. Novocaine just doesn't seem to work very well on me."

No surprise there. Whatever electrochemical circuitry is involved in putting painkillers to work had likely been seriously compromised by Marla's years of alcohol and THC consumption.

It was clear, as she picked at her meal, that she was far more interested in the Mojito. She had ordered another one before I'd finished my beer.

Chidingly, "You've been pretty quiet today. Sad that I'm leaving?"

"Just trying to put things together. Sure, I'll miss you, but it's good that you're going now. The time is right."

"I guess."

We were halfway through lunch when Marla took a big gulp of her second Mojito, wiped her mouth and said, "Look...about this thing with Sasha. You surely can't think I put him up to it."

I put my cards on the table. "You believe that you have rights to the glass in my possession. I disagree. About that same time...knowing that I'm here with you...Sasha breaks into my house. And then, when he comes up empty-handed, who does he call? Please, Marla...please, tell me what I should think."

Her face became a fist. "Did you just call me a thief?"

"I just asked you a question."

"Take me home...now. And when we get there, I want you out within three minutes or I'm calling the police to remove you." I was gratified that she was not screaming. Maybe it was something about the two of us in restaurants together.

"I'm going to finish my lunch."

Eyes burning and red-faced, "Fuck you. I'll get a cab."

I'd had all of it I could handle. "I think you're overreacting, but if you're in a hurry...suit yourself."

As if she'd waited her whole life to do it, in truest Drama Queen fashion, Marla tossed the last of her Mojito in my face. She grabbed her purse, leaned over to hiss loudly, "Everything I whispered in your ear was a lie," and dashed out of the dining room.

I went to the men's room to wash the drink from my face. Returning to the table, I apologized to my waitress and asked for the check. Leaving the restaurant, I saw Marla on the other side of the street, smoking a cigarette, pacing and talking to herself. I started to cross the street. She spotted me and said loudly, "Don't come over here!"

"Let me drive you home, Marla."

"Stay away from me! I mean it!"

I smiled weakly at an elderly couple staring bullets at me as they walked past.

"You could stand there for an hour before your cab comes. Let me take you home."

"I want you out of my house!"

"Fine. Then shouldn't we both get there at the same time? C'mon, Marla...let me drive you home. The goddamn cab fare from here to your house will be fifty bucks."

Right on cue, the taxi rolled up. Marla glanced in my direction and got in.

And as I watched that cab pull away, all the tumblers in my jostled brain clicked neatly into place.

With a new perfect clarity, I knew exactly what I had to do. And it would involve a radical change in my travel plans.

First, though, I went back and bought that black cowboy hat. I took my time, looking in some of the shops we'd skipped over. I bought a colorful serape for my friend, Miriam. I found a friendly little tavern with a comely little barmaid and had another beer in Old Town. I would miss San Diego. There was something about the place that felt right.

The California sun was setting when I pulled into the alley behind the bungalow, and Marla's car was not there. Coming through the gate, I saw she wasn't parked out front either. The front door was locked. Maybe she'd taken her laundry to the cleaners. There was a parking space on the street, so I moved the convertible around front and took a seat in the garden.

Twenty minutes later, Marla came through the gate from the back.

"Please move your car so I can park in front of my house."

I stood up and did what she'd requested. She pulled her car around and went inside, straight to the bedroom and closed the door. She came out ten minutes later, wearing the famous green get-up, red-eyed and drinking what looked like the second half of a gin and tonic, lime slice on the rim.

Sitting down in the kitchen, "What are you waiting for? Pack up." The old bartender in me could tell by her voice and facial muscles that she'd had several drinks since leaving the restaurant. She'd probably gotten high as soon as she got home.

"Can we talk about it?" I knew what she'd say, but I needed to hear it.

"There's nothing to talk about. I want you out of my life...now."

I started for the bedroom. "Do you want to come along…make sure I don't take anything that isn't mine?"

"Just get your crap and go. Don't be an asshole."

I got my carry-on from the closet and, starting with my shaving kit, packed. I heard her go into the kitchen and shortly, the sound of cabinet doors and the distinctive clink that ice makes as it ricochets off good crystal.

And then, "Hurry up!"

She came in to use the bathroom. When she was done, she sat at the desk, filled the pipe to the top and lit it. I went into the living room to get the things in that dresser. Marla slammed the bedroom door. I did a quick inventory, looked in the bag to make sure my papers were in order and touched all my pockets. I was done packing.

I got a drink of cold water from the fridge. Marla called out from the desk, through the closed door, "What are you waiting for? Just go, already." This was followed by a paroxysm of coughing.

Standing in the middle of the living room, I said, "Thanks for everything. I had a good time…except for the shitty times. I'm glad I got to meet the rest of the cast…Ben, Sasha, Enid, the landlady…Barry. Can't forget the millionaire. Good luck with that, too. You were right about one thing…I do like it here."

No sound from the bedroom but for the faint sloshing of ice in a near-empty glass and the striking of a cheap lighter.

Keys in my hand, bag on my shoulder, I couldn't resist.

"Sorry I didn't get a chance to meet your Marine."

Silence. Then a groan that started low and rose in volume and pitch. Her chair pushed back from the desk. A long, high-pitched moan followed and the sounds of papers and weightier objects being moved around. Then quiet again.

I put my bag on the floor. I took three steps and tapped on the door. "Are you..."

The door swung open and I was staring down the barrel of a revolver. Beyond it, Marla's bleary eyes and shaky hand. From three feet away, she had a bead on my sternum.

Her words a nasty stiletto whisper, she said "You're the thief, you selfish bastard. You stole my love. You stole my glass. You stole my grief." Her finger firmly on the trigger, she kept poking the gun at me to punctuate her words.

I slowly backed up two steps and Marla followed. The hum of the freeway seemed to be in the room right behind me. The tick of the tiny clock in the kitchen sounded like a hammer. I put my hands shoulder high and froze in my shoes.

I'm no firearms expert, but I know a thirty-eight-caliber revolver when I see one. I was all but certain this one was not loaded. The cemeteries are crowded with people who were "all but certain", but I could see that the chambers on either side of the hammer were empty.

"Please put that down, Marla. All I want to do is walk out of here and leave you to your life. Please. Don't do this." She had a tight grip on the gun and looked awkward holding it.

A revolver can be fired two ways; if you just pull the trigger, the cylinder rolls to the next chamber, the hammer drops and the bullet is discharged. If you cock the hammer first and then pull the trigger, the cylinder does not move and the hammer falls where it is.

In a louder voice now, "You're the dirty fucking thief." She put her other hand on the gun, supporting the growing weight. "You stole my money, you stole Neil's clothes, you robbed me of the time I needed to mourn for him and *now I'll never get it right!*"

Would Neil have left the gun loaded or empty? Maybe, in his pain and delirium, he considered suicide and had put in only one round. Either way, Marla would probably not take the added step of pulling back the hammer.

The air went out of everything. My heart twitched. My bladder turned to ice.

With her small thumb, she was pulling back the hammer.

Screaming now, "I hate you so much right now. I'm mad enough to kill you. The Marine is none of your fucking business! You left me in so much pain and he was just there." She was gritting her teeth.

Arms trembling and face as red as a convertible, in silent slow motion Marla's eyes closed tight. The barrel of the gun tilted upward half an inch. She was pulling the trigger. I had time only to think, "No way."

The hammer came down with a loud, authoritative snap. No explosion. I wasn't on the floor.

Her eyes flew open. Turning the gun slightly, she looked at it in confusion.

With my right hand I pushed the gun to the left and gripped it hard at the same time, twisting it away from me and out of Marla's hand. She swung at me and punched me hard on the right ear. I pushed her backwards onto the loveseat.

"I'm calling the cops, you son of a bitch!" she shrieked.

"You're not calling anybody. You're shitfaced and your fingerprints are all over this thing. They've been here before and they'll lock you up for assault. Don't be an idiot."

She buried her face in a throw pillow and howled into it. Hair a tangled mess, a shiny ribbon of snot running from one nostril, spit flying, she shrieked, "I hope you die! I hope your fucking plane crashes! You stole from me and you stole from Neil! Get out! Get the fuck out of my house!"

I picked up my bag and placed the revolver on the kitchen table. "I'll leave this here."

She picked up one of Neil's small pieces, a glass sombrero, and then put it back down. She threw a book that rustled just past my head, hit the TV and sent a potted plant crashing to the floor...just glancing off Neil's urn. She threw one of the pillows at me as she screamed into the other, her eyes huge and fierce, veins bulging on her lobster-red forehead and neck.

With one ear ringing, (for a tiny woman, she had delivered one hell of a left hook), I walked backwards out the door and up the sidewalk. I climbed into the convertible and started the engine. I heard her front door slam as I pushed down on the accelerator.

I was no more than fifteen feet from the curb when I heard behind me, "Die, you prick!" The image in the rearview mirror was Marla, standing in the middle of the street. In the halogen glare of the streetlight, I watched her throw something. At the same instant that I heard, "You piece of shit!"...the revolver tumbled past my ear, thudded heavily off the dashboard and fell onto the passenger's seat.

Instinctively, I grabbed it, did a quick survey of the surroundings and tossed it over my shoulder, back into the street towards Marla. Maybe she'd see it, maybe not. I didn't want it anywhere near me.

Quickly up on the freeway, the sun setting orange and violet on the vast Pacific made a striking backdrop. Top down, with a pint of adrenaline still to burn off, I sliced through the tepid air of the falling night. An unfamiliar mixture of remorse and emancipation came over me. My guts unclenched just long enough for me to taste bile.

So…this was it.

Best-laid plans shot down and burning…this time I did it right. I got a ninth-floor suite at the Doubletree with a spectacular view of the city. I took a long shower, lined up a movie on cable and ordered dinner from room service; Caesar salad, New York Strip medium, baked sweet potato, gelato and Guinness.

After eating, unable to get interested in a light comedy, I stood at the window for a long time and absorbed the movement and lights of the San Diego night. I breathed deeply and recalled the sage advice of Mike Nichols; "Cheer up. Life isn't everything."

Pushing their way past all considerations and distractions were a thousand thoughts of Marla. Poor, crazy-ass Marla. Immune to logic or reason, vengeful and irresistible, she used sex as currency. In pursuit of the pleasures of the flesh I had let her play me like a pawnshop ukulele. I fell in love with her and I had very much wanted her to love me.

Beautiful and brutal, she was lost when I found her, drowning in grief and co-dependency. We had used each other up.

Two voluptuaries in purgatory, we would have to figure it out on our own.

5

Hindsight is blind. Days are layered, one atop the other. Week upon week, events are prioritized to establish a hierarchy of impact. Month following month, the kidney punches and finger sandwiches that constitute our lives conspire to occlude our ability to see them. The past becomes mere imagery and rumor.

We strain to peer back into days distorted by the pernicious urgency of the clock. Evanescent, our memories are diminished, fuzzed, eventually becoming opaque. The good times seem richer. The bad times soften at the edges, but never fail to break our hearts.

Three years after returning the rented red convertible, my time with Marla had been hammered into perspective and I was living a full, albeit studiously single, life. I had not spoken to her since that last night in Olinda.

Three years. Looking back, it does not seem possible. Warren Zevon was right; the hurt gets worse and the heart gets harder.

On that Wednesday I left San Diego, I got a later start than I originally planned. I had unfinished work.

At eight PM that same night, I arrived in Flagstaff, Arizona. It had taken nine hours to cover five hundred miles. Physically and emotionally trashed, I got a room at a clean, moderately priced motel, grabbed a bite and fell asleep watching local news.

The inescapable downside to the new plan would be the long hours filling with thoughts of Marla. I called Miriam, telling her I'd decided to drive home from California, that I needed time alone to clear my head. I repeated the story for family, work and editor.

I thought about how the beautiful Marla had landed in my lap. It had ended badly and now I needed to do those things necessary to salvage my sanity and get back on track.

Out of the motel at seven the next morning, a small cooler stocked with bottled water, granola bars and three vending machine sandwiches, I gassed up and left Flagstaff and struck out for Amarillo. With bathroom and fuel stops, I wanted to cover the six hundred miles in eight or nine hours. That was as long as I was willing to drive in a day.

When I dropped my bag on the motel bed in Amarillo around five o'clock that Thursday evening, I was tired of thinking about Marla. My back was kinked up and aching. My eyes were fried. I had pushed myself to drive ten hours, struggling to stay awake the last hundred miles. I showered and slept for an hour. I drove a couple of miles back up the road to a little diner for a proper meal. I made sure to sit where I could see the SUV.

I ate one of the best meatloaf dinners I'd ever tasted and washed it down with an ice-cold beer. At the register, I picked up the issue of Time magazine with the piece about Neil's glass.

Back in my room, I read the article. It presented Neil as "a revolutionary" and "explosive", describing his work as "mind-blowing" and "unmistakable." I fell asleep with the magazine on my chest.

The price of glass had just gone up.

Meatloaf and back spasms kept me up most of the night. I got back on the interstate at ten AM and struggled from the outset. Exhausted and sore, I took extra breaks along the way to get out of the vehicle and move around. It was a grinding, tedious ride. I listened to country music and farm reports. I sang Talking Heads songs at the top of my lungs so I wouldn't fall asleep. I assigned names to people in passing cars.

Getting fuel at a truck stop, I struck up an exchange with a guy who was also on his way to Ohio for a wedding in Urbana. He rolled his eyes and shook his head. "My sister. Number *four*. Idiot."

I abandoned my plan to drive six hundred miles. After little more than four hours and two hundred seventy-five miles, I looked at the stingy skyline of Oklahoma City with relief. I treated myself to a room with a whirlpool tub and let the jets of hot water pound the knots out of my back and neck for an hour. I took a Vicodin and a three-hour nap. I woke up thinking about how much I missed the Pacific.

I've played a lot of bit parts...cameos in the lives of others. This is a character flaw and five days on the road seemed like an opportune time to work on it. I tend to give exaggerated weight and inflated importance to my role in relationships. Looking back, it seems I am never as important in other people's lives as they are in mine. So it had been with Marla.

I ate well and sensibly at a vegan restaurant. I took a swim in the hotel pool and then spent another hour in the whirlpool. I showered and fell asleep at eleven.

Early Saturday morning, after a light breakfast and taking time to stretch my back and leg muscles thoroughly, I put Oklahoma City behind me and headed for St. Louis, five hundred miles to the east. I felt a little better. The day was cloudless.

I stopped in Springfield for lunch and gas. I couldn't look at any more packaged food. I had lunch at a picnic table outside an ice cream stand. An older Canadian couple, Seth and Liz, sat down with me. They were bound for New Mexico to thaw out after a "pretty ragged" Nova Scotia winter. After chili cheese dogs and milkshakes, we wished each other safe travels and I took a short walk around the nearby neighborhood to get my blood moving again. I opened the back of the SUV to make sure nothing had shifted and then got back on the highway.

I called Miriam to tell her I'd be home Sunday and asked her to open some windows before I got there. The place had been sealed against the winter for six months and I'd developed a liking for fresh air.

"At least this time you stuck it out for the duration, Scanlon."

"Pretty much, yeah. It's finished."

"She tossed you out?"

"I'll tell you all about it later. It's for the best."

"Sorry to hear your little Tantric melodrama has ended. You alright?"

"It's not so much that I want to lie down and die. I just want to not be alive for a while."

"So…sex or money? It's usually one of the two. Or is it another guy?"

"All of the above. Apparently she'd boinked a Marine out of spite the day after I left last time. Will you let some air into the place in the morning? I'll be home tomorrow night. I don't want to talk about this shit now."

"Jack, from what blessedly little you've told me…she is a model of self-destruction. Most likely she was overwhelmed and she cheated to sabotage herself. That might not make sense to you or me, but for some people sabotaging a good thing is a way of punishing themselves, and then they blame others."

"Thanks, Mrs. Freud. I'll call when I get home tomorrow night."

I drove to the western side of St. Louis. Around five, another ten-hour day ended at a Holiday Inn. I got a ground floor room and parked near my door. There was a restaurant and bar on the premises. I cleaned up and went to get a bite.

The crowd in the bar was well on their way to a wooly Saturday night. Local girls in tight jeans and low-cut tops, some with body glitter on their décolletage, looking for a good time. They dry-humped and sparred with young men in ball caps, looking for a non-binding motel memory. I sat in the restaurant. I ordered fish and chips and VO on the rocks.

Back in my room, I spread out on the bed but couldn't concentrate on TV. I hit the "off" button, closed my eyes and tried to relax my back and neck. One more long push to Cleveland tomorrow. Five hundred fifty miles and I'd be home.

The concept of gathering the Seven Deadly Sins together had never entered my mind until that night during Marla's visit when she told me Neil had, indeed, finished all seven pieces. The impact of seeing "Lust" for the first time had shaken her. I recalled thinking how many points I would score if someday I could make that happen for her, but then…she was in front of my fireplace, putting lotion on those well-turned legs and I didn't think about glass again for a long time.

We'd talked about it in her garden once, when she asked what I thought they were worth, but quickly moved on to other things.

When I purchased "Greed" in Chicago, it was partly in the delusional hope that one day Marla and I could enjoy them together, in our living room.

It was the confrontation over lunch at Balboa Park that forced me to see the true improbability of any such plan.

The trigger was the vision of Marla stepping into that cab, the smell of her drink still drying on my shirt. I was compelled to initiate a simple solution.

In St. Louis that night, I dreamed I was walking barefoot with Marla along the beach at Torrey Pines. The sun and surf were stainless. She was happy, holding my arm tightly, grinning and consoling me. "It's going to be fine, Sweetie. Please don't worry about it. Everything's going to be fine. You'll see."

The next morning…in that surreal landscape when I am no longer sleeping, but not yet truly awake…I rolled toward where she would have been…reached across a mile of empty, white sheets.

With sunny weather all the way and light Sunday traffic, I made good time. It was seven PM, dark and getting frosty outside. I felt like someone had worked me over with an ax handle. I needed a hot bath and a drink.

Ten hours and five hundred and fifty-six miles after leaving St. Louis, I unlocked my front door, dropped my bag in the hallway and limped to the bathroom. It seems that the closer you get to home, the more distressed your bladder becomes. Until, by the time you reach your door, you are in agony…cramping and thinking about just doing it in the driveway and screw the neighbors.

On the dining room table, under a fresh lime and a paring knife, was a note from Miriam; "*Opened six windows for thirty minutes. Bottle of Stoly in the freezer. Tonic below. Mucho gusto.*"

Vodka tonic in hand, I soaked in the tub. Repeatedly having to add hot water started to irk me, so I drained the tub and took a shower.

Downstairs, I turned the music on low and made myself another drink. The Big Chair was calling out to me and did not disappoint when I finally sat down. Too tired to build a fire, I closed my eyes and imagined one. It would take another day for my body to stop vibrating, my eyes to stop wobbling and my brain to unclench. It was good to be home. Trying to not think about Marla was proving more painful than thinking about her.

Conceived piecemeal and executed with mixed emotions, my plan to reunite The Seven Deadly Sins had never been perfect. But it was as solid as I could make it and I was committed to it. I had done what groundwork I could and coincidence had taken care of the rest.

When I think back to that Wednesday morning three years ago in San Diego, I can recall the smallest details.

I had the buffet breakfast at the Doubletree and checked out at eight AM. I drove to the airport car rental to return convertible. Pleading ignorance about the small dent in the dashboard and having purchased the extra insurance package, I was forgiven. I then negotiated the one-way rental of a sport utility vehicle, to be dropped off in Cleveland six days later.

I headed for the nearest "big box" home improvement store. I bought two rolls of heavy packing tape, a hundred feet of bubble wrap, five medium-sized cardboard moving boxes and five cinder blocks. I grabbed a dozen bottles of drinking water and a pack of gum and paid cash.

My purchases loaded in the back, I looked at the dashboard clock. A minute before nine, I considered calling Marla about my watch. It wasn't on my wrist or in my bag. While I dithered, she called me. I let it go to voicemail.

"Johnny, you forgot your watch and your toothbrush here. I will send them to you first thing tomorrow. I'm leaving to go to the dentist. I'm so sorry about everything. I'm sorry I'm such a mess." She never sent them.

It seemed impossible, unacceptable, that this would be the last time I'd hear her youthful, alluring voice.

Wearing shades and a cap, I headed toward the bungalow. I drove down her street and then the alley behind. Her car was gone. It was nearly a two-hour drive to the dentist's office. She'd be in the chair anywhere from thirty minutes to an hour. I had at least four hours to do my thing.

Enid was in Denmark. Ben never rose before noon. Sam, the guy who lived behind Marla, was at work until three, but I still made sure his car wasn't around. I parked the SUV next to the garage in Marla's spot. No stranger to this neighborhood now, I didn't anticipate raising the suspicions of whoever lived across the alley.

I quietly opened the gate and went to the garage door. On a recent errand to pick up cleaned and folded clothes, I had a copy of Marla's house key made at the hardware next to the laundry. It was the same key that worked the knob and deadbolt on the door to the garage.

Once inside, I closed and locked the door behind me and turned on the lights. I gently opened the heavy overhead door long enough to move my stuff from the vehicle into the garage and then closed it. The boxes were identical in size to the ones in repose four feet above my head. I folded them into shape, sealed the bottoms with plenty of packing tape and stacked them aside. I got the stepladder and began very carefully bringing the five heavy Sins down from their loft to the garage floor.

They were more difficult to handle without help. Sweating now and a little arm-weary, I got them all down. I smiled at Neil's bright, childish markings on the boxes and the value of their contents. I promised him I was doing the right thing. I cut the tape and opened them.

One by one, on a space I'd cleared on my old friend's bench, I gently removed each piece of glass from Neil's boxes and placed them into their new boxes, adding more bubble wrap as needed. I taped them generously and put them back on the floor. It was a reverential, almost tender exercise. All the glass now ready for transport, I took a break and grabbed a bottle of water from the SUV. It was ten thirty. Marla would be close to the dentist's office.

It was getting stuffy in the garage. I took some deep breaths and another long drink of water.

I lifted the first cinder block onto the bench and swaddled it in bubble wrap. Taking one of the old boxes, I put the dead weight into it and taped it shut. I did this four more times. The Deadly Sins were not all of identical weight. But they were all close enough to the weight of one cinder block that whoever next lifted these boxes would have no questions.

I huffed and cursed the five old boxes with their worthless contents up the ladder and into the nest I'd constructed for them just days before. I was careful to position them exactly as they had been, covered with the same tarp. I put the ladder back in its place and walked around the garage. Marla would surely notice anything out of place. Satisfied that I'd left no traces of my presence, I stood directly under the boxes one last time to make sure there was no sign of tampering.

I opened the overhead door, opened the rear of the SUV and carefully placed the new boxes, heavy with sin, inside. I had lowered the rear seats to avoid having to stack one box on top of another. I closed the hatch and then went inside the garage to close and lock the overhead door.

Taking a quick peek through the shade on the door and finding no one in the backyard, I stepped out, closed the door behind me and locked it. I double-checked the deadbolt. Marla was paranoid of a break-in.

It was eleven o'clock. Marla was in the dentist's chair.

I was headed east.

In the three years post-Marla, I published two reasonably well-received books and was content with my career's course.

I wrote two magazine articles about my friendship with Neil and about his extraordinary glass. I mentioned him frequently on my website and whenever I found myself in galleries or in the company of artists. Rumors abounded regarding The Seven Deadly Sins. They were in Europe. They were in China. They did not exist. They were five feet tall and weighed hundreds of pounds apiece. Neil had been buried with them.

Neither Marla nor Neil had taken pictures of them. The only proof of their existence was the photos I had taken with my cell phone in that sepulchral storage unit.

A former student of Neil's had spent a year compiling photos and interviews for a book about him. I lent him photos of some of Neil's older work, not the ones I'd taken at Marla's storage space. He interviewed me and included my remembrances of Neil in his book.

I was quoted as saying, "I own the first of the Seven Deadly Sins...'Lust.' Neil told me to consider it a permanent keepsake. I have seen the complete set of 'The Seven Deadly Sins' and there are others who can verify that Neil absolutely did complete them. No, I will not give you their names."

His book sold few copies, but enjoyed some popularity in the art world and served to further bolster Neil's growing legend and to increase the value of his work.

Two of his life-sized glass and copper figures appeared in *Architectural Digest*, prominently on display in the living room of the hottest movie producer in the world.

Just six weeks ago I spoke with a gallery owner in New York who had known Neil and often showcased his work. He was convinced that the seven pieces, as a collection, could be worth easily a quarter of a million, probably considerably more "in the right auction setting."

Speculation that the unaccounted-for Sins were in the hands of one person led to further speculation that they were in the hands of multiple owners. Rumors spread that these owners, unaware of the glass's value, were allowing them to gather dust on bookshelves and windowsills, in barns and garages...or worse...that they were simply gone.

My immediate plans for The Seven Deadly Sins ended at a nondescript corrugated metal storage facility in Richfield, Ohio, where I put them three years ago. After, I returned the SUV to the Cleveland airport and took advantage of the complimentary ride home. I have not set foot in the storage space since, mailing a money order annually.

But before I stashed them away, I allowed myself a singular and unique pleasure. After picking up 'Lust' and 'Greed' from

Miriam's, I opened all of the boxes and set The Seven Deadly Sins on the long workbench in my garage.

I was the first and only person to ever see them together. It was a very emotional experience. Neil's genius shone through and within each piece.

I took time to look at them closely. I photographed them individually and as a group, shooting a whole roll of film with my old thirty-five millimeter Nikon.

I did not see it as a noble plan to liberate great art from barbarians. I did not consider it a statement about Marla or Neil or me. It was never an act of payback or vindictiveness. I wanted to believe that by virtue of my actions, Neil's masterpiece would not end up sold off to buy weed and wine and to support deadbeats. They would not be turned into objects of sociopathic worship or idols for hustlers.

In order to protect the integrity of my old friend's masterwork, I chose to sacrifice a significant portion of my integrity.

Marla had gotten one thing right. I had, indeed, become a thief.

Epilogue

Two years ago, just a year after leaving behind Marla and The Bungalow of Busted Hopes, I got a call from a familiar area code.

"Is this Johnny?"

I felt an unsettling twinge in my chest as, for a split second, I thought it was Marla. But the voice, though familiar, was wrong.

"This is Jack. Who's this?"

"It's me, Enid…Marla's neighbor."

Disappointed relief. "Enid. How was Denmark?"

"It was fine…should I call you Jack or Johnny?"

"Whatever you're comfortable with. Is something wrong?"

"I thought I should let you know a few things."

"Enid, if this is about Marla, I really don't want to deal with it anymore."

Plunging on, Enid said, "She's drinking a lot…everyday…and running out of unemployment. She won't let me mention your name. I made her sit down one night and told her that she had made a big mistake…that she had a guy who truly loved her and she shit on him. She cursed me and cried and that was the last time we talked about you. If I bring you up, she goes inside and shuts the door."

"I hope that's not what you called to tell me."

"I called to tell you that Sasha stole her glass." I was uncomfortable and confused. I had thought all connections to that time and place had been severed.

"What glass? Marla has a lot of glass."

"The big glass. The ones you put in the garage. The Deadly Sins. After all of your hard work and the terrible things she put you through, I thought you should know."

"You know about that? She was going to keep that top secret."

"She told me about it as soon as I got home from Denmark. She told me how you guys had put them up there. She got really drunk one night a couple weeks ago and took Sasha back there to show him. I went along."

"How do you know Sasha stole them?"

"Sam, the guy who lives behind Marla. A week ago he saw Sasha go into the garage. About an hour later, Sam was taking his trash into the alley and saw Sasha and another guy taking boxes from the garage and putting them in a car. He told Sam he was putting them back into storage for Marla. Nobody has seen him or the glass since."

We talked for a few minutes more, when I said I had to go.

"I appreciate the call Enid, but I won't need any more updates. You take care of yourself."

"You too, Johnny. Any message for Marla?"

"No. No message for Marla."

That evening I listened to Pavarotti sing *"E lucevan le stelle."*

It was the verse, "she came as fragrant as a flower and fell into my arms" that pried open a window in my mind.

For me, it was always about simply *being* with Marla.

We are beings, not portraits, not performers. Ram Dass counsels us to "Be. Here. Now."

Those times when I have ignored this counsel, my life has become bewildering and unmanageable.

Those times of living fully, in the moment, have been filled with wonder and newness. They are as near to perfect joy as I will ever know.

Not sex. Not euphoriants. Not things tangible. Not the beach or the sunshine.

Being with a person so uniquely alluring, one who carried and projected so much wild energy and then trading energies with that person, had opened new worlds for me.

Marla Stone laid waste to everything I thought I knew about love and trust. She gave me new standards for joy and sorrow, for pleasure and pain.

Every day I imagine the look on Sasha's face as he opened those boxes.

Made in the USA
Charleston, SC
06 August 2013